Where DID WE GO *Wrong* <u>AGAIN?</u>

MONICA MATHIS-STOWE

Copyright © 2013 Monica Mathis-Stowe

Cover designed by: Dzine By Kellie
Cover photos by: Roy Cox Photography

All rights reserved
Printed in the United States of America

The Literary Publishing Group
P.O. Box 1370
Temple Hills, MD 20757
www.MonicaMathisStowe.com

13 Digit: 978-0-9852209-3-8
10 Digit: 0985220937

DEDICATION

This book is dedicated to all the wonderful women who have been a true friend to a sister in need.

ACKNOWLEDGMENTS

First and foremost, I would like to thank God for guiding me during this journey. This book would not have been possible without the support and encouragement of my husband, Reggie, and our son, Shane. My party planning sister, Tonya Miller, has helped me more than words can express. Sometimes my lips forget to say, "thank you," but my heart always holds you near and dear. To all my relatives and friends who offered emotional support as this book went from rough draft to completed novel, I thank you. My love for each of you has no boundaries.

My sincere gratitude to all the test readers who started out with me, but were unable to finish. It's a demanding job and I thank you for your time and contribution. Tina Salahuddin and Sharnetta Latimore stayed the course and read every single word of this novel. Your encouragement and brutal honesty made me step my game up and for that, I thank you with all my heart.

Working with every author is a dream team of people who work diligently to get the novel ready for the readers. Talented editors, Judy Roth, Noël Higgins, Faydra Deon, and Tina Nance provided their expertise and time in polishing my manuscript. Thank you ladies for not only editing my novel, but also teaching me along the way. Thanks Kellie of Dzine by Kellie for using your invaluable skills to design another book cover that will stop people in their tracks.

Hats off to my beautiful cover models, Jasmin Burman, Lauren Dillard and Wendy Mackall for allowing me the honor of using their beauty for another book cover. Thanks to Roy Cox Photography for shooting the book cover image and make-up artist, Monica Cook, for highlighting the models' beauty with her skills.

Words cannot express my gratitude to you, the readers. You hold a special place in my heart. Because of your support, I was able to accomplish my dream of becoming a bestselling author. I have nothing but respect and appreciation for each and every one of you. For all the book stores, independent and chain, thank you and your staff for allowing me the privilege of hosting a book signing in your store.

Please forgive me in advance if I neglected to include anyone who contributed to this novel. It's not intentional. Thanks to you all and I look forward to hearing from you soon.

www.MonicaMathisStowe.com
www.twitter.com/MMathisStowe
Facebook: Author Monica Mathis Stowe

Chapter 1

"Oh, my God! Where did all this blood come from?" Joy wondered just before everything went black.

Bea and Juan rushed past the toppled Christmas tree to their daughter's side. Sobbing, Bea dropped to her knees and tried to wake Joy.

"Don't move her, Bea." Juan took his cell phone out of his shirt pocket and dialed 911.

Trent slammed and locked the front door, then rushed to Maxine's side, moving his hands all over her body to check for injuries. "Are you hurt? Are you okay, Maxi?"

"No! No! No! This isn't happening!" Maxine cried as she stood paralyzed with fear, watching the chaos unfold in Joy's living room.

"You're not hurt! Everything's gonna be okay! Help is on the way!" Trent put an arm around Maxine, trying to comfort her.

Maxine didn't respond. Her eyes were focused on what was happening in front of her. It looked like a scene from a war movie. Everybody was hysterical. The living room was filled with echoes of people crying and screaming.

The dead weight of Allen's unconscious body had Gabby pinned to the floor in a puddle of blood. "Get him off me! I can't breathe!" Gabby screamed as she tried to wiggle herself free.

Allen's sister and brother, Tyesha and Tyrese, quickly lifted Allen off Gabby and gently laid him on the floor.

"Oh, my God! Help me!" Tyesha screamed. Her entire

body shaking, she stared at Allen with bulging eyes. Blood gushed from his chest as she pressed down to stop it.

"Somebody get some towels! Quick!" Tyrese bent down to see if he could help Tyesha with Allen.

Trent ran upstairs and grabbed all the towels he could carry from Joy's linen closet and rushed back down. He gave the towels to Tyrese, went into the kitchen, fixed an ice pack for Joy's head, and gave it to Bea.

After Juan ended his 911 call, he helped Gabby to the couch. Blood dripped down her right arm and off her fingers. Juan rolled up her sleeve and found an open gash. Snatching a dinner napkin off a nearby table, he wrapped it around her arm to stop the bleeding. She winced from the pain as tears trickled down her face.

Three loud knocks made everyone stop and look at each other with uncertainty. A deep voice yelled, "Police! Open the door!"

Trent left to open it.

"No, Trent! Don't! It could be Dean coming back to kill us!" Maxine screamed.

"No, Maxi. It's not Dean," Trent responded in a calm tone. "You can see the flashing lights in the window."

Maxine quickly turned her head to the living room window, and then whispered, "Okay."

A few minutes later, Prince George's County police officers and detectives were scattered everywhere. Some were inside the house taking pictures and gathering evidence, while others were outside searching the neighborhood and surrounding areas for Dean. Maxine and Trent answered questions while paramedics brought in stretchers and medical equipment to treat the injured. Allen was quickly put on a stretcher and taken to the hospital with Tyesha and Tyrese trailing behind in tears. Two police officers escorted them to the hospital.

Another paramedic was on the sofa with Gabby. She glared at him as he cleaned her cut, put a bandage on it, and then examined her. She couldn't believe how close Nadia came to losing her mother tonight. She was going to make Dean pay for what he did to them.

"Maxi, you're trembling," Trent said as he put his arms around her.

She was too devastated to talk anymore. With so many emotions running through her, she didn't know which one was going to come out if she spoke. As if feeling her pain, Trent held her closer and kissed her forehead. *Thank God for Trent,* she thought as she wrapped her arms around him and buried her face in his chest. He had risked his life and freedom to save them. Although he'd done his share of bad things to her, right now, she needed him more than ever. Having him by her side was the only way she was going to make it through this tragedy.

Maxine turned her head to look at the paramedics taking Joy out on a stretcher. She released Trent, ran to Joy's side, and grabbed her friend's hand. Maxine gasped when she saw the brace around Joy's neck and a knot the size of an orange on her forehead. Unable to stop the tears flowing from her eyes, she tried to speak, but the words wouldn't come.

"Maxine, please move! We need to get Joy to the hospital so the doctors can examine her and the twins!" Bea yelled as she pulled Maxine away from Joy.

Trent stepped forward and held Maxine back. "C'mon, Maxi. She needs to go."

The paramedics, escorted by two police officers, pushed Joy out the door with Bea walking closely behind, giving them instructions on how to care for her daughter and unborn grandchildren.

Juan turned to Trent before he left. "Can you get Maxine and Gabby to the hospital?"

Trent looked at Gabby and then Juan with a puzzled expression. "Isn't she going by ambulance?"

"She refused to go with the paramedics," Juan explained with a smirk. "The bullet grazed her skin and cut her arm. Nothing serious."

"But, she was bleeding so—" Trent said before Juan cut him off.

"She was bleeding so much because she was overheated and upset. Now that she's calmed down, it stopped." Juan frowned and shook his head. "I need to go before Bea carjacks the ambulance and drives Joy to the hospital herself."

After Juan left, a detective, overdressed in an Armani suit and wearing too much cologne, approached Trent and Maxine. "Hello, I'm Detective Briggs. I understand the officers talked to you earlier, but I need to ask you a few more questions about what happened here tonight." He pointed at the dining room table for them to have a seat.

After they sat down, Trent put his hand over Maxine's for support. She broke down crying earlier when the police questioned them. She gave him a nod and half-smile to let him know she was okay, then turned her attention to Detective Briggs.

"I know it's been a rough night for you, but we need to find..." Detective Briggs looked at his notepad, then continued, "...Dean Bennett before he hurts someone else. Why don't you start by telling me your names?"

"My name is Trent Anderson, and this is my, um..." Trent looked at Maxine for permission to call her his wife.

She nodded her approval.

"Okay and this is my wife, Maxine Crawford-Anderson," Trent continued.

Detective Briggs wrote their names down on his notepad and excused himself from the table. Maxine's eyes followed him. He ripped a sheet from his notepad, gave it to a police officer, and whispered something to him before he returned to the table. Maxine wondered what he was doing, but was too upset to question him about it.

"Sorry about that; so tell me what happened. What made Mr. Bennett target you folks tonight?" Detective Briggs asked as he sat back down at the dining room table.

"A few months ago, Dean found out the twins Joy is carrying weren't his, so he left her," Maxine said before she wiped her cheeks with a tissue she took out of her handbag.

"And Joy is his wife, correct?" Detective Briggs wrote notes in his pad.

"Yes, she is. Joy told me Dean came over this morning, but when he saw she had moved on with her ex-boyfriend, Allen, her twins' biological father, he was upset." Maxine immediately regretted telling the detective this information because she could tell by his expression that he was judging Joy harshly. She decided to stop talking and let Trent answer the detective's questions.

It took Trent twenty minutes to recap the night's events. The whole situation was bad, but it could've been a lot worse, especially with Gabby's interference. Nobody expected her to leap from the floor and run toward Dean, too. Allen tried to push her back to keep her safe, and that's when Dean pointed the gun at them and fired.

"What did Mr. Bennett do after he fired the gun?" Detective Briggs asked, continuing to take notes.

"He looked shocked. He ran out the front door with the gun still in his hand," Trent answered.

Detective Briggs stood and asked Trent and Maxine to show him where everything happened. They followed him into the living room where the paramedic was still treating Gabby. He was putting a blood pressure cuff on her left arm. Maxine could tell by the look on Gabby's face that she was ready to kill the enamored paramedic who was obviously going the extra mile with his exam.

Trent pointed at the two steps leading into Joy's sunken living room. "This is where it happened. Allen was standing here and Gabby was right behind him."

"Uh-huh... so the bullet struck him in the chest, exited his back, and grazed her arm." He walked to the back of the living room and stuck his pen in the wall where the bullet was still lodged. He called one of the crime scene investigators over to remove the bullet.

"Trent! Oh my God, Trent!" Maxine gasped.

"What's wrong, Maxi?" Trent looked around, expecting to find Dean had returned.

"I just realized, almost an hour ago, I was standing in front of the same wall they're digging the bullet out of. What if the boys..." Maxine started crying again.

"Don't think about it, Maxi. You're safe now. Let's finish up here so we can go to the hospital and check on Joy and Allen, then go home to our kids," Trent said as he held Maxine tightly in his arms.

Detective Briggs excused himself to speak with the officer he had been talking to earlier. Maxine left Trent to get Gabby so they could leave for the hospital right away. As Maxine and Gabby approached Trent, two uniformed officers were walking towards him from the opposite direction.

"Are you Trent Anderson?"

Trent cleared his throat and answered, "Ummm… Yes, I am."

"Put your hands behind your back," the cop instructed.

"What! Why? What's going on?" Maxine questioned.

"Don't worry about it, Maxi." Trent gave her a comforting smile.

The officer handcuffed Trent and read him his rights.

"What's wrong with you people? The real criminal is out there running the streets with a loaded gun, and you arrest my husband for saving our lives?" Maxine's tone grew louder with each word.

"Since you're divorcing him, he's no longer your problem," Gabby interjected.

Detective Briggs stepped forward to explain. "I'm sorry, Mrs. Anderson, but your husband violated the terms of his house arrest and we have to take him in."

"You should've never let him out." Gabby glared at the detective.

"Be quiet, Gabby!" Maxine snapped. "I want to talk to your boss. He shouldn't have to spend one second in jail. He saved our lives."

Detective Briggs stared at Maxine, hunched his shoulders, and released a deep sigh. "Let me call the chief and see what I can do."

Gabby sighed loudly to show her boredom with the whole situation. "C'mon, Maxine. Let's go to the hospital."

"No. Not until I help Trent," she snapped at Gabby, then looked at Detective Briggs who was dialing his boss.

"Let's go now, Maxine. Let his family deal with him. He's not your responsibility anymore," Gabby yelled.

"How can you say that? He's my sons' father and the reason we're all alive tonight."

"Don't be a fool! He almost killed you! Do you remember he cracked your head wide open in two places over some packing supplies you left on the floor? Have you forgotten your five-day stay in the hospital because of him?" Gabby shouted.

Maxine looked down at the floor and said in a low voice, "He served his time for that."

Gabby smiled seductively at the police officers. "Please take him back to jail. If you ask me, it's karma and since she's not smart enough to think for herself, I have to do it for her."

Maxine ignored Gabby and stared at Trent, pleading with him not to get upset.

He shook his head and frowned at Gabby. He had never liked her, and now he could honestly say he hated Gabby. How Maxine and Joy had stayed friends with her for so long, he could never understand. He always thought they were too good to be associated with Gabby's hateful ass.

A few minutes later, Detective Briggs returned with a smile. "This is your lucky day, Mr. Anderson. My boss has agreed to let you go home." He glared at Trent. "You have to go straight home. No hospital visit for you tonight."

Maxine started to protest, but Trent stopped her. "Don't worry about me, Maxi." He raised his arms behind his back so the cops could remove the handcuffs.

"That's the smartest thing he's ever said. Now let's go," Gabby ordered. She reached in her purse to get her ringing cell phone, then walked toward the front door.

When Gabby was out of sight, Maxine kissed Trent and whispered, "I'll call you later from the hospital."

He smiled. "Stay as long as you need to. I'll take care of the boys."

"Thanks for everything, Trent." Maxine caressed his cheek lovingly.

Gabby rushed back in the room looking pale and visibly shaken. "Maxine, let's go! Bea just called and said Allen might not make it!"

"Oh, Jesus!"

Detective Briggs gave Gabby and Maxine a ride to the hospital because he needed to question everybody who had attended the Christmas dinner at Joy's house. Gabby stared at Maxine as they sat in the backseat of the detective's car. Visibly trying to hold back tears, Maxine peered out the window with her arms crossed over her chest. They hadn't said a word to each other since they left Joy's house.

Gabby knew their lives would never be the same after this evening, but she had a plan to fix it. She was going to make Dean pay for everything he put them through tonight. There was no way he was going to jail to possibly get out early for good behavior like Trent. If everything worked out the way she planned, Dean Bennett wasn't going to live to see another day.

$\mathcal{C}$hapter 2

"Dean, I know you didn't mean to kill Allen. I don't blame you."

"You mean it, Joy? Because I still love you and it was an accident," Dean slurred.

"I know and I still love you, too. Where are you? The doctors are releasing me and I can come get you. We're going to put our family back together, Dean."

"Really? Now that their father's dead, the twins need me to be their daddy." Dean was sobbing between gulps of vodka. "I wanna see you, Joy."

"I want to see you too, Dean. Where are you?"

After a brief pause, Dean sighed, then said, "I'm at the Red Roof Inn in Lanham."

"What's your room number?"

"Call me when you get here and I'll come outside. We need to get out of Maryland as soon as possible."

"I agree. I'm on my way. Dean?"

"Yes, Joy."

"I love you so much. Please don't leave. I need you. The twins need you. Promise me?"

"I promise, Joy. I love you, too, and our babies. This is how it was supposed to be."

"You're absolutely right. See you soon."

Gabby smiled wickedly as she punched the End Call button

on Joy's cell phone and looked at Allen's two oldest brothers, Bo and Chuck. They were standing in front of her with their mouths half open. She could tell by the shocked expressions on their faces she had done her best-ever Joy impersonation.

"Damn, girl! You sounded just like her!" Allen's oldest brother, Bo, exclaimed.

"Of course I did. Who do you think covered for her in college when she snuck off to visit Allen in Atlanta?" Gabby bragged with a conceited smirk. What they didn't know was that Dean was so drunk, she could've used her own voice and still gotten away with it as long as she used Joy's phone.

"I don't like this shit! My baby brother layin' up in the hospital fighting for his life and this bitch talkin' about him being dead. That's some bad luck shit right there and I ain't feeling it," Chuck, the second-oldest of the six Johnson brothers, complained.

Bo grabbed his brother's shoulder. "He'll make it. Allen's tough and ain't shit gonna keep him away from Joy and his twins. Now let's go get this mother-fucker and make him pay for what he did."

They stared at Gabby, eager to know where Dean was, but she stared back full of attitude.

"Where he at?" Bo asked eagerly.

Gabby rolled her eyes and shifted her body weight from one leg to another as she tightened the belt on her wool coat. She didn't want the Johnson brothers to think she was afraid of them. They had a reputation for being career criminals and cold-hearted thugs, but she was determined not to let them intimidate her.

"He's at the Red Roof Inn in Lanham."

"What room?" Chuck snapped. He glared at Gabby like he wanted to kill *her* instead of Dean.

"He didn't say. He's expecting me to call him when I get there. When you arrive, I'll call him and get him to come to the parking lot," Gabby explained.

Bo and Chuck looked at each other. Bo tilted his head for Chuck to follow him. They walked a few feet away to talk in private. Every few seconds, Chuck glanced back and scowled at Gabby. She stood in the cold December air, wondering what was going on. After a few minutes, they rejoined her. Searching their faces, she tried to figure out their mood, but they showed no expression.

Chuck grabbed Gabby's arm. "C'mon, you goin' with us!"

Gabby snatched her injured arm from Chuck's tight grip and moaned in pain. She didn't want to be caught anywhere with the Johnson brothers. Even standing in the hospital parking lot was too close for her comfort, but she was willing to make a sacrifice to get them to take care of Dean.

"Keep your hands off me and I am not going! I gave you everything you need to get him. I don't want anything else to do with it. Just let me know when the problem has been taken care of," Gabby ordered.

"Who the fuck you think you are, bitch?" Chuck lunged toward Gabby, but Bo blocked him.

"Gabby, I understand what you saying, but we need you to go. I think we all want the same thing, so we need to work together to make it happen. If you don't go and help us, we can't do this." Bo sighed. He didn't trust her and needed her to go to make sure this wasn't a set-up.

"Don't reason with her dumb ass!" Chuck interjected angrily.

Gabby ignored Chuck as she thought about what Bo said. She knew he was right and she needed to see her plan through. She looked Bo in his eyes and announced, "I'll go."

"Thank you." Bo pointed across the parking lot. "My truck is over there."

"What you thanking her ass for? I still don't trust this bitch," Chuck barked.

Gabby rolled her eyes at Chuck, then looked at Bo and pointed to her SUV a few cars away. "I'm not riding with you. I'll be driving my Lexus. You can follow me."

"No problem," Bo agreed. He was willing to do whatever was needed to get Dean.

Gabby left the Johnson brothers and sashayed across the parking lot to her Lexus. She knew they were used to getting their way, but so was she. Before the end of the night, one of them was going to have to give in and she had no intentions of it being her.

Earlier that night, Maxine's father had picked Gabby and Maxine up from the hospital. Maxine agreed to watch Nadia so Gabby could return to the hospital to support Bea. After changing out of her bloody clothes, Gabby took a couple of Advil for the pain in her arm and drove back to the hospital. She needed face-to-face time with the Johnson brothers to make her plan work.

After she arrived, she joined Bea at Joy's bedside. Even though the twins were fine, Bea had been micromanaging the hospital staff all night and prevented anybody from telling Joy that Allen had been shot. Joy was in so much pain, she probably wouldn't have remembered it anyway. She finally fell asleep after the doctors gave her some medicine.

Hoping for a moment alone, Gabby suggested to Bea that since Joy was asleep, she should go check on Allen. The second Bea left, Gabby reached into Joy's purse and pulled out her cell phone. When she turned it on, there were thirteen missed calls from Dean. She didn't know who was dumber: Dean for calling so many times or the police for not checking Joy's phone. Their stupid actions worked in her favor.

When Bea returned, Gabby went downstairs where the Johnson family was waiting for Allen to get out of surgery. She whispered to Bo that she could help him find Dean. Bo told Chuck, and they met Gabby outside in the hospital parking lot where she gave her Oscar-worthy performance.

A few minutes after her encounter with Bo and Chuck, Gabby was behind the wheel of her Lexus pulling out of the hospital parking lot. A silver Toyota Camry with Pennsylvania tags pulled in front of her and cut her off. To avoid hitting the car, she slammed on her brakes so hard her purse slid off the passenger seat, and all its contents spilled on the floor. She blasted her horn and the car sped away. "Stupid non-driving idiot!" she screamed, before proceeding out of the parking lot with the Johnson brothers following close behind in a black Suburban. Merging onto the Baltimore-Washington Parkway, she relaxed and smiled as she thought about how her plan to have the Johnson brothers kill Dean was falling into place.

Thirty minutes later, they pulled in the parking lot of the Red Roof Inn. The Johnson brothers jumped out of the Suburban and ordered Gabby to call Dean. Bo and Chuck paced around their truck looking like hungry pit bulls circling a piece of raw meat.

Gabby reached on the floor of the passenger side, picked up Joy's phone, and dialed Dean. She cleared her throat and took a deep breath. "Dean, I'm in the rear of the back parking lot."

Dean looked out his motel room window. "I don't see your car."

"Gabby let me borrow her truck in case the police followed me," she lied.

Dean hung up abruptly. Gabby wondered if he believed her. Minutes later, her concerns disappeared when she saw him stumbling down the steps wearing a black skullcap and a shearling coat. Waving the Johnson brothers away, she watched Dean zigzag across the parking lot. She knew he was intoxicated by the way his words slurred on the phone, but seeing him like this showed her he was drunker than she thought. Anger overcame her when she saw his face. The thought of him putting his gun to Joy's head and shoving it at her pregnant belly made Gabby want to put her gear in drive and run him down. The only reason she decided against it was that he might survive. She was depending on Bo and Chuck to torture Dean with a slow and painful death.

Before Dean reached her vehicle, Bo and Chuck grabbed him from behind, covered his mouth, and in one swift motion threw him in the back of their Suburban. *They've done this before,* Gabby thought. She tried to see what was going on inside the truck, but the windows were tinted. The truck rocked side to side and bounced up and down for what seemed like an eternity.

When the rocking finally stopped, Bo got out and approached Gabby's SUV with his chest heaving. "Give me Joy's phone and leave!"

"Don't raise your voice at me!" Gabby snapped back.

He looked angrily at Gabby as he moved closer to her SUV. "You starting to piss me the fuck off! Go home or go the same place he's going! Your choice." Bo snatched Joy's cell phone from her hand. The force caused some of her fingernail polish to chip and a couple of her nail tips to break off. "I'll take care of the phone. You were never here and this never happened. If I find out you talked to anybody, I'll break your fucking neck myself! Now get the fuck out of here!"

Gabby decided it was time to go home. All night, she'd had Bo on her side, and if he turned on her, there was nothing stopping him and Chuck from killing her, too. Besides, she could tell by the way they handled Dean; her presence was no longer needed. "I'm leaving," she snapped back, full of attitude.

As she rolled up her window, a car pulled in front of them. Breaking into a sweat, she looked at Bo with a tense expression and silently prayed for the car to drive away. The last thing she needed was somebody who could place her with the Johnson brothers at this motel tonight.

"Excuse me, but can you tell me which direction of the Beltway will get me back to downtown D.C.?" a male's voice asked.

Gabby was too nervous to look at the man. She didn't want him to see her so she kept her face turned to the side and her eyes on Bo.

"What the fuck we look like, tour guides? Get your ass out of here!" Bo shouted.

She watched the car drive away. It was a silver Toyota Corolla with Pennsylvania tags, just like the one that cut her off in the hospital parking lot earlier. Somebody was in the backseat looking back at them. *This was too much of a coincidence. Why would somebody follow me here, and what did they see?*

Chapter 3

The next morning, Joy woke up in the hospital with a pounding headache. She removed the oxygen mask covering her nose and exhaled slowly. The hospital monitors annoyingly echoed in the background, making her head hurt even more. Wires were attached to her stomach and fluids flowed into her arm through an IV. She tried to sit up, but the pain in her head wouldn't let her.

"What's wrong?" she asked in a groggy voice.

Bea and Juan ran to her bedside.

"You're okay, honey. You're at Washington Hospital Center," Bea explained in a soft, motherly tone. "The twins are fine, but you have a concussion."

Joy closed her eyes to process what Bea had just told her. *Why am I in the hospital and how did I get a concussion? Was I in a car accident?* She opened her eyes and looked around the room. Maxine and Gabby were sitting in chairs near the door with solemn looks on their faces. The memories of last night came flooding back.

Remembering the blood on the floor, Joy again tried to sit up, but the pain defeated her efforts. "Oh, my God! Where is Dean? Who did he hurt?"

Bea put her hand on Joy's shoulder and gently pressed her flat. Joy pushed her hand away. "Easy, Joy. Think about your babies."

Joy rubbed her baby bump. "Where's Allen? He should be here with me! Where is he?"

15

"I can't be in here for this. I'll be back," Maxine whispered to Gabby then stood to leave.

Gabby grabbed Maxine's arm, pulled her down, and whispered in her ear, "Get yourself together. We need to be strong for Joy."

Maxine yanked her arm from Gabby's grip. "I'll be in the hallway," she replied in a low tone, then left the room with tears in her eyes.

"Gabby, what's going on? What are you whispering about? Where's Allen? Oh, my God, where is he?" Joy broke down crying.

"Joy, I need to tell you something." Bea swallowed the hard lump forming in her throat and held Joy's hand between hers. "Last night, Dean shot Allen in the chest."

Joy gasped and coughed as she tried to catch her breath. "Not my baby! Not Allen! No!"

"Joy, stop and listen to me!" Bea insisted.

"No, I don't want to hear it! How am I going to live without Allen?" Joy cried.

"No, Joy! Listen to me, baby! He made it through surgery last night," Bea continued.

Joy froze in place and stared at Bea, desperate to hear more. "He did?" Although her head was pounding, she was more concerned about Allen than herself.

"Yes, baby. Allen is alive. He had a collapsed lung, but the bullet just missed his heart. He's already out of ICU and resting in his room. The doctors said he was lucky." Bea had tears in her eyes.

Joy closed her eyes and prayed. "Oh, thank God! Thank you!"

"Tyesha and Tyrese have been by his side all night and we've been checking on him, too," Bea added.

"I want to see him." Joy yanked the covers off her body.

"No, Joy! You need to let your doctors check you and the twins before you try to get out of this bed," Bea ordered.

"Not now, Bea. I need to see him. I need to be with Allen right now," Joy demanded.

"Let her go, Bea," Juan said. He hugged his daughter and kissed her cheek. "He's been asking for you since he woke up."

Bea protested, but when she saw how determined her daughter looked, she called a nurse to help unhook Joy from the fetal monitor and other wires connected to her body. The nurse and Bea helped Joy into a wheelchair and then they proceeded to Allen's room.

Detective Briggs and a police officer were standing outside of Joy's room. They looked eager to talk to her as they rushed to follow her wheelchair.

"Can she answer a few questions now? We still haven't been able to locate her husband," Detective Briggs said.

Juan positioned himself between Joy's wheelchair and Detective Briggs. "We answered all your questions last night. She's in this hospital because of what her sorry-ass husband did. Leave my daughter alone and go find Dean. He's the one you should be questioning." Juan turned around and walked with Bea and Joy to Allen's room.

Joy wondered where Dean could be and if he would be bold enough to show up at the hospital. She wanted to talk to the cops after she saw Allen, because they needed to find Dean as soon as possible. She wanted him captured before he hurt anyone else she cared about.

Bea pushed Joy into Allen's room. Tyesha and Tyrese were asleep in chairs, dressed in the same clothes they had on for the Christmas dinner. The creaking sound of the door opening and Joy's squeaky wheelchair woke them up. Joy's eyes searched the room for Allen. Tears flowed down her face when she saw him lying motionless in his hospital bed. The guilt she felt was unbearable.

"Is it alright for me to spend some time with him?" Joy asked Tyesha and Tyrese. She wasn't sure how they felt about her since she was the reason Allen got shot.

"Girl, why are you asking that? Of course, Joy." Tyesha hugged her. "I'm glad to see you up."

"Me too. He's been asking for you," Tyrese said before he hugged Joy.

Bea pushed Joy's wheelchair to Allen's bedside. Everyone left to give them some privacy.

Joy touched his cheek gently. She stood and kissed him lightly on his lips then sat back down because she felt dizzy.

He opened his eyes and smiled when he saw her. "Hi, beautiful," he whispered.

"Hi, baby. I'm so sorry."

"No, not your fault. You okay?" Allen talked as if every word was a struggle.

"Yes, I'm fine." He had been through too much for her to whine about her headache.

"Babies?"

Joy stood and placed Allen's hand on her baby bump. "They're fine. It feels like they're playing soccer right now."

"Good. Love you." He closed his eyes and fell asleep with a smile on his face.

Joy spent the next twenty minutes in her wheelchair staring at Allen as he slept. She told him repeatedly how much she loved him and couldn't wait to spend the rest of her life with him. She let him know that the second her divorce from Dean was finalized, she was going to marry him and spend the rest of her days making him happy. She caressed his arm and face and smiled as she thought about her future with Allen and their twins.

A nurse entered the room and smiled at Joy. "Hello. Sorry to interrupt your visit, but I need to replace his fluids and take his vitals."

"No problem," Joy replied as she used her legs to push her wheelchair back to give the nurse access to Allen.

Joy and the nurse talked while she performed her duties. The way she cared for Allen and her pleasant personality made Joy instantly like her. For the first time since she woke up, she relaxed a little, knowing Allen had someone taking good care of him. When the nurse pulled the covers back to check his wound, he opened his eyes.

"How are you feeling, Mr. Johnson?" the nurse asked in a caring tone.

Allen smiled. "I've been better."

"I know you have. The doctor will be in to check on you soon." She changed Allen's bandage and put the covers back over him. "Alright now! I have other patients to tend to, Mr. Johnson, so you behave yourself or your lady friend will have to leave." She winked at Joy. "I just gave him something for pain, so he'll probably fall asleep soon. That'll be a good time for you to get some rest, too."

"I will, and thanks for taking good care of him." Joy rolled her wheelchair back to Allen's bedside.

"You're welcome, sweetie. That's why they pay me the big bucks," the nurse joked then left the room.

Joy chuckled as she stood to give Allen another kiss on his lips. "I'm not leaving your side, baby, until they kick me out."

Allen looked Joy in her eyes and whispered, "Good." He closed his eyes and fell asleep.

A cell phone rang on the table near the chairs where Tyesha and Tyrese were sitting earlier. She could tell by the ringtone it was Allen's phone. She didn't want it to disturb him so she rolled her wheelchair over to answer it.

"Hello." Joy could hear a lot of background noise, but no one said anything. "Hello."

"Is Allen available?" a female voice asked sharply.

"No, he's not. May I take a message?" Joy asked, curious to know who it was.

"Is this Joy?" the female asked in an annoyed manner.

"Who wants to know?" Joy answered abruptly, irritated by the woman's tone.

The call ended.

Joy wanted to call the number back to set the rude female straight, but Allen called out to her from his bed. She changed her mind because she wasn't going to let anyone interfere with her precious time with Allen. She knew Bea would be back in the room any minute demanding she go back to her bed. She turned the phone off and put it back on the table. Since the caller knew her name, she assumed it was one of Allen's outspoken ghetto nieces calling to check on him and the call was dropped.

By the time Joy had rolled back to Allen's bedside to see

what he needed, he had fallen asleep again. She watched him, continuing to think about their future together with a big smile on her face. She was massaging her temples, trying to relieve her headache, when Bo walked in the room and hugged her.

"Wassup, Joy? How is he?"

"Hi, Bo. He's doing better than I thought. Did you talk to Tyesha?"

"Yeah, she told me everything that happened and I was here when the doctors came out after his surgery." Bo sat in a chair and watched Joy as she rubbed Allen's face.

"Oh, okay." She nodded and continued to stare at Allen lovingly. "They haven't found him, Bo, and I'm sorry this happened."

Bo rubbed Joy's back. "Nobody blames you for this. You a victim just like Allen. That motherfucker was sick in the head."

Joy nodded in agreement with tears in her eyes as she thought about everything Dean did to them. She was still concerned for Allen's safety, and needed to make sure someone was with him at all times. Dean was persistent and she knew he wasn't going to give up until she and Allen paid for hurting him.

"The police are downstairs waiting to talk to me. Bo, what do you think about me asking them to place an officer outside of Allen's door in case Dean comes here? They can't find him, and I don't want him to do anything else to Allen." Joy wiped her tears.

"That's not necessary, girl. We'll be here to protect him. Now, how you and my niece and nephew doing?" Bo changed the subject to take Joy's mind off Dean.

"We're fine. I'm more concerned about Allen's safety. Can you promise me somebody will stay with him until they catch Dean? He looks so weak..." Joy fought back her tears.

"I got you. No problems, no worries," Bo said reassuringly as he hugged Joy.

"Thanks, Bo. I'll probably have to go stay with Bea or Poppy until they catch him. He's crazy enough to come back to my house, and I can't risk anything happening to my babies." Joy looked down and rubbed her stomach. "I won't feel safe until they catch him."

Bo looked at Joy's worried face and knew he needed to tell

her the truth to put her mind at ease. He pulled his chair closer to Joy's wheelchair and whispered, "Allen's safe and you're free now, Joy. No more problems from your ex. Trust me, no worries. You can thank me by keeping that happy smile on my lil' bro's face."

Joy felt relieved. She smiled and said, "That's what I live for, Bo. Thank you."

"I always got your back, lil' sis. Later." He kissed Joy on her cheek, patted Allen's arm, then left.

The Johnsons must be rubbing off on me because I wasn't affected at all by Bo hinting to me that he killed my husband. Now she understood why the police couldn't find Dean. There was no way the Johnson brothers were going to let him just go to jail after what he did to them. Allen was their golden child and Joy was carrying his twins. Hurting them the way Dean did was a guaranteed execution. *I'm finally free from Dean*, Joy thought as she stood to kiss Allen's lips again. She couldn't stop smiling because there was nothing stopping her and Allen from getting married now. Finally, she could look forward to her future.

MONICA MATHIS-STOWE

Chapter 4

The following morning, Maxine sat up in bed, stretched her arms over her head, then cursed under her breath when she looked at the alarm clock. It was almost eleven o'clock, and she hadn't planned to stay long. She spent yesterday at the hospital with Joy. On her way home late last night, she stopped by to visit her sons, but they were with Trent's mother, Gloria. She decided to stay for a quickie that lasted almost three hours and put her in a semi-coma.

Getting out of bed without a stitch of clothing on, she went into the bathroom. When she opened the door, a cloud of steam floated into the bedroom and the shower radio was on full blast playing the latest Beyoncé song. She shook her head and sighed as she stepped over a pair of boxers and a T-shirt to get to the toilet. After she released her morning pee and rinsed with mouthwash a couple of times, she pulled the shower curtain back and stepped in the bathtub.

"Maxi? That you?" Trent asked as he used his fingertips to massage shampoo in his hair.

"Of course it is. Who else would it be?" She reached up and turned the volume down on the radio hanging from the showerhead.

He rinsed the shampoo from his head and face before he answered. "Oh... I thought you were sleeping in after I wore you out last night."

She laughed as she pushed him aside so she could get under the running water. It was hot, just the way she liked it. "Is that right? Since you were up before me, does that mean I didn't handle my business last night?"

"I wouldn't say that." Trent gave her a seductive smirk before he pulled her close to him and rubbed a bar of soap over her wet skin. She moaned with pleasure when he slid the soap over her erect nipples while he massaged her clitoris with his fingers. She reached behind her and stroked his hard manhood. Trent dropped the soap, turned Maxine around, and picked her up. She wrapped her legs around his waist and kissed him passionately as the water cascaded over their bodies.

He pressed her up against the back of the shower wall and thrust himself inside her. His feet slid from under him and they fell to the bottom of the tub. Without skipping a beat, Maxine lay on her back and stretched her legs out toward him. He raised her legs in the air and entered her again. He stroked her slowly and pinched her nipples between his fingers as the warm water fell on their naked bodies. With each stroke, Maxine groaned and begged for more. Her pleas made him move faster and deeper inside her. The feeling of warm water falling on them and the sound of their naked bodies smacking together had them wild with ecstasy. Maxine cried out in pleasure as her body shook from the impact of her orgasm. A few seconds later, Trent's body stiffened as he released his juices inside her and fell back in the tub, barely missing the faucet.

They showered and returned to the bedroom to get dressed. Maxine smiled at Trent as she put on the same pair of blue jeans and Morgan State University sweatshirt she had on the day before. She made a mental note to pack an overnight bag to leave here in case this happened again. She couldn't stand wearing the same underwear more than once, and the thought of using somebody else's toothbrush made her gag. As she sat on the bed and tied her tennis shoes, she realized how much she still loved Trent.

"Thanks for a wonderful visit, but I need to get out of here." She went to the dresser and used Trent's brush to wrap her damp hair around her head.

Trent put his arms around her narrow waist. "Don't go. I called in sick so we could spend the day together." He slowly kissed the side of her neck.

"I wish I could, but I have a lot to do and I haven't talked to anyone since I left the hospital last night." She put the brush on the dresser and turned around to hug him. "I'll try to come back later."

"Can you stay for breakfast?" Trent poked out his bottom lip and stared at her with pleading eyes.

Maxine looked at her watch. "It's almost one o'clock. You mean lunch, don't you?"

Trent chuckled. "Let me cook you something before you go." He gave her a quick peck before he left for the kitchen.

While he was cooking, she changed the sheets and made the bed because she knew he wasn't going to do it. The smell of bacon filled the apartment and she couldn't wait to eat. Trent cooking instead of expecting her to do it was a definite sign of how much he had changed. Good sex and cooked meals still weren't enough for her to take him back, but he was heading in the right direction.

Trent had just finished scrambling eggs when he heard a knock on the door. Turning off the burner, he dropped two slices of wheat bread in the toaster, and pressed the lever down. At the door, he looked through the peephole and immediately frowned. *Oh, shit! This is not good*, he thought before he unlocked and opened the door.

Dr. Jim burst through with a tight face and squinted eyes. "Where is Maxine? And don't tell me she's not here because I saw her minivan out front."

"She's in the bedroom, Dad." Trent pointed toward the bedroom.

Dr. Jim wrapped both his hands around Trent's neck and squeezed as tight as he could. "Don't ever call me your dad. No son of mine would ever do to a woman what you did to my daughter!"

Maxine was in the bathroom sprinkling Comet in the tub when she heard the scream. She dropped the can and ran toward the living room to find out what all the commotion was about. When she saw her father's hands around Trent's neck, she screamed, "Daddy, stop! Stop!"

Trent tried to loosen Dr. Jim's grip, but he was no match for

25

the older man's strength. Trent felt his eyes rolling back in his head and his body going limp. At the sound of his daughter's voice, Dr. Jim let go. Trent fell to the floor, coughing and gasping for air.

Dr. Jim got in Trent's face again. "In the future, you are to call me Dr. Crawford and address my wife as Mrs. Crawford. Maxine may be willing to forgive you, but her parents aren't."

Maxine stood in front of her father. "Stop it! What are you doing here?"

"You need to ask yourself that very question," Dr. Jim snapped. "When you didn't come home last night, we were worried. Nobody had heard from you and your phone went straight to voicemail."

"I'm sorry. My battery died and I didn't plan on staying here." She looked down and swallowed hard.

"You should know better after all the mess that went down with Joy's husband. He's still on the loose and you don't think to call to let us know you're okay!"

"I'm sorry, Daddy." She reached out to hug him, but he stepped back.

"I don't wanna hear it." He pointed at Trent. "To be with a man who beat and almost killed you is utter foolishness! Think, Maxine!"

Trent stood. Struggling to control his coughing, he rubbed his neck. "I would never hit—"

"Shut the hell up, Trent! You already did," Dr. Jim shouted. "Starting today, I'll pray and ask God to show my daughter what kind of weak son of a bitch you really are! My daughter and grandsons are better off without you."

After Trent took several long, deep breaths, he felt strong enough to confront Dr. Jim. He turned toward him and declared, "I love my family, sir. I mean, Dr. Crawford."

Trent's words angered Dr. Jim even more. Rage ripped through him as he grabbed Trent by his shoulders and forcefully raised his knee to Trent's groin, twice. Trent fell to the floor like a sack of bricks. He curled up in a fetal position with his face twisted into a combination of fury and agony. Holding his stomach, he gagged, then vomited on the carpet.

Maxine dropped to her knees to help him. "Oh my God, Daddy! Stop this!"

Dr. Jim stood over Trent with his hands balled into fists. "If you hurt my daughter or my grandsons, I'll kill you. If I see that she's unhappy, I'm coming for you. Not for an explanation, but to end your life."

Trent raised his hand and tried to speak, but the pain in his groin wouldn't let him.

"Daddy, why are you doing this? Just leave!" Maxine pleaded as tears rolled down her cheeks.

"I wanted him to pay ever since I watched you in the hospital having seizure after seizure because of him." Dr. Jim stared at Trent with pure hate. "Why, Maxine? Why would you go back to him?" Dr. Jim asked, full of rage.

"Because he's my husband and I love him." Maxine used her sweatshirt to wipe the vomit from Trent's lips. "He's a good man, Daddy. He saved our lives yesterday."

Dr. Jim shook his head as tears formed in his eyes. "As your parents, we gave you everything. We raised you up in the church, paid for not one, but two college degrees, and even purchased you a house after you got married to give you a good start in life. But what do you do? You go back to a man who caused you nothing but pain! What about the almost $300,000 worth of debt he's saddled you with? You'll never be able to retire!" Dr. Jim let out a deep sigh. "I guess we forgot to teach you some goddamn common sense. I don't support this reconciliation. As a matter of fact, I want you out of my house. You have until tomorrow evening to remove your things. I'm not going to let your poor judgment upset your mother."

Tears streamed down Maxine's face as she watched her father yank the door open and stomp out of the apartment. She sat on the floor stunned and silent as her father's words sunk in.

"Don't worry, Maxi. You and the boys can move in here with me," Trent mumbled.

Maxine's stomach did somersaults at the thought of living with Trent again. She was content with the occasional booty-call and short visits, but a permanent living arrangement with him terrified her. She took a few minutes to think about her options and had to stop herself from screaming when she realized she didn't have anywhere else to go.

$\mathcal{C}$hapter 5

The day before New Year's Eve, Gabby stood in the middle of Joy's living room, dressed in black, boot-cut jeans and a peach V-neck sweater. She tapped her black-leather boot on the mahogany floor and snapped her fingers as she looked around the room. "This doesn't work for me either." She pointed at two green and beige armchairs. "Place one on each side of the fireplace. I like them better over there."

"Damn, lady! We moved these same two chairs six times already. Make up your mind," the furniture delivery guy with dreads snapped.

Gabby gave him a cold stare. "Do I have to remind you that I own you until six o'clock? Maybe I should call your boss and tell him how unsatisfied I am with your service."

"Naw, we good," he replied quickly. He needed his job. He exhaled deeply before he had one of his co-workers help him move the chairs by the fireplace again.

Gabby tossed two throw pillows in each chair and wondered if Joy would like it. After the crime scene investigators left Joy's living room in shambles, she asked Gabby to help Juan redecorate. Gabby looked forward to finally giving Joy's house some much-needed style. Interior decorating was her passion, and nothing made her happier. She immediately came up with an all-white theme for Joy's living room at a cost of about ten thousand dollars. Joy quickly nixed the idea. She gave Gabby a check for twenty-five hundred dollars and told her to make the room family-friendly with a sleeper sofa and darker colors. Gabby wasn't happy, but she made it work. She even spent a thousand dollars of her own money to get the look she wanted. It was the least she could do since she'd been living there ever since her husband, William, committed suicide a few months ago.

It took forever, but she finally picked a furniture arrangement. The delivery guys left two hours later. Juan stopped by briefly to install a flat-screen television he bought Joy for Christmas and to hang some pictures Gabby purchased. She added a few accessories to complete the room and stood near the living room's entrance to inspect her work.

The doorbell rang. She ran to answer it because Nadia was napping upstairs. Looking out the peephole, she gasped when she saw Rayshawn standing there. She quickly opened the door.

"What are you doing here?" Gabby stared at him with both hands on her hips and her head cocked to the side.

Rayshawn pushed past her and marched in the house with a white, plastic bag in his hand. "I'm here to see my daughter, you lying bitch."

Gabby rolled her eyes and followed him. "Be quiet, Rayshawn! Nadia is napping."

Rayshawn got close to Gabby's face. "Fuck that! Wake her up 'cause I'm here to take her with me."

Gabby took a couple of steps back and placed her hand over her nose. "First, go get a mint for your stinkin' breath, and then go get a life."

"Go get my daughter," Rayshawn ordered.

Gabby was angry, but she needed to remain composed because Rayshawn had every right to be mad at her. While she and Nadia were in Baltimore the week after Thanksgiving, she promised him visitation with his daughter, but didn't keep her word. Instead, she'd been ducking his calls, and when she did answer, she lied to him about Nadia being sick or them having other plans.

"You didn't answer my question. Why are you here?" Gabby asked calmly.

"I'm here for my daughter! Where was she at when you was getting shot at?" Rayshawn asked with the veins in his temples throbbing.

Now Rayshawn had Gabby's attention. She was at a loss for words, wondering where he got his information, because she hadn't told him or anybody else about the shooting, and her name wasn't mentioned in the newspaper article. "Somebody gave you some wrong information. I've never been shot."

"Bullshit!" Rayshawn dropped his bag and grabbed Gabby's arm. "Which arm is it?"

She snatched her arm from Rayshawn's grip, narrowed her eyes at him, and pointed at the front door. "Get out!"

"I ain't going no damn where until I have my daughter with me!" He picked the bag off the floor and took a book out of it. He handed it to Gabby. "You need to look at this."

Gabby studied Rayshawn like he had just lost his mind, then she turned her attention to the book.

He cleared his throat. "It's called a dossier. Do you know what that is?"

Gabby crossed her arms over her chest and continued to stare at the book he was pointing at her. "I know what a dossier is, Rayshawn. Why do you want me to see it?"

"Because it's all about you," he announced with a devious smirk.

She grabbed the book from him, went into the living room, sat down, and opened it. The first picture was of her dead husband, William, hanging from the ceiling in her old bedroom. After news broke of her affair with Rayshawn, his marriage ended, and he decided to tell William that Nadia was his child, not William's. She struggled for breath as memories of that horrible day came flooding back. Behind William's pictures were sworn affidavits from William's family stating he killed himself after he found out Nadia wasn't his daughter. Gabby slammed the book shut and threw it at Rayshawn who was now sitting beside her on the couch.

He blocked the book with his hand and it landed on the floor. He picked it up and said, "My lawyers hired this private detective from Pennsylvania to get information on you after you lied about letting me see my daughter."

That's who was following me in the Toyota with Pennsylva-

nia tags. "Okay, you have a book full of lies. Now, get out!" Gabby shouted.

He let out a deep belly laugh. "I got a lot of interesting information on you." He handed her the book again. "You need to look at this if you wanna keep full custody of my daughter."

Gabby refused to take the book again. "Okay, Rayshawn, you have a few pictures and people telling lies about me. What is that going to accomplish?"

"I have proof of every horrible thing you did since I met you," Rayshawn bragged. "I told you one day I was gonna get your ass back for all the shit you put me through, and today is the day, bitch!"

Gabby rolled her eyes. "Oh, really?"

"Oh, yeah. You know, I never figured you for a Red Roof Inn type of chick."

"What!" Gabby froze.

Rayshawn opened the book again and showed her a picture of Allen lying on the living room floor after he had been shot, then another picture with Allen's brothers standing outside the hospital talking to her; the last picture was Bo standing beside her Lexus in the Red Roof Inn parking lot.

"How did you get these pictures?" Gabby asked as she snatched the book from Rayshawn to look through it more closely.

"Didn't you know emergency personnel take pictures of everything these days? My private detective was very thorough. He took some pictures of you and used his connections at the police department to get the other copies. The shit he got on you blew my mind." Rayshawn laughed and pointed at Dean's picture. "Check it out. The private detective thinks you took these thugs to the guy who shot you and your girl's man and that's how he ended up missing."

Gabby swallowed hard, shaking inside. "What do you expect me to do? Give you custody of Nadia? I'll never do that," she stated firmly.

"I have the power. I can have the private detective call the police right now and give them this information. They'll bring you in and question you about it and being questioned about a man's disappearance won't look good for your ass in court. My lawyers already told me with everything I have on you, I can get full custody with no problem, but I'm not as heartless as you. I know Nadia needs you. All girls need that bond with their mothers."

Tears formed in her eyes. Her involvement in Dean's disappearance was the only thing in Rayshawn's dossier that had her concerned. Everything else could be explained away by her attorney if they went to court, but she didn't want it to go that far. She feared what the Johnson brothers would do to her if they knew she was questioned by the police.

"Rayshawn, don't underestimate me. When you push me in a corner, I come out swinging." Gabby stared at him angrily.

"I know that from experience; that's why I told everybody and their momma, if anything ever happens to me, to look for you. You might have those same thugs do something to me, too, but you'll definitely go to jail for it."

Tears rolled down Gabby's face. "Is this your way of trying to get me back in your bed?"

Rayshawn laughed out loud. "Fuck that shit! I don't want you! Your pussy cost me too goddamn much!"

Gabby wanted to snatch his tongue out of his mouth and choke him with it. She knew he wouldn't pass up sleeping with her again if she propositioned him, but she wasn't that desperate. "What do you want then?"

Rayshawn rubbed his hands together. "Thanks for asking. First, I want my baby girl to go to Georgia with me. I'll bring her back in three weeks when I come back to town on business. Next, I wanna drop the child support payment in half starting next month. Finally, I want a set visitation schedule."

"I'll think about it," Gabby said quietly.

"You don't have a choice. You have more to lose than I do. I'm smarter than you. My lawyers are smarter than your lawyers. Remember when you said that shit to me? And if you don't do what I want, I'll give this information to the police and get custody of my daughter when you go to jail. Either way, I win." Rayshawn smiled smugly.

Gabby was speechless. She dropped her head in her hands,

closed her eyes, and thought about everything Rayshawn said. *I don't want to lose my daughter and I don't want Allen's brothers to think I talked to the police.* She didn't see a way out of this without losing her daughter or her life. After a few minutes, she pulled herself together and shouted, "I'm tired of fighting you, Rayshawn!"

"Then stop doing it 'cause I ain't going no damn where. She's my daughter and I love her." He patted the book to remind Gabby she was in no position to call the shots. "C'mon, Gabby. You making this shit harder than it needs to be."

Gabby sighed. "Okay. She can go, but you better take care of my baby and I'm gonna call you every day."

Rayshawn hunched his shoulders. "Oh, I take care of all my children so your phone calls aren't necessary."

"Just answer my phone calls. I'll go get her ready."

As she walked upstairs to get Nadia, she knew her days of trying to keep Rayshawn away from her daughter were over. After all this time, he finally had control and she had to figure out a way to get it back. After she packed Nadia's clothes, she sat on the bed and thought everything over. Within a few minutes, she smiled to herself because she knew exactly what she needed to do to put Rayshawn back in his place.

Chapter 6

Joy stepped out of the front passenger seat of her father's car and looked at the red brick building across the parking lot. Her legs shook so badly she could barely stand straight. Her parents looked at her with concern as they got out of the car. It was New Year's Eve and she had been on bed rest since her release from the hospital two days ago. Although she was supposed to remain in bed until her doctor appointment next week, she received a call she couldn't ignore.

After Juan locked his car, they started the dreadful walk across the parking lot to their destination. Bea held Joy's shaking hand in hers as Juan opened the door for them to enter the building. It was times like this that made Joy appreciate her parents. She was so glad that even though her mom never forgave her dad for cheating on her all those years ago, they both still understood the importance of being there for Joy. Actually, it was remarkable, considering they were only teenagers when Joy was born.

An elderly man at the front desk looked over his glasses at them as they approached his desk. "How can I help you?" he asked.

Joy's cell phone rang before anyone could answer. She released Bea's hand and pulled the phone out of her purse. She frowned and hit the Ignore button.

"Ma'am, no cell phones are allowed in the building," the man said as he looked at Joy with squinted eyes.

"Sorry," Joy replied.

"Who was it?" Bea asked, eagerly.

Joy looked at Bea with tight lips and sighed. "It was Allen."

"We can wait a few minutes while you go outside and call him. He should know about this," Bea stated firmly.

"I'll call him when we leave," Joy replied as she turned off her phone and gave it to the man at the desk.

Bea looked at Juan and shook her head disapprovingly. He ignored her and gave the guard his phone after he turned it off.

"I'll call him for you. Of all the people in the world, he should be the one to hear about this," Bea said, staring directly at Joy.

"No, Bea! I don't want to worry him until I know for sure!" Joy snapped as she looked at her mother with an annoyed glare.

"Bea, let Joy handle this her way. We're just here to support her," Juan added in his thick Puerto Rican accent.

Bea sighed and smacked her lips as she turned off her phone and gave it to the man behind the desk. Although she didn't agree with Joy and Juan, she wasn't going to make an already stressful situation worse by insisting Joy tell Allen about this.

The man behind the desk called a security guard to escort them to their location. As they followed him down a long, wide hall, Bea took Joy's hand in hers again and held it close. Juan walked quietly beside them.

When the elevator doors opened, the guard said, "I'm taking you to the basement where one of the assistant medical examiners will help you. I suggest you keep your coats on 'cause it gets quite nippy down there."

The strained smile on the guard's face only made Joy more nervous. It was like he knew after she left here today, her life would never be the same. The elevator shook slightly and came to an abrupt stop. When they stepped out, a man in a white lab coat was standing there. He introduced himself as Felix and asked them to follow him. They walked a few feet down another wide hall and turned a corner. Dean's parents were sitting in one of the offices. When they saw Joy, they came out and gave her a reserved hug and barely spoke to Juan and Bea.

"Thanks for coming, Joy. I know you're still recovering, but it's the law here for the spouse to identify the body..." Mrs. Bennett turned her head to hold back her tears.

Joy rubbed her arm. "It's no problem."

"Are you ready to go in or do you need a few minutes?" Felix asked.

"We're ready," Joy answered in a quivering voice.

"This way, please," Felix instructed.

Everyone followed him. He pushed a button to open two swing doors, and they entered a room. The strong scent of chemicals had them all covering their noses and mouths with their hands. Gleaming steel tables were lined up neatly across the back and side walls. He showed them where to stand, then walked to a table in the middle of the room. A large figure covered by a white sheet was on the table. Felix looked at them before he slowly pulled the cover back.

Joy unconsciously moved closer to get a better look. Bea and Juan stayed by her side. The further he pulled the cover back, the more nauseous Joy felt. As she looked down at the body on the table, she felt her stomach in her throat. She refused to scream or cry. After everything he did to her, she refused to play the grieving wife or act like she wasn't happy he was dead. *He deserved this.*

She couldn't take her eyes off his corpse. The right side of his face was black and purple and swollen beyond recognition. His right eye was the size of a large egg, the bone around it shattered, and the left side of his face drooped down as if he'd had a stroke. Brain matter and fluids leaked out. His curly, black hair was matted with dried blood. Joy got light-headed and the room started spinning. She lost her balance as she turned to hold the wall for support. Juan caught her and with Bea's help, they took her in the hallway and sat her in one of the chairs.

"It's Dean. He's dead," she whispered, repeatedly.

From inside the room, Dean's mother let out a loud shrill sound and cried Dean's name over and over until her husband dragged her kicking and screaming from the room. He sat her in one of the chairs near Joy and held her until she didn't have the energy to scream anymore.

Forty minutes later, after they regrouped, everyone was escorted into a conference room. Joy didn't need to see Detective Briggs seated at the head of the large conference table to know he was there. Since her release from the hospital, he had visited her every day at Bea's house with updates on the case. After he left, Bea would open all the windows to air the house out. Joy swore he worked alone, because nobody wanted to smell his stinky cologne. They took their seats around the table and looked at him.

"First, let me say how sorry I am for your loss," Detective Briggs said.

"Ummm," Bea muttered, then cleared her throat.

Juan and Joy shot her a look to behave.

"Who did this to our son?" Mr. Bennett asked.

"Your son's death has been ruled a homicide." Briggs looked at Joy and her parents for a reaction.

Juan rested his elbows on the table and glared at Detective Briggs. "Maybe I should call my lawyer."

Detective Briggs gave Juan a half-smile. "That's totally up to you, but Mr. Bennett's murderer has been arrested," he announced.

Joy's heart kicked in her chest as her pulse raced. She didn't want Bo or any of the Johnson brothers to go to jail for killing Dean. She swallowed the lump forming in her throat as she tried to hold back her tears. Her marriage to Dean screwed up so many lives. *How is Allen ever going to forgive me if one of his brothers goes to jail for killing Dean?*

Detective Briggs took two eight-by-ten photos out of a manila folder. He slid one toward Mr. and Mrs. Bennett and another in Joy and her parents' direction. They stared at the mug shot with furrowed brows.

"Is this who killed our son?" Mr. Bennett asked.

"Do any of you recognize him?" Detective Briggs asked.

Joy recognized him immediately. She had seen him a few times with Chuck but had never talked to him. She assumed Bo did it after they talked in Allen's hospital room the day after the shooting. *Why would this guy be willing to go to jail for it?* Joy had a lot of questions, but she knew not to ask any of the Johnson brothers.

She knew about their criminal reputation, but this was proof they were more powerful and dangerous than she ever imagined.

When everybody answered no, the detective sat quietly for a few seconds and looked at each one of them before he resumed talking. "Based on our investigation, Dean Bennett checked himself into the Red Roof Inn in Lanham after he fled his wife's house."

"You mean after he shot Allen!" Joy interjected angrily.

Detective Briggs nodded, then continued, "The motel cameras show him leaving his room, but he didn't go to his car. Since there were three empty vodka bottles in his room, we assumed he walked to the closest liquor store, which was across the street from the motel. The store's surveillance cameras weren't working, but a clerk remembered seeing him because he paid with a fifty-dollar bill and forgot his change."

Mr. Bennett tossed the picture at Detective Briggs. "How did this man end up killing our son? That's what we need to know."

"Your son never made it back to his motel room. The assailant, Marques Brown, also known as Peanut, was pulled over on a routine traffic stop last night. He had two guns in his possession; one was registered to Mr. Bennett. The arresting officers also discovered Mr. Bennett's wallet in the stolen vehicle."

"How did he know Dean?" Mrs. Bennett asked, anxiously.

"He didn't. During Mr. Brown's interrogation, he admitted to seeing Dean leave the liquor store and followed him with every intent to rob him. They got into a fight. Dean pulled out his gun but dropped it. Mr. Brown picked it up, shot Dean in the head, and disposed of his body in a stream a few miles away."

Mrs. Bennett started crying again. "Like a piece of trash."

Bea chuckled. "Isn't that something? He was murdered with the same gun he held to my daughter's head. God is good."

Mr. and Mrs. Bennett shot daggers at Bea with their eyes.

Detective Briggs cleared his throat. "I'm sorry. Mr. Brown has been in and out of jail for most of his life. He was released a year ago after serving time on a home invasion charge and was out on bail awaiting trial for a felony theft charge when he killed your son."

"Unbelievable! Doesn't the Three Strikes Law apply in this state?" Mr. Bennett asked.

"Yes, and he's going away for a very long time, Mr. Bennett." Detective Briggs stood and gathered his things to leave. "Again, I'm sorry for your loss. If you have any questions, you can reach me at any of these numbers." He gave everybody his business card before he left.

Mrs. Briggs wiped her eyes and regained her composure. "I'm sorry my son hurt so many people." She looked at Joy. "I know you said the children you're carrying aren't Dean's, but we would like to get a paternity test done to make sure."

"Why?" Joy stared at Mr. and Mrs. Bennett with wide eyes.

Bea bristled with outrage. "These aren't your grandchildren. Dean wasn't their father. Your son shot their father and now he's in the hospital recuperating." She pointed at Juan and herself. "We are the only living grandparents these children have."

Mrs. Bennett ignored Bea and spoke directly to Joy. "I don't trust you. You'll hear from our family attorney. We want a paternity test done as soon as possible. If they are our grandchildren, we're going to sue you for visitation."

"What!" Joy screamed.

Bea pointed her index finger at Mrs. Bennett. "You better be careful, lady! Threatening my child will get you a permanent spot in that room with your son. He knew these weren't his children and like you, he didn't want to accept it."

Juan banged his fists on the conference table. "Enough! Hasn't your son put my daughter through enough already! Now you threaten to take my grandchildren!"

"Everybody calm down! I'll agree to a paternity test, but only after the twins are born. Doing one now will put them at risk for a premature birth and I'm not going to do that." Joy rubbed her temples trying to stop the migraine she felt coming on. It was shocking to see both her parents this upset at the same time. Bea was always fussing and threatening somebody for one reason or another, but Juan was usually low-key and mellow.

Mr. Bennett looked at his wife and nodded. "Of course. We

don't want to risk our grandchildren's lives any more than you do, but if you change your mind, you will hear from our attorney."

"Didn't I just tell you about threatening my daughter!" Bea yelled at the Bennetts.

"Let's go!" Joy grabbed Bea's hand and followed Juan out of the conference room.

During the hour-long ride back to Bea's house, Joy begged her mother not to tell anyone about Dean until she talked to Allen first. As they walked in the house, Bea kept telling her to call Allen. Joy ignored her and went straight to her old bedroom and lay across the bed to stop the pounding in her head. Every time she closed her eyes, visions of Dean's corpse appeared. She sat up, ate a few crackers she had in her purse, and took a couple of pain pills her doctor prescribed.

Bea pounded on the bedroom door.

"What is it, Bea?" Joy asked impatiently. Whether Juan and Gabby were finished redecorating her house or not, she was definitely going home tomorrow.

"It's Allen. He wants to talk to you," Bea yelled through the door.

No, she didn't! "Didn't I tell you I was going to call him, Bea? Hang up and I'll call him on my cell."

"Hurry up. Tyesha said he was leaving the hospital against medical advice because he thought something was wrong when we didn't answer our phones. Um-hum, I told you to call him earlier."

"I'm calling him now, Bea." Joy rushed to use the bathroom first.

She sat on the edge of the bed and reached for the house phone, but changed her mind, because she knew Bea would be on the other line listening. She turned on her cell phone and dialed Allen's hospital room.

"Hello," Allen answered in an irritated tone.

"Hey, baby! How you feel?" Joy asked in a calm voice.

"What the hell is going on? I've been calling you for the past three hours. When you didn't answer your phone, I thought something had happened to you, especially when Juan and Bea didn't answer theirs either." Allen pushed himself to a sitting position, because he was getting agitated.

"I'm sorry. I didn't want to upset you until I knew for sure," Joy explained.

"Too late for that. Bea told me everything. I'm glad that motherfucker is dead! Good riddance!" The pain in Allen's chest caused him to grind his teeth and lie back in his hospital bed. "And why would you agree to do a paternity test on my children without talking it over with me first?"

"Everybody was so upset and it happened so fast. I—"

"You can let them know that the paternity test is not going to happen and if they have a problem with it, tell them to come see the man their son shot!"

"Allen, please calm down, baby," Joy pleaded.

"Calm down? It's hard to calm down when my children aren't even born yet, and they're already caught up in your drama. Is this shit ever gonna end, Joy? Look, I'll talk to you tomorrow. I got company." He slammed the phone in Joy's ear.

Chapter 7

Maxine hesitated before she rang the doorbell. She shifted from one foot to the other as her fingers gripped the handles on her purse and a bag of food she was carrying. It was Joy's first day back home, so Maxine had cooked some food and planned to spend the day with her girlfriends. Now she was having doubts. She wanted to tell Joy and Gabby about the changes in her life since the last time they saw her, but she knew they were going to be just as upset as her parents.

Maxine jumped when Gabby opened the door.

"Maxine? I saw you pull up a few minutes ago. What took you so long to get out of the car?" Gabby looked Maxine up and down before she stepped back to let her enter.

"Oh, girl, I was just trying to make sure I had everything before I came in. That's all. Happy New Year!" Maxine stepped inside, set her purse and bag on the floor, and hugged Gabby.

"Thanks, but what's so happy about it?" Gabby crossed her arms over her chest and frowned as she watched Maxine take off her coat and hang it in a closet near the front door.

Joy had warned Maxine that Gabby had been in a bad mood since Nadia left with Rayshawn. Maxine hoped spending the day together would put them all in better moods. "Has Rayshawn returned any of your calls?"

"No! When I call him, he texts me back that Nadia is fine. When I see him, I'm going to choke the life out of him," Gabby fumed.

Payback is a bitch, Maxine thought as she followed Gabby into the kitchen. Maxine was delighted Rayshawn finally got to spend time alone with his daughter. As hard as he fought Gabby to see Nadia, he deserved this time alone with her. She never agreed with the way Gabby had handled her situation with Rayshawn and William. Still, as Gabby's friend, Maxine had put her opinions aside and supported Gabby.

When they entered the kitchen, Joy was sitting at the table with a cordless phone to her ear and tears in her eyes. She smiled at Maxine, blew her a kiss, and returned to her phone call. Maxine looked at Gabby with furrowed eyebrows.

Gabby shook her head. "She's been arguing with Allen about the paternity test with Dean's parents since she left the morgue yesterday."

"Oh." As Maxine listened to Joy pleading for Allen to understand her side, she took the herb-roasted chicken, rice pilaf, green beans, and crescent rolls out of the bag and set them on the stovetop for later.

Gabby carefully examined each dish. "Too many carbs. All you needed to cook was the chicken and green beans. A salad would've been nice, too."

Maxine rolled her eyes at Gabby. "Well, the next time, you cook what you want."

Joy ended her call and tossed the phone on the table. "Oh, my God! He's so fucking stubborn! He's driving me crazy!" Joy stood and hugged Maxine. "What's going on, Maxine? Happy New Year, girl! Mmmm, that food smells good."

Maxine rubbed Joy's swollen stomach. "Happy New Year, Joy. I understand why you agreed to do the paternity test. Dean's parents thinking the twins are their grandchildren is your last connection to him. Once the test proves he's not their father, you're finally done with him and his family," Maxine reasoned.

"Exactly! And that's what I was trying to get Allen to understand, but he refuses to even discuss it," Joy exclaimed.

"I don't blame Allen for being upset. Dean is dead, so Joy is already done with him. What does she have to prove to his parents? A paternity test is a waste of time and money. Everybody, including his parents, should move on!" Gabby snatched her bottle of water off the kitchen table and marched to the living room.

Maxine looked at Joy, who seemed just as shocked by Gabby's outburst as she was. They followed Gabby to the living room.

Maxine stopped at the entrance and gasped. She couldn't believe this was the same room where they had been held hostage a week ago. "Oh, my God! I can't believe this."

The blood-stained oak floors had been replaced with mahogany. The walls were painted a soothing green hue with a bright, white trim. Two green and beige chairs beside the stone fireplace made it look like a separate sitting area. The colors from the dark beige sofa and loveseat across the room blended everything together. There was a green, black, and beige area rug under a black coffee table. Accessories in the same colors sat on two end tables and the fireplace mantel. The room was picture-perfect and looked too nice to use.

"Thanks," Gabby replied with an arrogant smirk as she sat on the loveseat.

"The chick is talented. She got skills. What can I say?" Joy kicked her slippers off, sat on the couch, and put her feet on the coffee table in front of her.

"Great job, Gabby! This is your calling." Maxine sat on the couch beside Joy.

Gabby leaned back on the loveseat and crossed her legs. "It's okay. It's the best I could do with limited funds. Buying furniture in a warehouse and getting it the same day is not my style, but it's what Joy wanted."

"It's what her money could afford." Joy laughed.

"I know that's right," Maxine added with a giggle.

Gabby crossed her arms over her chest, squinted her eyes, and glared at her friends. She thought about telling Joy how she spent a thousand dollars of her money but changed her mind. She wanted to save it for when she really needed to make Joy feel guilty.

"Why you looking at us like that, Gabby? I know you're

worried about Nadia being with Rayshawn, but she's fine." Maxine got up, sat beside Gabby on the loveseat, and put her arm around her friend's shoulders. "What can I do to make you feel better?"

"She knows Nadia's fine. That hussy needs some dick." Joy laughed. "She hasn't had sex since William died, and she all backed up."

Maxine quickly took her arm from around Gabby's shoulder and scrunched her face. "Girl, I can't help you with that."

"Joy, sex is not a cure-all, but I have decided to start dating again," Gabby said.

Joy laughed out loud. "I told you, Maxine. Our girl is horny. She had Nadia demanding all her attention, and now that she's gone, her vajayjay is screaming for some attention."

Gabby couldn't help but laugh with Joy and Maxine because she knew they were right. Although she was missing Nadia, she was missing the comfort of a man, too. Gabby had already reconnected with a couple of her exes. As soon as Joy was taken off bed rest, she planned to let one of them give her body some much-needed attention.

Gabby looked at Maxine. "So, I hear you've been busy. Why didn't you tell us you moved out of your parents' house?"

"Huh? I, I, um." Maxine frowned because she hated it when Gabby and Joy used her to change the subject.

"I talked to Dr. Jim and Ms. Pat this morning and they told me you moved out. Why would you do that?" Gabby stared at her for an explanation.

"That's what adults do, Gabby. They leave the nest and move into their own place. You should try it sometimes," Joy said with a smirk.

"Oh, don't worry. As soon as your big butt is off bed rest, I'm moving in with Bea until I find my own place. I have no plans to stay here and listen to you and Allen moaning and groaning," Gabby replied.

"Um, good luck with that." Living with Bea for the past couple of days drove Joy crazy. She wondered how long Gabby and Bea would last under the same roof. "Maxine, we talked every day and you never told me you moved."

"I didn't mention it because you were recovering from your concussion and Gabby was busy helping Juan get your house together. It's no big deal." Maxine rubbed her sweaty palms together.

"Your parents didn't give any details so where did you move and why the secret?" Gabby asked with squinted eyes leveled on Maxine.

Joy was staring at her, too. Maxine knew her parents wouldn't tell Gabby or anybody else why they evicted her, because they were too embarrassed. She took a deep breath, looked them in their eyes, and decided to tell them the truth. She cleared her throat. "I moved back into my townhouse. When my tenants moved out in November, instead of renting it again, I moved in with the boys and..."

Gabby snapped her fingers in Maxine's face. "Why did you move out, Maxine? This better not have anything to do with Trent! I hate him!"

"Stop the drama, Gabby! Maxine is smarter than you give her credit for. After what Trent did to her, nothing would make her go back to him. We all hate Trent, now let's go eat." Joy said.

"How can you say that, Joy, when he saved your life?" Maxine asked angrily.

"I thanked him for saving my life, but I'll never forgive him for almost taking yours," Joy replied.

"Are you back with Trent?" Gabby asked in disbelief.

"She knows Trent is bad news." Joy grunted as she tried to stand up.

"You didn't see her after the shooting. She was defending him. Oh, and I didn't tell you the cops were going to arrest him, but she stopped them," Gabby stated.

"Excuse me! I'm standing right here, still in the room with y'all!" Maxine yelled.

"You defended him, Maxine?" Joy asked with eyes bulging.

"Of course, I did. He saved eight people from a crazed gunman. The police were wrong and they knew it so they let him go home." Maxine stared at them with tight lips. After Trent risked his life to save them, she thought they would be willing to forgive him.

47

It broke her heart to hear her friends talking about him in such a negative way. They were no better than her father.

"Maxine, I know you're grateful for what Trent did, but don't let it change your mind about him. Once an abuser, always an abuser," Joy advised.

"I can't believe how judgmental and unappreciative you two are! Neither of you would be standing here if it wasn't for Trent! I'm leaving!" Maxine stomped in the kitchen and grabbed her purse.

"You can't be serious!" Gabby yelled.

"C'mon, Maxine. Don't go," Joy pleaded.

Maxine didn't respond to her girlfriends because she knew they wouldn't understand. *Trent was not the same man he had been when he abused me. He made a lot of good changes in his life.* She pulled her coat out of the closet near the front door, and left seconds later.

Gabby and Joy stared at each other, surprised by Maxine's reaction.

———

On the drive home, Maxine thought about all she had accomplished in the five days since her father kicked her out of his house. After the initial shock wore off, she decided it was the perfect time for her and the boys to move back into their townhouse. She and the boys had stayed with Trent that night, and she made plans to move the next day.

With the help of a full-service moving company, she and the boys were moved in and completely unpacked within two days. Even though she didn't want to rush their reconciliation, she agreed to allow Trent to move into the townhouse with them on a trial basis. She, however, told him not to break his lease on his apartment. After his address change was approved by his parole officer, Trent moved in with them two days later.

She purposely avoided telling her friends about the move, because she didn't want their help. Organizing the move herself made her feel stronger and more independent. She also wanted to give herself time to break the news about Trent being back in the house.

Maxine backed her minivan into her garage and proceeded into the house. When she opened the side door, the boys ran and jumped in her arms before she had a chance to step in the house.

"Mommy, Mommy!" they screamed.

"Hey, boys!" She gave them each a big hug and kiss. They ran back into the living room to play.

Trent approached her while she was hanging her coat in the closet. "How did everything go?"

Maxine scowled.

"That bad, huh?" Trent knew Gabby and Joy weren't going to be happy about their reconciliation, but he had to step back and let Maxine see for herself.

"They didn't give me a chance to tell them we're back together," Maxine looked at Trent with tears welling.

He moved closer and put his arm around her shoulder.

"Mommy, you sad?" TJ asked.

"Mommy sad!" Maxwell yelled as he jumped up and down.

"Okay, group hug to make Mommy feel better," Trent said.

He let Maxine go and scooped his boys up in his arms and hugged them.

"Wait!" TJ yelled. "We forgot Mommy!"

"We sure did! Come on over here, Mommy, and get some of this group hug," Trent teased.

Maxine stood in front of Trent and wrapped her arms around her family. She looked in Trent's eyes, and in that instant, she saw the man she fell in love with years ago. A good man who adored his family. She leaned in, closed her eyes, and kissed him.

"Awww, Mommy kissed Daddy!" TJ pointed out, laughing.

"Do it again!" Maxwell demanded.

Trent put the boys down, took Maxine in his arms, and kissed her long and hard. "I love you, Maxi."

Maxine smiled and touched his face gently. "I love you, too." In that moment, Maxine knew Trent and her boys were all she needed.

Her cell phone rang. She took it out of her pocket and looked at Joy's name bouncing on the screen. She immediately hit the Ignore button and turned it off. If her family and friends couldn't put the past behind them and see the good in Trent, she didn't need them. She was prepared to cut ties with all of them to have her family back together again.

Chapter 8

It was the first Monday of the New Year. Gabby sat in the office of her lawyer, Jim Conman, dressed in a navy-blue suit with her hair pulled back into a simple bun. She stared at Jim with a tense expression as he talked to Detective Briggs on the phone. She prayed he would believe her explanation for being at the Red Roof Inn on Christmas night and hoped it was enough to stop Rayshawn from thinking he could control her. Rayshawn had stopped texting her a couple of days ago and she felt she had to do something drastic. Not knowing where Nadia was or even if she was still alive terrified Gabby. Her only thought was bringing her daughter back home.

Jim hung up his desk phone and sighed. "Detective Briggs believes you should've called the police when you found out the fugitive was at the motel, but he's not going to charge you with anything. Based on his investigation, the victim was at a nearby liquor store when you and your acquaintances arrived at the motel."

Idiot. "Really? So he doesn't need to question me or my, um, acquaintances?" Gabby crossed her arms over her chest and smiled wickedly.

"No. They have a signed confession and evidence that proves they have the right person. He had no desire to reopen the case. Next time someone calls you with a tip, give it to the police and let them do their job. As a matter of fact, just stay out of it," Jim said as he looked at Gabby with a stern face.

"There won't be a next time. Now, what about my other problem?" Gabby snapped her fingers and stared at Jim with a scowl.

Pulling a thick folder from under a pile of papers on his desk, he frowned. Gabby was his most difficult and demanding client. She didn't call him every day, like some of his other clients, but when she did call he knew it was something major that required his immediate attention. The dossier she brought to his office this morning made him suspect that Rayshawn and his lawyers were planning something, but he didn't want to worry Gabby until he had all the details.

Jim picked up the phone, dialed Rayshawn's lead attorney, and put the phone on speaker so Gabby could hear. His secretary answered and put them on hold. After a brief wait, Rayshawn's attorney got on the line and informed Jim that two of his partners were on the call as well. Jim sat upright in his chair, cleared his throat, and told Rayshawn's lawyers about his conversation with Detective Briggs and how the private detective they hired didn't have information to cause Gabby any serious harm. They agreed unanimously. The little hairs on the back of Jim's neck stood at attention. He'd been representing Gabby for over a year, and Rayshawn's attorneys never agreed with him about anything without a fight.

Before he ended the call, Jim threatened to call the police and media if Rayshawn didn't phone his office within the next ten minutes so Gabby could talk to her daughter. They assured him Rayshawn would call immediately.

Five minutes later, he did. Jim put him on speaker.

"This Rayshawn Robinson. My lawyers asked me to call you about my daughter." Rayshawn's southern accent was stronger than ever.

"Why haven't you returned my calls? Where is Nadia?" Gabby yelled across the desk.

"She right here, chewin' on a chicken bone as happy as she can be," Rayshawn sang in a baby's voice.

"What?" Gabby and Jim stared at each other with furrowed eyebrows.

"She cuttin' teeth, so that bone feel good on them gums," Rayshawn explained.

"I know that, Rayshawn! That's why I packed her teething toys in her bag, you fool!"

"We ain't using that shit. All 'em plastic toys made in China cause cancer and other diseases. I gave my boys chicken bones when they were teething and they turned out fine."

"You are so ignorant! Where is she? I want to hear her voice. And take that bone away from her, Rayshawn! It's ten o'clock in the morning and you have her chewing on a bone instead of feeding her a real breakfast," Gabby snapped.

"Oh, she eatin' real good. She like her daddy, love that southern food. We puttin' some meat on her bones."

"Oh, my God!" Gabby gasped and covered her mouth with both hands as a vision of a fat little girl sitting on Rayshawn's front porch popped in her head. The little girl was chewing on a chicken bone, wearing dirty clothes with no shoes on her feet and her hair all over her head. She needed to get Nadia away from Rayshawn before he turned her into an Ebonics-talking, fat slob like him.

"Go 'head and talk. I got the phone to her ear," Rayshawn ordered.

Hearing Nadia babbling and giggling on the phone made Gabby smile. Tears filled her eyes as she listened to her daughter's voice. "Nadia, it's Mommy. I love you, Nadia." Gabby struggled to talk as she tried to hold back her tears. She missed her daughter so much.

"She 'bout to eat the phone. We gots to go. She'll be back in two weeks," Rayshawn said.

"No! I'm coming to get her now!" Gabby snapped.

Rayshawn was silent for a few seconds before he responded. "Oh, you forget real fast, don't you? She's staying with me until I come back to Maryland."

Gabby reached across the desk to grab the phone.

Jim grabbed her hand and stopped her before she picked it up.

"Rayshawn, this is Jim Conman, Gabby's attorney. I spoke with your legal team earlier and explained to them that whatever you were trying to blackmail my client with wouldn't hold up in court. Now, I don't think Gabby has a problem with Nadia staying with you for an additional two weeks, if you agree to a daily phone call for her to check on her daughter."

Gabby's eyes shot daggers at Jim. She had no intentions of letting Nadia stay another day with Rayshawn, let alone two weeks. She shook her head no, crossed her arms over her chest, and stared angrily at Jim.

"Hell, no! That bitch ain't give me that courtesy when she had Nadia all this time."

"Mr. Robinson, I need you to hold the line for a second, please." Jim pressed the hold button and looked at Gabby.

"Absolutely not! I want my daughter back now!" Gabby jumped up and paced Jim's office with her arms crossed and lips poked out.

Jim walked from behind his desk and went to Gabby's side. "Gabby, be reasonable. You already agreed to let her stay with him and if we ever went to court, we can prove you tried to let her spend time with her father, but it didn't work out."

"Court?" Gabby asked with wide eyes.

"Lawyers don't hire private detectives without a reason. They're planning something and letting her stay for two more weeks will make you look like you're trying to work out custody with Rayshawn. Trust me on this," Jim reasoned.

Gabby thought about it for a few minutes then agreed to let Nadia stay. Jim had never let her down and she trusted his judgment.

Jim returned to his desk and pushed the speaker button. "Mr. Robinson, I'm sorry to keep you waiting."

"Yeah, I was 'bout ready to hang up."

"I'm glad you didn't. I just want to remind you that Gabby has full custody of your daughter. She is free to pick her up anytime she wants. The choice is yours, Mr. Robinson. Is she picking Nadia up now or are you going to agree to a daily phone call for the next two weeks?"

Rayshawn mumbled something to someone in the background. "Aw'right? One call a day."

Jim nodded for Gabby to agree.

"One missed phone call, Rayshawn, and I'm on the first flight to hicktown to get my daughter from you and your country bumpkin family," Gabby snapped.

"I hear you, bitch!"

"Now you hear me, Rayshawn. I want my full child support amount deposited into my account as usual. Since you blackmailed me into reducing the amount, whatever I agreed to doesn't count. You will continue to pay child support and my legal fees like we agreed."

"I'll let my lawyers handle it," Rayshawn said angrily.

"Good to know. And, Rayshawn, make sure you take good care of my child. For every scratch, bump, or bruise I see on her body, I'm going to take it out on you. And you better have her looking cute at all times. That means taking the chicken bones out of her mouth and feeding her fruits and vegetables and dressing her in the nice outfits I packed for her. I know you're used to raising fat, unattractive children, but Nadia doesn't fall into that category. Her beauty comes from my side of the family."

"What the hell, you..."

"Save your breath. I don't want to hear it." Gabby reached across Jim's desk and hung up on Rayshawn before he could say anything else.

Jim looked at Gabby and shook his head.

She clapped her hands and laughed. "Thank you, Jim. If you didn't smell like an ashtray and look like a baby sumo wrestler, I would kiss you."

"If you really want to show me your appreciation, stay out of trouble and try to get along with your daughter's father. Is that too much to ask?" Jim walked over to the coat stand in the corner and lifted Gabby's coat off the hook.

Gabby stood. Jim held her coat behind her as she slid her arms through the sleeves.

"I can definitely stay out of trouble, but getting along with Rayshawn is never going to happen. When Nadia comes home, he'll never see her again." Gabby put two fingers to her lips, kissed them, and placed her fingers on Jim's forehead. "See you next time."

Jim had a feeling the next time was going to be sooner than she knew.

———————

Gabby left Jim's office, smiling ear to ear. She had Rayshawn back where she wanted him, somewhere between pitiful and defenseless. She took the elevator down to the lobby and frowned when she saw Bo Johnson sitting there skimming through a *Sports Illustrated*. Tall, dark, and handsome described him perfectly. He was about 6' 2" with perfectly smooth, milk-chocolate skin, and every feature on his face looked like it was handpicked and placed by God, especially his light, hazel eyes.

She had contacted him after Rayshawn showed her the pictures of them together at the Red Roof Inn. He had been giving her advice on how to handle things and met her here this morning to make sure everything was taken care of the way they planned. Although he wasn't her type, the more time she spent with him, the more curious she was about what he could do in the bedroom.

She sashayed to where he was sitting and stood in front of him. She removed a few hairpins and let her long hair fall past her shoulders. "Everything has been taken care of, thanks to my lawyer."

"Not in here." Bo stood, put his fingers around her arm and led her to the parking garage.

"Not so tight. Didn't anybody ever teach you how to treat a lady?" Gabby snatched her arm from him and walked a couple of steps ahead.

"You ain't no goddamn lady," Bo barked.

"I'm more of a lady than any of those ghetto-project chicks you sleep with." Gabby laughed.

When they reached Gabby's Lexus, she opened the driver's door and threw her handbag in the passenger seat. Bo pushed her to the side and slammed the door shut. He grabbed the back of her hair, turned her around, and pushed her against the SUV.

"Don't keep playing fucking games with me. What happened?" Bo snapped.

"Are you flirting with me, Bo?" Gabby smiled as she locked eyes with him.

The tension between them was explosive. Gabby got in his face and told him what he wanted to hear in whispered tones.

He gripped her chin with his hands. "I don't want any more shit from you."

Gabby pushed his hands off her face and kissed him hard. Their tongues explored each other's mouths as their bodies pressed together as one. Minutes later, they separated, gasping for air.

"I'm not the man for you. You need to stick to them weak-ass, college boys you like to fuck over 'cause if I fuck you, you'll be the one committing suicide, not me." Bo lifted her skirt, pushed her underwear to the side, and stuck his finger inside her.

"Ummm, nice," Gabby moaned.

Bo pulled his finger out and pointed it at her face. "Look how bad you want me to fuck you."

Gabby put the same finger in her mouth and sucked it.

"Can you handle being fucked by a real man?" Bo whispered in her ear.

"You're not my type and I don't think you're man enough to satisfy me." Gabby put her palm on his jeans and rubbed his erection. "You're a little too rough around the edges for me."

"I can tell you like it rough." Bo bit her bottom lip.

"How rough can you give it to me?" Gabby licked her lips seductively.

"You know I'm married, right?" Bo pulled her closer to him.

"If you don't care about your wife, why should I?" Gabby pulled her thong off and slowly rubbed it across Bo's face.

"I'm just lettin' you know what's gettin' ready to happen between us is just sex. Nothing more. You understand?" Bo explained as he stared into her eyes.

"Uh-huh." She put her hand under his shirt and rubbed his chest.

Bo opened the driver's door and back passenger door to give them some privacy. He unbuttoned Gabby's shirt and turned her around so her back faced him. He bent her over, lifted her skirt, and smacked her hard on her butt. "You been wanting this since we met, haven't you?"

"I'll let you know after we finish." Gabby reached in her purse and gave Bo a condom.

He pulled his pants and boxers down, slid the condom on, and pushed himself inside her. Gabby moaned. He grabbed a handful of her hair and stroked her slowly.

"Harder!" Gabby urged. "I thought you knew what you were doing."

Bo pulled her hair tighter, rammed himself deeper inside her, and smacked her butt with his other hand. "Is that what you want?"

"Yes! Harder!" Gabby begged.

Bo let her hair go and grabbed both of her breasts as he thrust himself further inside her.

"Oh yeah, baby!" Gabby squeezed her internal muscles in a pulsating rhythm.

"Don't do that!" Bo warned.

"I knew you couldn't handle me," Gabby panted.

"Fuck!" His knees buckled.

They came together and collapsed in the driver's seat, exhausted.

Once they caught their breath, Bo pulled his pants up and looked at her. "This won't happen again."

Gabby laughed. Sex with Bo was better than she'd expected. He thought it was over, but little did he know, it wasn't over until Gabby decided they were done, and she was just getting started.

*C*hapter 9

For Joy, Wednesday couldn't have come quickly enough. She was ecstatic as she walked in the Washington Hospital Center, anxious to see Allen. She stepped in a waiting elevator and pushed the button for the fifth floor. With each passing floor, her heart beat faster in anticipation of seeing her man. She couldn't wait to smell him, touch him, and kiss his juicy lips. When the doors opened, an attractive white woman with the brightest, aqua-blue eyes Joy had ever seen tried to step on before Joy was completely out. The woman intentionally bumped Joy's shoulder, knocking her off balance.

"What is your fucking problem?" Joy shouted, incredulously.

"You're the problem, you fat pig. Try dieting, big girl," the woman snapped as the doors closed.

Oh no, that bitch didn't just call me fat. Joy quickly pressed the button to stop the elevator doors from closing, but she was too late. It was already going down. She thought about taking the next elevator downstairs to kick the woman's ass but changed her mind. Seeing Allen and keeping her unborn children safe were more important than choking the life out of that rude white bitch. She took her coat off and inhaled several deep breaths to calm herself before she proceeded down the hall to Allen's room.

When she got there, the small room with a single hospital bed was empty. The television was mounted to the wall near the ceiling and several chairs were lined up against the wall under the window. There was also a more comfortable-looking loveseat in the room, too. Every surface had a greeting card, plants, and flowers. His laptop was on the table beside his bed along with a framed eight-by-ten picture of Joy and another of Allen and Joy together.

Allen opened the bathroom door, walked into the room, and stopped dead in his tracks when he saw Joy.

"Hi, baby. Guess who's off bed rest?" Joy squealed as she tossed her coat on a chair near his bed. It had been a week since she last saw him and she wondered how he could look so damn sexy after getting shot in the chest. He stood there wearing black sweatpants and a matching zip-up hoodie with a white T-shirt under it. His freshly shaved head and trimmed goatee made her body ache for him. She wanted to run and jump in his arms but didn't because she was enormous and didn't want to hurt him or their twins.

"Hey, beautiful." He smiled as he walked toward her with his arms stretched out in front of him.

Walking into his waiting arms, her body relaxed and she hugged his waist. As their lips met, she tilted her head back and opened her mouth slightly to allow his tongue to slide in. Without thinking, she pulled him closer and tightened her grip around his waist so their bodies pressed together as one.

"Ouch! Not too tight, baby." Allen flinched and removed his arms from around Joy.

"Oh, my God, Allen! I'm so sorry. You look so good, I forgot." Joy pulled back and looked at Allen with frightened eyes. "Did I hurt you?"

"I'm good." While holding her hand, he led her to a loveseat near the window. Fearing she might hurt him again, she sat as far away from him as possible, but he put his arm around her shoulder and pulled her closer to him.

"Stop, Allen. I don't want to hurt you." Joy tried to move back over but he wouldn't let her.

He touched his chest gently as he stared into her eyes. "My stitches are here and you're going to be over here, so you're good."

"I'm too big. Some woman just told me to go on a diet."

Joy cautiously moved closer to him but didn't rest her head on his chest like he wanted.

Allen laughed out loud as he rubbed her belly. "You're beautiful, Joy. That woman was probably having a bad day."

"She was right. Look at me." Joy stood and frowned as she turned around in her Pea in the Pod navy-blue, wrap dress. "I'm not even going to tell you the number on the scale today."

Allen pulled her in front of him and planted small kisses on her belly. "C'mon, baby. Don't do that. I have never seen you look as beautiful as you do right now. As long as your doctor isn't concerned about your weight, don't worry about it."

"Mm-hmmm. Just remember you said that after I give birth and still have a few extra pounds on my ass." Joy sat back down on the chair.

"Oh, that's the best place for it to be." Allen laughed. "Bea called me earlier after your doctor's appointment."

"Of course she did. Right after I specifically told her I wanted to talk to you myself about what the doctor said." Joy shook her head disapprovingly. *Will Bea ever learn to stay out of my business?*

"It's all good. I was glad to hear my babies are healthy and growing." Allen rubbed Joy's belly lovingly. "She offered to help us out financially since the doc won't let you go back to work."

Joy braced herself for Allen's response. She knew he was too proud to accept financial assistance from anyone. He probably cursed Bea out and told her to mind her damn business.

"I told her we didn't need her help. I'm a man and I can take care of my family." Allen smiled at Joy as he twirled one of her curls around his finger. "The twins will be here in three months and neither one of their parents is working, but we'll be okay."

"If you're not worried, I'm not worried. I know we'll be okay. I'll still get eighty percent of my salary," Joy said proudly. Her teacher's income wasn't a lot, but the excellent benefits made up for it. Once she completed her doctorate in education, she knew her salary would increase.

Allen took his finger out of Joy's hair and pulled her face close to his. He kissed her softly. "I missed you."

"I missed you, too, but we still need to discuss the paternity test, Allen."

"No, we don't. We've been arguing too much about that. Now that I know you and our babies are okay, let's make the rest of your visit about us. Let's not talk about Bea, your girlfriends, my family, paternity tests, finances, nothing but us." He planted several soft kisses on her lips.

The nurse Joy met the morning she found out Allen was shot walked in the room. "Good morning. Long time no see, Ms. Lady. How are you and those babies doing?"

"Wonderful! How are you?" Joy smiled.

"Good. I'm sorry to disturb y'all but the doctor scheduled you for a chest x-ray in thirty minutes, Mr. Johnson. If everything looks good, he plans to discharge you tomorrow." She smiled. "Let me check your vitals and I'll be out of your way in a few minutes."

"Free at last," Allen joked.

While the nurse checked Allen's blood pressure and vitals, Joy walked around the room and read some of Allen's get-well cards. Most of the names she recognized and the few she didn't were probably Allen's work colleagues or fraternity brothers. One name caught her attention though. There was a large floral bouquet, balloons, and several cards from someone named Diana. Joy searched her brain trying to remember if she ever met a friend of Allen's named Diana. She took the card out of the floral bouquet and read it: *Allen, I've watched you get stronger every day. Continue your recovery so you're at your best when your twins are born. With much love and respect, Diana.*

Joy trusted Allen. Both of them had friends of the opposite sex, but there were never any secrets about it. Still, she wondered why there was so much in the room from Diana. After the nurse left, she watched Allen close his room door and turn his attention back to her.

"Who is Diana?" Joy asked with a blank stare.

Allen hunched his shoulders. "Just a friend. She was in a play at the Warner Theatre so she stopped by a few times."

"Every day?" A hollow feeling in the pit of her stomach gripped her when she realized another woman had been there for

Allen when she couldn't be.

"She didn't stay long. She stopped by this morning on her way to the airport to go back to New York," Allen explained.

Joy put her hands on her hips and glared at Allen.

"Oh, come on, baby. Don't even go there," Allen pleaded.

"Don't go where, Allen? If she was here every day, why am I just hearing about her?" Joy snapped.

"Because she's not worth telling you about," Allen replied in a calm tone. He held her hand and led her back to the loveseat. After they were both seated, he leaned over and kissed her as he opened her dress and lifted her bra to expose her breasts.

"Stop, Allen! Somebody might walk in here," Joy protested.

"The door is closed. And if they do come in, it won't be the first time somebody walked in on us." Allen kissed her breast.

Joy tried to stop him, but when he put his mouth on her breasts and sucked her nipples, her body relaxed and she began to enjoy it. She reached between his legs, but he pushed her hand away so he could focus on her. He pulled her dress up to her thighs and stuck his hand inside her underwear. Joy let out a soft moan when she felt Allen's touch.

"Did you miss my hands on your body?" Allen whispered in Joy's ear.

"Yes, but I really miss you *in* my body," she murmured.

They stared into each other's eyes. Allen gently massaged her clitoris, searching for the right spot. He planted a trail of kisses from her collarbone to her lips.

"Ooh...baby." Joy grabbed the arm of the loveseat, arched her back, and opened her legs wider. A deep groan from the back of her throat escaped her lips.

"Is that it, baby? I want you to come on my fingers." Allen continued to stimulate her clitoris until her entire body shook and she cried out in ecstasy. He put his mouth on hers to muffle her sounds.

Joy laid her head back on the loveseat and tried to catch her breath. She looked at Allen with seductive eyes. "Your turn, baby."

Someone knocked on the door. Joy quickly pulled her bra

down and adjusted her dress before Allen told them to come in. A male orderly entered the room with a wheelchair. His eyes went straight to Joy's exposed thighs. Allen pulled down her dress.

"Wassup, man?" Allen looked the guy over.

"Oh, I gotta order to pick up Allen Johnson for a chest x-ray," he said in a deep voice.

"I'm Allen." He stood and walked toward the bathroom. "I'll be ready in a minute, man. She got something on my fingers. I need to go wash my hands right quick."

Joy gasped and burst out laughing.

The orderly fidgeted with the handles of the wheelchair and looked out the window to avoid eye contact with her.

A few minutes later, Allen returned from the bathroom and kissed Joy goodbye. "I'm ready," he said as he sat in the wheelchair.

"Can I go with him?"

"You pregnant?" the orderly asked as he stared at her belly. "'Cause pregnant ladies can't be near the machines. Something about it not being good for the babies."

"Come here." Allen held his hand out for Joy. "I won't be long. Why don't you relax, and we can finish playing that game when I get back."

"I'm looking forward to it." Joy blushed as she thought about what she was going to do to Allen when he returned.

The orderly propped Allen's door open, then pushed his wheelchair out of the room. Joy looked around for something to do while he was gone. She pushed a chair to the table beside his bed and turned on the laptop. She wanted to check her email and search the web.

Once the Wi-Fi was connected, Allen's email appeared on the screen. Joy was getting ready to click the red box in the corner to close it until something caught her attention. There were two emails from DirtyDiana2U@yahoo.com. Joy clicked the first email, Subject: DON'T YOU MISS THIS? Joy gasped when images of a naked white woman in different poses flashed across the screen. It was the same woman who almost knocked her down in the elevator earlier. Her hair was a different color, but Joy would recognize those piercing blue eyes anywhere. The screen kept flashing non-stop pictures of a naked Diana in the most revealing positions. Joy closed the laptop. Her stomach lurched and she ran to the bathroom to vomit.

Once her stomach settled, she returned to the laptop and opened the other email from Diana. The subject line read, CAN WE DO THIS AGAIN? Joy almost knocked the laptop off the table when she saw a video of Allen and Diana in bed having sex.

Thirty minutes later, Allen returned and watched Joy as she paced back and forth. As he got out of the wheelchair, she glared at him with a tear-stained face and then abruptly turned her back to him until the orderly left the room.

"Babe, you okay?" Allen asked as he approached her.

"Do you remember earlier when I told you a woman called me fat?" Joy asked as she stood in front of the laptop.

"That's no reason to be upset, Joy." He tried to embrace her, but she pulled away.

"That same woman shoved me and almost knocked me down when I got off the elevator," Joy said with tears in her eyes.

"What! Did she come back and do something to you?" Allen turned Joy around to face him. "Baby, what's going on? Talk to me." Allen wiped the tears from her face.

"This is the woman!" Joy pushed his hand away from her face and hit a button on the laptop.

The sounds of Allen and Diana having sex filled the room. Joy stared at him with tears streaming down her face. Allen covered his face with both hands briefly, then looked at her with pleading eyes. She stood with her arms crossed over her chest and her eyebrows raised, waiting for his response.

"Joy, that's old. It happened in China. She sent me the email a few days ago. I talked to her about it." Allen reached around Joy and turned off the laptop.

"But you didn't talk to *me* about it. What was she doing here every day? Were you playing with her pussy, too?" Joy sighed.

"Baby, you know me better than that. I didn't do anything wrong. I was a single man when I made that video. Nothing is going on between Diana and me. We're just friends." Allen reached out to hold her hand, but she snatched it away.

"What kind of friend sends you a PowerPoint presentation of her pussy? A fuck friend, that's who." Joy wiped the tears from her face and shook her head.

"Where is the trust, Joy? Don't you trust me, baby?"

"NO! She sent you the pictures first; you didn't tell me. She sent you the video next; you still didn't tell me. She's been in your room with you every day bringing you gifts and you never said a word to me." Joy stared at him with cold eyes. "Whatever trust I had in you is gone." She stomped past Allen and picked up her coat and purse.

"Baby, don't leave like this. I'll be home soon and I don't want this fucked up mistake to interfere with us. C'mon, let's sit down and talk it out," Allen begged.

"I don't want to talk to you. You should go stay with Tyesha when you're released because I don't want to see you." Joy stared at Allen with pure hatred.

"I'm coming home to you when I leave here, not Tyesha. I walked away from my career in China to come back here to be with you. I took a bullet in my goddamn chest to protect you and our children. Why? Because I love you and our babies. I wouldn't jeopardize that by sleeping with another woman."

"Your secrets about Diana are just as bad as you sleeping with her. Give me some space and time to think this through." Joy walked toward the door.

"Fuck that! No! I'm coming home to you. We've been through too much, baby." Allen stood in front of Joy and blocked her from leaving.

Using the palms of her hands, she pushed Allen's torso. While clutching his chest, he stumbled back with a stunned expression. The pain was so intense, he dropped to his knees moaning.

"Stay away from me, Allen!" She walked around him and left.

Chapter 10

Maxine awakened Saturday morning with every intention of going for an early morning run before her family woke up. When Trent opened his eyes and saw her changing clothes, he pulled her back in bed and made love to her. An hour later, Trent was in a deep sleep and she no longer had the desire or energy to go for a run. Instead, she took a shower, put on a pair of sweatpants and a T-shirt, then checked on her boys. They were sleeping peacefully in their rooms, so she went downstairs to make breakfast.

While breakfast cooked on the stovetop, Maxine sang along with Jill Scott on the radio, thinking how happy she was these days. Other than Trent still being under house arrest and having to be home before eight o'clock every night, she had no complaints. She loved teaching, and her boys were doing well at school and daycare. She was finally living the life with Trent she always wanted and was looking forward to their future together.

The doorbell rang and startled her. After she flipped the pancakes over and turned down the flame, she ran to answer the door with the spatula in her hand. The sight of Joy and Gabby standing on her front porch smiling ear to ear took her breath away.

"Hey, girl!" Joy said as she hugged Maxine and walked in the house.

Gabby held up a bag of food for Maxine to see. "We bought you salmon cakes from your favorite restaurant to apologize."

"We?" Joy raised her eyebrow. "It's a peace offering. I

know Gabby pissed you off on New Year's Day."

Maxine pointed the spatula at her girlfriends. "Actually, both of you heifers pissed me off. I need to check on my food and then we'll talk. I have something important to tell you."

Following Maxine into the kitchen, Gabby and Joy looked forward to catching up and making amends with their friend. Maxine didn't get upset with them often, but when she did, she usually had a good reason for it.

"Girl, we must've really pissed you off. We haven't heard from you since you left my house a week ago." Joy removed her coat and tossed it on an empty chair beside her. She pulled a chair out from the kitchen table and sat down.

"You did piss me off, but I'm glad you're here because I need to tell you about some changes I made in my life." Maxine turned off all the burners and sat in an empty chair.

Gabby stood at the head of the table with her arms crossed over her chest and her lips pursed. "I don't appreciate you not returning my calls. What if something happened to Nadia while she's with her idiot father? What if I needed something? What if I—"

"Shut up, Gabby! This is about Maxine, not you! Now sit your ass down and listen to what she has to tell us," Joy interjected with a deep frown.

Gabby sighed. "Don't think you get to tell her about Allen's sex tape before I tell about the good sex I'm having." Gabby took off her coat and placed it on the back of her chair before she sat down.

Maxine eyed her friends with an arched brow. "Allen has a sex tape? Who are you sleeping with, Gabby?"

"Oh, Maxine, we need to catch up. When Allen came home from the hospital Thursday morning, he couldn't get in the house because Joy had the locks changed and refused to answer any of his calls. He's staying with Tyesha." Gabby shook her head in dismay.

"That's harsh, Joy. Why did you do that to Allen after all he's been through?" Maxine stared at Joy with sad eyes.

"I don't want to talk about Allen or Gabby's latest victim. What's going on with you?" Joy half-smiled at Maxine.

The sound of heavy footsteps coming downstairs silenced them because all three women knew those feet didn't belong to Maxine's sons.

Maxine thought it was best to stay silent and let this play out on its own. It was too late to do anything about it now, and it was time for her girlfriends to know the truth. Whether they accepted it or not, it wouldn't change anything for her.

"Maxi, is breakfast ready yet? You made me work up an appetite this morning." Trent entered the kitchen wearing his boxers and a white T-shirt.

"What is he doing here?" Gabby yelled as she jumped up.

"Maxine?" Joy stared at Maxine with bulging eyes.

Maxine ignored Joy as she rose from the table.

Gabby got in Trent's face and poked her finger in his chest. "Get out. I will not let you hurt her again."

Maxine and Joy followed Gabby as she backed Trent into the living room.

When his back hit the living room wall and he couldn't move any further, Gabby made a fist and punched Trent in his nose. A stream of blood poured from his face.

"Stop it, Gabby!" Maxine ordered.

Trent grabbed Gabby's wrists and held them with a tight grip. "I'm not going to allow you to come in my home and try to turn my wife against me, so get the hell out."

Gabby kicked Trent's shin, twisted her wrists out of his grip, and slapped him hard across his face.

"Make that the last time you put your fucking hands on me, bitch." Trent raised his hand to strike Gabby.

Joy rushed to Gabby's side. "I wish you *would* put your goddamn hands on her. We'll kill your ass in here."

"Go ahead, Trent. Hit me." Gabby teased with a smile.

Maxine planted her petite body between her girlfriends and Trent. "Don't, Trent. It's what they want. Gabby, keep your hands off my husband."

Crimson-faced, Gabby stared at Maxine. "He almost killed you! You can't be so stupid you would take him back."

"She's not. This was just a one-time slip-up. Right, Maxine?" Joy chewed her bottom lip, praying that was the case.

"No, it wasn't. Trent still has his apartment, but he moved in with us temporarily so we can work on our marriage." Maxine held Trent's hand as he used his other one to wipe the blood from his nose with his T-shirt.

"You are incredibly ignorant when it comes to men, Maxine. He's using you, just like Kevin Bradley. Remember the married man you were screwing who told you nothing but lies to get between your legs. You believed everything he said, no questions asked." Gabby shook her head to show her disappointment.

"Shut the hell up, Gabby! She told us that in confidence," Joy snapped.

Trent focused his evil glare on Maxine. "What married man, Maxi?"

Maxine looked down at the floor and swallowed hard. "That was a mistake."

"You are stuck on stupid, Maxine." Gabby again pointed her finger in Trent's face. "Go upstairs and pack your bags. I'm kicking you out today because she doesn't know any better."

"He's not going anywhere. He's my husband. We're back together and he's staying right here!" Tears streamed down Maxine's face.

Gabby looked straight in her eyes. "It's either him or me. If you reconcile with him, you end our friendship."

"No. Stop it. This is getting out of hand. We promised to never let a man come between us," Joy exclaimed.

"He's not a man," Gabby said in an eerie tone.

"You're wrong, Gabby. He's my man and I'm staying with him."

Gabby moved closer to Maxine's face and shouted, "He's going to kill you."

"Like you killed your husband," Maxine screamed back.

Gabby gasped, then slapped Maxine hard across her face.

"Oh, my God!" Joy shrieked.

Without skipping a beat, Maxine slapped Gabby back. "I choose my husband. So I guess we're no longer friends."

"You heard her, now get the hell out!" Trent yelled.

"No! We're still friends! We'll always be friends. We're sisters," Joy cried as she put her arms around Maxine and Gabby and tried to bring them together in a group hug. "Please don't do this."

Gabby pulled away immediately. She went in the kitchen, snatched her coat off the back of the chair, grabbed the bag with the salmon cakes in it, and walked toward the front door.

"Gabby, don't do this!" Joy pleaded with her.

Gabby opened the front door and left without saying another word.

Maxine stared at Joy with tears running down her face. "You can leave, too."

"I'm not going anywhere," Joy said, hugging Maxine.

"You should go," Trent suggested.

Joy faced Trent. "Fuck you, Trent. If you put one goddamn finger on Maxine or those boys, I know people who can make your ass disappear. You better think twice before you get the urge to use her as your fucking punching bag again."

"That's enough, Joy. Just go," Maxine advised with a sob.

Joy took Maxine's hand. "I don't agree with what you're doing, but I won't end our friendship over it." She glared at Trent. "As a matter of fact, I plan to make sure I spend more time over here with you and the boys. You better get used to it, Trent."

He started to say something, but Gabby's loud car horn stopped him.

The noise and all the arguing had given Joy a headache. She didn't want to leave Maxine alone, especially with Trent looking like he was ready to take his anger out on somebody, but she couldn't stay either. She decided to go home, get rid of her headache, and come back.

"I'll be back later," Joy said as she got her coat.

Trent ignored her and went upstairs.

"I'll be okay." Maxine wrapped her arms around Joy and laid her head on Joy's shoulder.

Joy held Maxine in her arms and caressed the side of her face to reassure her that everything was going to be okay. She could feel Maxine's body trembling in her arms. When Maxine heard Trent coming back downstairs, she stepped away from Joy, wiped her face, and tried to smile. Joy looked at Trent, then Maxine, and wondered if she should stay after all.

Deciding for her, Maxine opened the door. "Bye, girl. I'll call you later."

TJ and Maxwell ran downstairs and asked for breakfast. With a gentle nudge, Maxine helped Joy out the door before the boys saw her. Because she didn't want them to see her upset, Joy left reluctantly. Watching the door close and hearing the latch lock had her frozen with fear. She closed her eyes and begged God to look over Maxine and her sons.

When Gabby saw her, she stopped blowing the horn and kept her eyes on Joy as she slowly walked down Maxine's front porch. Removing her coat and bag from the passenger seat, Gabby got out and put them in the back. When she saw how worried Joy looked, she shook her head disapprovingly before she got back behind the wheel.

"I can't believe you. How could you turn your back on Maxine like that? You need to—"

Gabby put her palm up to stop Joy from talking. "I don't need to do anything. Maxine is dead to me."

"Gabby! Why do you always have to take shit to the extreme?"

"You better get your head out of the clouds and prepare yourself for her death." Tears welled in Gabby's eyes as she stared at Joy.

Horrible memories of how she had found Maxine unconscious and bloody on her kitchen floor flashed in Joy's head. She didn't want to admit it, but she knew Maxine was in danger.

$\mathcal{C}$hapter 11

Gabby paced around Joy's living room Sunday morning with her cell phone to her ear. When Rayshawn didn't answer, she left him a message. "Rayshawn, where is my daughter? You haven't answered my calls for the past two days. I'm calling the police and reporting Nadia kidnapped."She went to her laptop on the dining room table and searched the Internet for the police department in Columbus, Georgia, where Rayshawn lived. As soon as she found it, her cell phone rang.

"Hello!" she said anxiously.

"Wassup?" Rayshawn asked calmly.

"Where is Nadia?" Gabby held the phone with shaking hands.

"She alright. Why?" he chuckled.

"That's not what I asked. Don't play games when it comes to my child!" Gabby yelled.

"She's not coming back to Maryland. I'm gonna let her stay here and raise her myself," Rayshawn announced.

"I'm going to kill you, Rayshawn! You better get on the next flight and bring her home right now."

"You should be happy I'm keeping her here. Now you free to fuck all the ex-convicts you want, but my daughter won't be around to see it."

Gabby paused. *He knows about Bo.* "I'm on my way to get her!"

"Come all you want, but she ain't goin' with you."

Rayshawn let out a deep laugh before he ended the call.

Gabby sat in front of the laptop with hot blood coursing through her veins. She was mad at herself for listening to her lawyer and letting Nadia stay with Rayshawn. Now he thought he had the right to keep and raise her child. She refused to ever let that happen. And he knew about her and Bo sleeping together, which meant he still had someone following her. That didn't concern her as much as Rayshawn thinking he could keep Nadia in Georgia. She looked up flights and the earliest available one was Wednesday morning. She wasn't waiting that long.

She ran upstairs, two steps at a time. When she reached her room, she yanked the closet door open, snatched her suitcase, and heaved it on her bed, throwing in clothes from her closet and dresser drawers. Driving to Columbus, Georgia, to get Nadia was the only thing on her mind.

Joy made her way to Gabby's room and stood in the doorway looking at her.

"Rayshawn thinks he's going to raise my baby in Georgia." Gabby slammed her suitcase shut and locked it. "There are no available flights until Wednesday, so I'm driving."

Joy took Gabby's arm and guided her to a clear space on the bed for them to sit. She put her arm around Gabby's shoulders and held her until her heavy breathing slowed down. After a few minutes, Gabby told Joy about the private detective Rayshawn had following her. She intentionally left out the pictures with Bo Johnson at the Red Roof Inn.

"That sick bastard! Have you talked to your lawyer? Does Rayshawn have a legal right to keep her?"

Gabby stood and took a legal-size envelope out of a briefcase beside her bed. She pulled out a sheet of paper and waved it in Joy's direction. "I still have the legal document he signed giving up his parental rights. I'm going to shove a copy down his throat when I see him." She smiled thinking about it. "It's a twelve-hour drive. If I leave now, I should be there before Nadia wakes up in the morning."

"You're not going by yourself. Give me a few minutes to pack my bag and I'll go with you."

"No, Joy! You have to pee every five minutes and that'll just slow me down. I need to get to Georgia as soon as possible." Gabby stood and took the suitcase off the bed.

"Say what you want, but I'm not letting you go alone. Who knows what Rayshawn has waiting for you?" Joy put her hands on her hips and looked at Gabby with an attitude. "If you go, I go."

Gabby rolled her eyes and sighed. "Hurry up, girl, and let's go bring my baby home."

———

Throughout the long ride, Gabby worried about Rayshawn taking Nadia somewhere else to try to keep them apart. It was a little after noon the next day when she pulled into the long driveway. She used her cell phone to call him as Joy watched anxiously from the passenger seat.

"Hi, Rayshawn. I'm here. Can you open the gate, please?" Gabby asked nicely. Her plan was to kill him with kindness, but once Joy and Nadia were safely in her car, she was going to beat him to death.

"I can see you on the monitor. Why didn't you use the intercom box like everybody else?" Rayshawn barked.

"You still haven't learned, Rayshawn. I'm not like everybody else. Now open the gate." She ended the call and stared ahead at the black iron gate with R&R centered on it. After a few loud clicking sounds, the doors opened. Eyes flaming with fury, Gabby pressed her foot down on the gas pedal and sped toward the main house.

Joy looked out the passenger window as Gabby drove ahead. The property was an old plantation, not modern as she had imagined. It was massive and somewhat tacky. She had never seen so many angel water fountains in one location. From the driveway to the iron gates alone, she counted four of them. Then she saw another six on the property before they reached the main house. The landscaping was lush and green, but someone planted plastic flowers instead of real ones. She burst out laughing when she saw some of the white price tags sticking out from under the dirt.

When they pulled in front of the house, the exterior looked

like it was in need of some serious repairs. Some of the bricks were missing from the front and sides of the house and the roof had missing shingles. Joy hoped the inside looked better because the outside could definitely be used in one of those haunted mansion movies. Gabby was out of the car and ringing the doorbell before Joy could take her seatbelt off. By the time she made it up the porch steps, an older, heavyset African-American woman opened the door and looked them up and down. She looked like a female version of Rayshawn, only fatter and with bigger breasts.

"Who are you? Never mind." Gabby rushed past the woman. "Where is Nadia? Rayshawn!"

Joy and the woman followed Gabby into the house.

"Rayshawn left, and for your information, young lady, my name is Mrs. Robinson and don't you come up in my son's house raising hell." She moved close to Gabby and pointed in her face.

"You have one second to get your arthritic finger out of my face before I break it!" Gabby threatened.

"You can try. I'll take this wig and my earrings off and whip you like your momma should have." Mrs. Robinson poked her finger closer to Gabby's face.

Joy backed Gabby away. "Let's get Nadia and go home."

"Where is my daughter, you old bat?" Gabby gave Mrs. Robinson an evil sneer.

"And this old bat 'bout to swing on your ass." Mrs. Robinson snatched her wig off and threw it on the floor.

"I'm not here to fight a senior citizen, so you better go sit down somewhere before you break a hip or have a heart attack." Gabby crossed her arms over her chest. "Where is my daughter? I'm not leaving here without her."

"There she is!" Joy called out.

A young Hispanic woman wearing a black-and-white maid's uniform entered the living room with Nadia in her arms. When the maid saw Mrs. Robinson's wig on the floor and Gabby's intense expression, she hesitated. Gabby screamed and snatched Nadia from the maid's arms. She held her daughter tight to her body until Nadia started crying.

Joy took Nadia from Gabby and kissed her. "Let's get her

things and go, Gabby."

"Don't bother, leave it. Rayshawn's child support just hit my account, so I'll buy her all new things." Gabby smirked at Mrs. Robinson.

"I know about women like you. Nothing but a home wrecker. You use your outer beauty to sleep with a professional ball player. You get pregnant, tear up their families, and then try to get all their money while using the innocent child as a pawn. It's sickening." Mrs. Robinson threw her hands in the air. "Lord Jesus, help us. The devil's spawn has entered our lives. We rebuke her, Lord Jesus. We rebuke her. Cast your angels around us, Lord, as we fight to save innocent Nadia from the devil who gave her life."

"Where is your holy water? Aren't you supposed to sprinkle that on me after you do your Indian dance and prayer?" Gabby laughed out loud.

With Nadia in one arm, Joy pulled Gabby toward the front door. "Open the door and let's go."

Gabby opened the door and Joy walked to the car with Nadia in her arms. Gabby followed them. While Joy was putting the child in her car seat, Gabby turned around and went back to the door where Mrs. Robinson was standing.

"Tell your son he's a coward. Any man who has his momma fight his battles is not worthy of being a father. He'll never see Nadia again." Gabby turned to leave.

"You are nothing but pure evil," Mrs. Robinson interjected. "If my granddaughter grows up to be anything like you, I'd kill her myself."

"That's a horrible thing to say, lady!" Joy glared at Mrs. Robinson over the hood of Gabby's SUV.

"If you ever say another word about my daughter being dead, the next time I shoot something at you, it won't be coming from my mouth." Gabby made a gurgling sound with her throat, then spit in Mrs. Robinson's face.

The old woman let out an ear-piercing squeal as she fell against the door clawing at her face. She dropped her head inside her shirt, wiped the spit off and then turned to face Gabby. With both arms pointed like loaded guns, she shot Gabby a hateful glare.

"Oh, my God! You're nasty! Rayshawn fucked up when he had relations with you. Ain't a mustard seed of good in you."

"And don't you forget it." Gabby smiled and waved as she walked down the steps.

She got behind the wheel of her Lexus, blew the horn at Mrs. Robinson, and drove away praying for the gate to be open. The last thing she needed was to be trapped on Rayshawn's property after what she just did. When they pulled up to the black iron gate, it was open. Gabby looked at Joy with arched eyebrows, then smiled. They breathed a sigh of relief as they drove down the long, narrow driveway.

"It's over. Rayshawn didn't stand a chance of keeping my baby. Let's go home," Gabby said excitedly.

"Not so fast," Joy stated with a trembling voice.

The end of the driveway was blocked by a Muscogee County Sheriff's squad car with flashing lights and sirens blaring.

"Um, can you go to jail for spitting in an old lady's face?" Gabby looked at Joy with frightened eyes as she chewed her bottom lip nervously.

"Oh, shit!" Joy's stomach did flips at the thought of having her twins in jail.

A white female police officer tapped on Gabby's window. Gabby rolled it down. "Hello, officer. Is there a problem?"

"Are you Gabrielle Roché?" she asked with a strong southern accent.

"Yes, I am."

The officer handed Gabby a thick envelope and said, "You've been served."

With her mouth wide open, Gabby ripped the envelope open. She moved her index finger and eyes across the pages.

"He's suing me for full custody. He claims I'm homeless and financially dependent on his child support because I'm unemployed. He's also claiming I have a promiscuous lifestyle that's a danger to Nadia."

Gabby quickly skimmed the rest of the six-page summons. She knew now that what she thought was the end was really just the beginning of her battle with Rayshawn.

Chapter 12

The next morning, Joy sat across from Gabby and Nadia at a Cracker Barrel restaurant in North Carolina. They'd slept late and missed the continental breakfast at the Holiday Inn. While Gabby strapped Nadia in a high chair, Joy had her cell phone to her ear checking her messages.

"Baby, I know you're pissed and you have every right to be. I was wrong. I should've told you about Diana. Please call me, text me, email me, anything to let me know where you are." Joy sighed, then deleted the message.

"Hey, girl. Call me back and let me know what happened with Nadia. You didn't tell Allen you were going to Georgia? He's been calling me looking for you. I didn't tell him anything." Joy smiled at the cheery tone in Maxine's voice.

"It's me again, baby. How long are you gonna make me suffer? You changed the locks. You won't answer my calls and you just disappeared without telling me. Joy, please call me. I couldn't handle it if something happened to you and the twins. I love you, baby. Please call me." She wiped the tears welling in her eyes and deleted the message.

Gabby looked across the table at Joy. "Are you okay?"

"I don't want to talk about it." Joy took a deep breath and exhaled to hold back her tears.

"Fine with me! I got enough problems of my own in case you forgot," Gabby replied in a sarcastic tone. "Oh, and since

Allen is out of the hospital, when we get back, I'm moving in with Bea until I can find my own place."

"Whatever." Joy looked around the restaurant for their waitress. She was starting to get a headache and her stomach was growling. They had been waiting long enough. She was ready to place her order and eat.

Gabby reached in her purse and pulled out her ringing cell phone. She looked at the screen and then Joy. "It's Allen again. Should I answer it?"

"No!" Joy snapped.

Gabby dropped the phone back in her bag and crossed her arms over her chest. "I thought I taught you better than this. You don't let some chick come in your house and take your man."

"Allen is *not* with Diana!" Joy stated with an attitude.

Gabby leaned across the table and grabbed Joy's wrist. "You're smarter than this, Joy. Are those twins using up your brain cells? Diana has staked her claim on Allen. She has made it known to you and Allen that she wants your man and is willing to do whatever it takes to get him."

"She's pursuing him, not the other way around," Joy replied angrily as she snatched her wrist from Gabby's grip.

Gabby rolled her eyes and sighed to show her disappointment. "Allen doesn't want her, huh? The truth hurts, but you need to hear it. Allen wants Diana."

Joy's cheeks turned red and her eyes bulged as she opened her mouth to protest. Gabby put her palm up to stop Joy from speaking. "Let me explain. Diana visited him every day at the hospital. Did he tell her to stop coming? No! Why? Because he enjoyed all the attention she was giving him. Diana emailed him naked pictures of herself. What happened between them to make her feel comfortable enough to do that? Ummm... he liked looking at her pictures and he told her. That's why later she sent the video of them having sex. Did he delete any of this from his computer? No! Why? Because he liked looking at it."

"I know! I hate him!" Joy covered her face with her hands and sobbed.

"No, you don't. You love Allen. He's a good man... for you,

anyway." Gabby poured milk into Nadia's bottle, screwed the top on, and gave it to her.

"What?" Joy dropped her hands and looked at Gabby with a questioning expression. She never had anything good to say about Allen in the past.

"Any man who's willing to risk his life to save his woman and unborn children is alright with me. And let's not forget he pushed me out of the way of Dean's bullet. If it wasn't for him, I might not be here right now." Gabby caressed Nadia's hair.

"He *was* a good man, now he's a fucking liar." Joy covered her mouth when Nadia stopped drinking her bottle and looked at her.

"He's just confused right now. He's been shot, and it made him feel vulnerable. Diana sees it and she's trying to swoop in and boost his ego to make him want her."

Joy looked down at her hands as the truth of Gabby's words sank in.

"You're to blame for some of this, too," Gabby added.

"I know it's my fault my husband shot him. I feel guilty about it every day." Joy massaged her temples and sighed.

"That's not what I'm talking about. You're always putting everybody before Allen. You should've learned your lesson when he left you for China, but you didn't. When you were on bed rest, you got out of bed to go identify Dean's body. He could've waited. It's not like he was going anywhere. How do you think that made Allen feel? You never went off bed rest to visit him. And don't get me started on the paternity test with Dean's parents. That's another example of how you're putting somebody else's wants before Allen's." Gabby watched Joy's expression to see if her words were getting through.

"I didn't think of it like that," Joy said in a low tone.

"Most women don't. Do you know how many married or committed men I've slept with because their wives or girlfriends put their children, work, family, friends, school, and whatever else before their man's needs. It's crazy how these men were willing to give me the world simply because I gave them what they wanted and showed them a little attention."

"I can see that happening, but I don't even know where to begin with Allen." She closed her eyes and rubbed her forehead.

"He wants to be a father to those twins. You can start there." Gabby pointed at Joy's belly.

Joy gasped and covered her stomach. "I'm not using my babies to hold on to Allen."

The waitress approached their table. "I'm sorry. We're busy this morning. Are you ready to order?"

"Yes, just one second, please," Gabby said.

"I'm ready to order." Joy looked at the waitress.

"Joy, this is my final bit of advice. Don't stay away from Allen too long. Every day Diana left the hospital, she went home and played with her pussy while thinking about your man. By now, she's tired of playing with herself and ready for the real deal." Gabby looked at the waitress and smiled. "Hello. I'll have an order of pancakes with fruit topping and turkey sausage on the side."

The waitress stared at Gabby with her mouth hanging open and her pencil in the air. "Oh... okay."

"I'll have the same thing but with maple syrup, please. Thank you," Joy added. She took her cell phone off the table and stood. "I'll be back."

Joy walked outside and sat in one of the rocking chairs lined up in front of the restaurant. She rocked as she stared at the cell phone and tried to gather the courage to call Allen. She wasn't ready to have a conversation with him about Diana, but he was the twins' father and deserved to know they were okay. She took a deep breath and steadied her fingers to dial his number. He answered on the first ring.

"Joy, baby, where are you?" he asked anxiously.

She shut down when she heard his voice. Tears welled in her eyes, she couldn't speak, and her heart kicked her chest.

"Please say something, baby," Allen begged.

"I need time away from you to think. Can you stop calling me and just give me some space?" Joy closed her eyes and swallowed the lump forming in her throat.

"You've had enough space. I've been out of the hospital for almost a week and we haven't seen each other or talked. Tell me where you are and I'll have Bo bring me to you."

"No," she whispered.

"Joy, you still there?"

"I need space and time to decide if I can still be with you after you cheated on me."

"I didn't sleep with Diana. I was in the hospital with a gun-shot wound in my chest. Tell me how you expect me to fuck some-body when I'm like that."

"Fucking somebody isn't the only way to cheat, Allen. You lied to me. You have secrets with her. I feel like I don't know you anymore." Joy sobbed. "How could you talk to me on the phone with her sitting at your bedside? What else were you two doing in your room?"

"Where is the trust, Joy?"

"My trust in you went away after I read your emails, Allen."

"I was wrong for not telling you about that. I'm sorry. I fucked up with that. Give me a chance to talk face-to-face so we can work this out."

"Bullshit, Allen! I don't want to hear how sorry you are. I want to hear the truth. Are you man enough to tell me the truth?"

Allen cleared his throat. "We kissed a few times, but that was it."

"You bastard! I don't have anything else to say to you!"

"Hell no! You wanted the truth and I told you. I love you, not Diana. Either we talk right now or I'll come by the house every day until you open the fucking door. Make a decision, Joy."

"Okay... I decide I don't want to be with you anymore."

"What are you saying?"

"I'm saying if I had to make a decision right now, I'd rather be alone than be lied to, cheated on, and disrespected by the man I love."

"Okay... um, shit. Don't, um, don't make a decision right now, baby. I'll give you your space. Call me when you're ready to talk. Just know that I love you, Joy."

"Goodbye, Allen." Joy pushed the End button, turned off her phone, and walked back into the restaurant.

*C*hapter 13

Maxine groaned as she hit her steering wheel. She pumped the gas pedal a couple of times, trying to start her engine. Nothing. She slumped over the wheel and sighed. It had been one of those days. Thank God, it was Friday and she had the weekend to rest at home with her family. Once she got home, that is. For now, she needed to find a ride. It was almost nine o'clock so calling Trent wasn't an option. She took her cell phone out of the cup holder to call Joy, but the battery was dead. *Shit*! If she had left work earlier as she planned, she wouldn't be in this situation.

She stayed late to see her students perform during a celebration in honor of Dr. Martin Luther King Jr.'s birthday. All twenty-five of the kids marched on stage in their Sunday best, locked arms, and sang "We Shall Overcome" as they rocked side to side. Even her problem students behaved for the performance and for that, she was grateful.

Someone tapped on her window. She turned her head, and seeing Kevin Bradley, rolled her eyes. He had been trying to get her attention all evening. She did everything in her power to avoid him. Since he was good friends with her principal, she knew there was a chance he would be at the program tonight, but that didn't mean she had to talk to him. He tapped her window again.

She swung her door open, trying to hit him with it. "What?"

He jumped back and laughed. "I see you're still mad at me."

"That's an understatement. How are your foreign-ex-change-students-slash-wife and kids doing?" Maxine beamed her narrow eyes on him.

He nodded his head and gave her a sly smile. "That's all in the past, Maxine."

"You got that right." Maxine closed her minivan door.

He tapped on the window again. "Do you need help?"

She looked around the parking lot. It was almost empty except for a few people she had never seen before. Common sense told her to take advantage of Kevin's help or she'd be stuck at the school for who knew how long. She opened her door. "My minivan won't start and my cell phone battery died. Can I use your phone?"

Kevin sighed. "I don't have my phone, but I can give you a ride home."

Maxine gave him a suspicious glance. She knew Kevin was trying to hook up with her again, but she did not intend to let that happen. Trent wouldn't be happy to see her coming home with the married man she'd slept with, but she didn't care. She just wanted to go home and see her family.

"You still live with your parents in Fort Washington? I can have you home in fifteen minutes," Kevin promised.

"I'm not with my parents anymore. I'll show you where to drop me off." She gathered her bags, locked her minivan, and walked with Kevin to his car.

A few minutes later, after they pulled onto the Beltway, Kevin reached across and squeezed Maxine's breasts. "Do you ever think about me?"

Maxine calmly brushed his hand off her chest. "I think about you every time I see a stray dog."

He frowned and put both hands on the steering wheel. "Would you consider letting me take you out to dinner to apologize?"

"No. We're both married and I don't think our spouses would like that." Maxine kept her eyes focused straight ahead and her hands in her lap. She didn't want to give Kevin any false hope of getting back between her legs.

"So you're back with the Magnum man, huh, the one who

beat you?" Kevin shook his head disapprovingly.

"Um-hum, and enjoying every second of it," Maxine bragged with a smile. "After you, I realized how much I missed my husband's big... you know. But I guess some women, like your wife, enjoy the smaller ones."

That was enough to shut Kevin up and keep his hands to himself. They rode the rest of the way in complete silence. As he took the exit off the Beltway, his cell phone rang. Maxine glared at him.

"Oh... I forgot I had it." He ignored the call.

"Liar," she murmured.

When Kevin turned into her development, she had him pull in front of her townhouse. After she gathered her bags and thanked him for the ride, she reached in her purse and offered him money for gas, but he refused to take it. Grateful to be home, she stepped out of his car and headed toward her front porch.

Kevin turned off his car and followed her. "Maxine, wait up."

"Go home, Kevin," Maxine ordered.

"I wanna apologize for what I did in the car and for lying to you before." Kevin shoved his hands in his coat pocket and looked down at the ground.

"Apology accepted, now go home to your wife and family." Maxine stared at him with pursed lips.

"Okay... take care, Maxine." He hugged her, kissed her cheek, and walked back to his car.

"Bye, Kevin." Maxine shivered as she walked up her porch steps.

She entered her house, closed and locked the door, then dropped her bags in the foyer. It was unusually quiet. She walked upstairs to find her family. When she reached the top step, Trent was sitting on the floor in the hallway. She jumped and almost tumbled back down the steps but grabbed the handrail to stop herself.

"Trent, why are you sitting on the floor? Where are the boys?" She bent down to kiss him, but he pulled away.

"With my mother. I wanted us to spend some time alone,

but I see you had other plans." Trent looked down at the floor.

"I didn't have other plans. The minivan wouldn't start and my cell died. I had to get a ride home. I should've left earlier, but the program was so good and my students did a wonderful job."

"I don't care about your students. Who was that mother-fucker who dropped you off and was kissing all over you outside?"

Maxine's stomach did a somersault. "It was Kevin," she answered in a low voice.

"Who?" Trent glared at her.

"It was Kevin Bradley. Everybody else was gone and he offered to give me a ride." Maxine shifted her body weight from one leg to the other.

"Bullshit, Maxine! You lying whore!"

"Trent Anderson, don't you dare call me that! He tried to hit on me and I set him straight. That was it. I'm not going to waste my energy arguing about it." Maxine stepped over Trent and went to her bedroom.

Trent followed her. "So it's a coincidence you ran into him after Gabby just mentioned him. I know that sneaky bitch had something to do with this. She would rather see you be in a married man's bed than with your husband, and you're falling for it."

"You sound like a crazy person right now, Trent. I haven't spoken to Gabby since she left here." Maxine removed her clothes, wrapped a towel around her body, and walked toward the bathroom.

Trent blocked her. "I will not have my wife whoring around with another man. Respect me! From now on, you better come straight home after work. No more teaching aftercare or participating in any after-school activities. When I get home, you and the boys better be in here waiting for me."

"I'm not under house arrest. You are. I'm not quitting my aftercare job. I enjoy it and it helps me pay all the debt you got us in. If you're not comfortable with that, you can move back to your apartment." Maxine walked around Trent and went into the bathroom.

Trent followed her and stood in the doorway. "I should whip your ass."

"I wish you would put your hands on me again. You'll regret it." Maxine slammed the bathroom door in Trent's face.

She turned on the shower, hung her towel on the rack, and stepped in the bathtub. While she was enjoying the hot water on her skin, Trent opened the door and yanked the shower curtain back. He stared at her with crazy eyes. Grabbing her hair, he pulled her out of the shower, and threw her to the floor. The impact knocked the wind out of her. He dragged her across the bedroom carpet by her ankle. The friction from the carpet burned her skin.

"Stop, Trent! You don't want to do this," she cried.

"You goddamn whore! You trying to wash his scent off you before you get in bed with me." He smacked her hard across her face, and Maxine felt her lip split.

"No, Trent." She tried to hit him back, but he sat on her chest and used his knees to pin her arms down.

"Don't you move. If you do, I'll choke you until you stop moving. Do you understand me?" He stared at her with his fist raised.

"Yes," she whispered, trying to remain still.

Trent kept his eyes on her as he moved off her chest. He crawled between her thighs and ordered, "Open your legs."

Maxine opened her legs spread-eagle.

He put his nose between her legs and sniffed. Spreading her vaginal lips open, he examined her. For what felt like hours, he alternated between touching, smelling, and inspecting her privates. When her legs dropped from fatigue, he smacked her hip hard with his open hand. The sting made her scream out in pain and she returned her legs to the position he wanted. Immediately, he rammed two fingers inside her and moved them around in a circular motion. When he pulled them out, he sniffed them.

"You cheating bitch. I can smell him all in you." Trent stood up and removed his belt from his pants.

Maxine dropped her legs and rolled under the bed. He caught her leg and pulled her out, but not before she grabbed the bat she kept hidden there. She flipped on her back and started swinging. The first swing caught the side of his head. The second hit his shoulder. He fell back into the dresser looking dazed and

89

confused.

Maxine jumped to her feet and kept swinging. Trent tried to run, but she hit him hard in his back and he fell to his knees. She raised the bat high over her shoulder and swung at his butt. He yelled out as he tried to crawl away from her. She beat his backside all the way to the hall, then used the handle of the bat to push him down the hardwood steps. His face was bloody and swollen by the time he reached the bottom.

"You better leave or I'll call the police and have you arrested." Maxine stood over him with the bat in the air, ready to strike again.

He spit a mouthful of blood on the carpet and crawled toward her, leaving a red trail. Moaning in pain, he reached out to touch her leg but she stepped back and swung the bat at his arm. A loud cracking sound echoed throughout the room. Falling on his back, he grabbed his arm, and screamed.

"You have one minute to get out or I'll call the cops," Maxine threatened.

"My curfew. Help me, Maxi. I'm sorry," he cried.

"Now you have thirty seconds." Maxine kept the bat in one hand and picked up her home phone with the other.

"No, don't call, please. I don't wanna go back. I'll leave." Trent stumbled as he stood to his feet. He held his arm and limped to the front door.

Maxine kept the bat pointed at him as she opened the door. He avoided eye contact with her as he staggered outside. After she closed and locked the door, she set her alarm. With her whole body trembling, she dropped the bat and reached for her phone. Praying for strength, she punched the numbers.

"Hello." Joy answered in a groggy voice.

"Trent hit me!"

"Did you call the police?" Joy jumped off her sofa, grabbed her handbag, and rushed toward her front door.

"No! Please don't call the police! Can you come?" She looked out the window and saw Trent driving away.

"I'm already in my car." Joy broke speed as she drove to Maxine's house.

90

Thirty minutes later, Joy followed Maxine around her townhouse as she gave a play-by-play of what happened between her and Trent. Joy was relieved that the blood on the carpet was from Trent and not Maxine. Other than a busted lip, Maxine didn't seem to have any injuries and she had calmed down a great deal.

"You need to have his ass locked up, Maxine." Joy frowned.

"No. I can't do that to my boys. They love Trent, and if he just went away, they would have a hard time," Maxine explained.

"They'll adjust, just like they did the last time." Joy shook her head because she knew her advice was wasted on Maxine.

The house phone rang. Maxine scowled then hit the speaker button. "Hello."

"I'm in the hospital. You dislocated my shoulder, you cheating bitch. I should press charges against you," Trent threatened.

"It was self-defense, and you'll be the one behind bars, not me. Either way, I'm filing for divorce."

"Bitch!" He hung up.

Maxine leaned her head on Joy's shoulder and sobbed. "Joy, I don't want to be alone."

"Girl, if you take his ass back, I'm through with you," Joy threatened.

"I'm not. I promise. I'm filing for divorce. After what he did tonight, there is no going back." Maxine cried. "Please don't tell Gabby about this. I don't want to hear her opinion about how stupid I am."

"I won't tell her, but you're not stupid. Keeping that bat under your bed and using it on his ass was genius." Joy put her arms around Maxine. "I'm gonna spend the weekend here in case he tries to come back."

"Thank you." Maxine wiped her eyes. "Will I ever find a good man to love me?"

"Don't rush it, Maxine. Take your time and get yourself together first, then the right man will find you."

"Joy, I need a man. I'm not independent like you and Gabby. I want a man to come home to every night. The right man is out there waiting for me; I just need to find him."

Joy rolled her eyes to the heavens. Ever since college, Maxine's desperation had always led her to the wrong men. Chills shot down her spine as she wondered what kind of asshole her friend was going to end up with next.

Chapter 14

It was Saturday morning. Gabby left Nadia with Bea and asked Bo to meet her at Joy's house. They sat beside each other in Joy's living room as he read the court summons from Rayshawn. Every time he frowned, moaned, or turned the page, her heart skipped a beat. The occasional angry gaze he threw her way told her he wasn't happy about her latest baby daddy drama. They'd been sleeping together regularly since their first encounter in the garage and she had learned to read his moods.

Bo folded the documents up and handed them to Gabby. "How do you plan to handle this?"

Gabby tossed her hair over her shoulders, smiled at Bo, and rubbed his thigh. "I thought you could help me with it."

"I've been helping you since this shit started." He brushed her hand off his thigh. "My suggestion, give him what he wants."

"What! He wants my daughter and he's not getting her," Gabby protested.

Bo rested his elbows on his thighs and leaned over in Gabby's direction. "You sure? Being a full-time daddy to a lil' girl is the last thing a professional football player wants, especially one going through a divorce. He's doing this because he wants something. Maybe it's you. Find out what he wants and give it to him."

"And you would be okay with me giving myself to him," Gabby snapped.

"You not mine. You can fuck who you want. Shit, I had sex with my wife before I came over here."

Gabby frowned and fire coursed through her body. Lately, she hated to hear Bo talk about his wife, Peaches. Gabby was never jealous of other women, but Peaches had something she wanted. Bo.

"I just want you to take care of this before it goes to court." Bo glared at her with a creased forehead.

"How am I supposed to do that? He tricked me into coming to Georgia to get my daughter so he could have me served with custody papers. I never saw it coming. It's getting harder for me to stay a step ahead of him. I don't—"

"Just shut the fuck up and listen! This shit has gotten out of control, private detectives with pictures, lawyers, custody fights. I'm sick of this shit. Do what you need to do to make it go away or you'll regret it."

"Are you threatening me?" Gabby asked with wide eyes.

"What do you think?" Bo gave her a cold, angry stare.

Her cell phone rang. She picked it up off the table and looked at the screen. "I need to answer this."

Bo nodded his permission.

"Hello."

"Good morning, Gabby. I just got a counteroffer on your bid."

"If they're not willing to accept my offer, move on and put a bid on the next property on my list," Gabby instructed.

"Before we do that, let me tell you about the counteroffer. It's—"

"Kate, when I hired you to be my real estate agent, you told me you understood what I wanted. I don't want to go back and forth negotiating on properties. I will pay fifty thousand below the asking price and half the closing costs. This is a cash transaction, so if we were dealing with intelligent people, they would accept my offer, but since we're not, let's move on."

"But I..."

"Don't waste my time with counteroffers! I want to be in my new home by next weekend. If you're not the agent to make that happen, maybe I should work with someone else in your firm."

"No, I'll go down your list until an offer is accepted."

"Good, and don't call me back until you have a firm offer and a closing date." Gabby ended the call and placed her phone on the table.

She'd been on a mission since her return from Georgia. Finding a home for her and Nadia to move into right away was a priority. She wanted to refute Rayshawn's claim that she was homeless if they went to court. Finding a job was going to be easier than she thought. She already had a couple of interviews lined up, but she needed to find a place to live first and then hire Nadia a nanny. Everything Rayshawn put in his summons to win custody of Nadia was going to be a non-issue by the time they went to court in March. She hoped it was enough for her to keep Nadia with her.

Bo observed Gabby while she was on the phone and watched her drastic change from a damsel in distress to a hardcore, confident businesswoman in a matter of seconds. After being around shady characters most of his life, he knew how to spot them a mile away. Since he started spending time with Gabby, he knew there was more to her than she let everybody see and it was time for him to find out who he was really sleeping with before he ended up being one of her victims. "What's your story? Everybody got a background. What's yours? Where you come from?" Bo asked with furrowed brows.

"What do you mean? You know I met Joy in college." Gabby rubbed her neck to release the tension.

"That's the PG-13 version. I wanna hear your real story before college and don't hold nothing back." Bo sat back, crossed his legs, and shot her a hateful glare. Based on her phone call just now, and what happened with Dean, he knew there was more to Gabby than what she told people.

Gabby hesitated. Some things were better left untold, but she'd seen this look on Bo's face before at the Red Roof Inn and knew he was serious. She trusted him. Since their entire relationship was built on secrets, she knew telling him about her past would stay between them.

"I'm the product of an affair my mother, DeeDee, had with

an Italian man she met in a bar while her husband, Leroy, was in jail. She tried to pass me off as Leroy's, but I was lighter than anybody else in my family. Leroy made her choose me or him. She chose him."

"That's fucked up!" Bo interjected.

"It happens more than you think. They had four daughters and a son together, so she decided to put me up for adoption. When my grandmother found out, she took me and raised me as her own. I had a perfect childhood until my grandmother died when I was sixteen. Then, my mother and her family left their two-bedroom apartment and moved in my grandmother's house with me." Gabby looked down and swallowed.

"What happened to you?" Bo moved closer and held her in his arms.

"They hated me. Leroy made his daughters fight me. They stole my clothes and money. Whenever DeeDee tried to protect me, Leroy would beat her up. Eventually, she stopped trying and left me to fend for myself." Gabby sighed. "Leroy made me live in the basement so his daughters could have my room. I got a job at a women's clothing store after school to stay away from them. I learned to keep my distance and things got better. Then one day, I went home and DeeDee had all my things packed up."

"Why?" Bo gently pulled her chin up to him.

"She overheard her daughters and Leroy talking about an attack they had planned for me. The girls were gonna jump me, cut my hair, and slice my face up with box cutters Leroy gave them. He told them to stick an iron pole inside me to make people think I was attacked by a man." Gabby sat up, wiped her eyes, and shook her head.

"Damn! Where'd you go?"

"My loving mother drove me to the house of one of the women my grandmother went to church with. They took me in, and the woman's husband raped me the first night I was there. He took my virginity. When I told his wife about it, she asked me to let him do it a few times a week so she wouldn't have to. In exchange for doing it, I didn't have to pay rent or do any chores. I didn't have a choice. I didn't have anywhere else to go."

Bo pulled her close and wrapped his arms around her. "That's enough."

"I wanna tell you. A month after I moved in, I found out I was pregnant. His wife took me to have an abortion and kicked me out the same day. I went to school early every day to bathe and kept my clothes in my locker or at the store. I slept wherever I could, fast-food restaurants, parks, and buses. Nobody knew and nobody asked any questions. Then one day when I was practically sleepwalking, a female customer I always helped asked me what was wrong. I broke down and told her everything."

Gabby took a deep breath and exhaled. "She folded a one hundred-dollar bill into my hand and left. When I got off work that night, she was in the parking lot waiting for me. She took me home with her and became like a surrogate mother, even though she wasn't much older than me. She taught me everything I know about men, how to survive on my own, and how to stand up for myself. She was fierce. After living with her for a few months, I found out she was a paid escort, but I didn't judge her because she was my savior. I don't know where I would be today without her. I never told anybody about my past, not even Joy and Maxine." Gabby wiped the tears from her eyes and looked away from Bo.

"Were you a prostitute?" Bo asked with compassion.

"No, I wasn't!" Gabby protested. Bo's question hurt her. "She was a paid escort, not me. She didn't try to force that on me. I kept my job at the mall, finished school, and went off to college. She said it was a fresh start for me and stepped back to let me live my own life."

"Damn! I'm sorry. It explains a lot." Bo looked at her with sad eyes.

"Don't feel sorry for me and don't analyze me either! I survived it and I'll get through this, too!" Gabby bit her bottom lip to hold back her tears. After reliving those awful years, her emotions were all over the place.

"I respect you. I know people who went through less than you and ended up on drugs and stripping, but look at you. You're beautiful, classy, educated, and street-smart. The full package." Bo stood and pulled Gabby to her feet. He held her tight as she cried

97

in his arms. She felt so much lighter and freer after years of keeping her past a secret. He wiped her tears and held her. Gabby raised her head up and kissed Bo.

He stepped back. "I can't have Joy walking in here on us, and I told you I just screwed my wife."

"Joy is spending the day with Maxine. She won't be back until later this evening." Gabby rubbed her hand on his erection. "And your wife didn't do a good job of taking care of your needs."

He grabbed her face between his hands and pressed his lips against hers. They stuck their tongues in each other's mouths and pressed their bodies together until there was no space between them. His erection throbbed against her stomach. He stopped kissing her and looked into her eyes.

"What are you doing to me? I can't get out of bed with my wife and jump into bed with you." Bo frowned and shook his head.

"I need this. I need you right now." She pulled his head to hers and put her lips on his.

They gasped for breath as they quickly undressed each other. Bo looked at her naked body and shook his head. He had never seen a more perfect body. He picked her up and carried her to the couch. She wrapped her legs around him as she placed small kisses over his lips and face. As he gently placed her on the couch, he stood over her and let his eyes move up and down her body, taking it all in. His manhood expanded with every glimpse of her.

Gabby quickly sat up, moved between his legs, and took him in her mouth. He grabbed the back of her head and pushed himself down her throat. She moaned as he stretched her mouth with his thickness. When he felt himself getting ready to release, he pulled out. Pushing Gabby back on the sofa, he wrapped his arms around her legs and pulled her close to his face. He kissed and nibbled her inner thighs while he flicked her clitoris with his fingers. When her vagina was dripping wet, he slid his fingers inside of her while he sucked her clitoris. She arched her back and pushed her hips closer to his face.

He raised his head and looked at her. "Damn, you wet! Girl, I'm ready to fuck the shit out of you!"

"Not yet!" Gabby pushed his head back between her legs.

"Finish what you started!"

He sucked her clitoris and curled his fingers inside her until he found her G-spot. Moving his mouth and fingers in the same rhythm, he took his time until Gabby let out a deep groan and her body twitched uncontrollably.

After wiping his mouth with the back of his hand, he took a condom out of his wallet and rolled it down his penis.

Gabby stood and pointed at the floor. "I need you to lie back and relax."

Smiling, he followed Gabby's instructions. She looked in his eyes as she slid down his manhood. The feeling of her warm and moist vaginal walls caused him to grunt while she exhaled deeply as he filled her insides. He immediately started moving inside of her.

"Stop it! Don't move!" Gabby ordered.

"Damn, ummm, okay." He clenched his teeth and tried not to move. While sitting on top of him, Gabby turned her whole body around, with him still inside her, until her back faced him.

Bo raised his head and watched in amazement. "Damn, girl. You'll make me come, just doing that shit." He put his hands on her hips and started moving inside her again.

"Stop moving, Bo!" She smacked his leg.

He squeezed his head between his hands. "Why you teasing me, Gabby?"

"Be patient. Trust me. It's worth the wait." She squeezed her internal muscles around his penis, leaned her upper body forward, and moved her hips in a circular motion until his manhood rubbed up against her G-spot. She moved her hips back and forth, enjoying the jolts of pleasure that shot through her body.

"Okay, Bo! Give it to me!"

He held her waist firmly and copied Gabby's pace. She stretched her arms out and squeezed his ankles as her orgasm caused her to convulse and moan. Bo stroked her until his body tensed and he released his juices. Sliding off him, Gabby lay between his legs completely spent.

"Damn! You felt good as shit!" Bo panted.

"I know." Gabby moved beside Bo, put her arm around

him, and closed her eyes.

Bo kissed her cheek and held her tight. This was the first time since they started sleeping together that he didn't rush out the door and run home to his family. She took pleasure in being in his arms and felt comfortable talking to him so freely. Common sense should have set off alarms in her head to stay away from Bo Johnson. If this continued, she might break her first rule. Never fall in love with a married man.

Chapter 15

Allen sat at the kitchen table and watched Joy as she took a bottle of water out of the refrigerator. It had been a week since they last talked. When she called yesterday and invited him to her doctor's appointment this morning, he thought it was a step toward working out their problems, but now he wasn't sure. They had been together for the last two hours, but she hadn't said a single word to him and refused to look in his direction. He was prepared to stay as long as it took for them to talk, but one of them needed to make the first move.

"Joy, can you stop ignoring me, please?" He walked to where she stood near the kitchen sink and put his arms around her. "A relationship is nothing without communication."

"A relationship is nothing without trust." She pushed his arms away and turned her back to him.

"Damn, I'm trying, baby. Can't you see that? I take full responsibility for the bad choices I made with Diana, but I'm here trying to work things out." He turned Joy around to face him. Guilt overwhelmed him when he saw how hurt she looked.

"Are you in love with her?" Joy tried to sound strong, but her voice cracked. She looked down at the floor so he couldn't see how upset she was.

"No! I don't love her and I never did, baby. I love you. Please believe that." Allen used his hand to raise her chin so he could look in her eyes.

"Why the secrets? What happened when she visited you every day?" Joy put her bottled water on the countertop and looked at him.

"I was wrong for not telling you about her. I'm sorry. I fucked up and I know it." Allen pulled Joy to him and held her close.

"I feel like I don't know you anymore." Trying to hold back her tears, she swallowed a lump in her throat. "How could you talk to me on the phone with her sitting at your bedside? And the emails? Why didn't you tell me?"

"I'm sorry." Allen sighed.

Joy stepped back from Allen's embrace and pointed her index finger inches from his face. "Tell me the goddamn truth about you and Diana or get out and don't come back."

"Okay," he relented. "You and my family didn't understand how I felt or just acted like everything was alright and it was rough. She saw me struggling and helped me through my bad days, but I stopped talking to her after you found the emails. I told her I love you and needed to focus on our relationship."

Joy's stomach did flips as she glared at him. "Why didn't you talk to me about your bad days? I couldn't be at the hospital with you, but I called you all the time."

"Bullshit, Joy! You weren't there for me. When I was in the hospital, I realized I would come back home to the same old shit with you." He paced back and forth in the kitchen with his fists balled. "I called you to talk about my setbacks and painful physical therapy sessions, but you would say some shit like 'let me call you back, I got Bea on the other line' or 'I can't talk because Gabby's upset about her daughter.' What the fuck, Joy? I needed you!"

"I didn't know I was doing that." Joy gasped and covered her mouth as she realized how many times she put her mother and girlfriends' issues before him while he was in the hospital. *Gabby was right; I don't put him first.*

"You never do, and that's how I ended up locking lips with Diana in the hospital. The first time was when I found out about the paternity test. She was right by my side and understood how hurt I was when you didn't." He stepped in front of Joy and looked at her.

"Why didn't you tell me how you felt? I would've..."

"You would've what, Joy? Why do I have to tell the woman I love how to love me back? Huh? Do you have to tell me how to love you?" Allen chuckled and shook his head. "You still don't get it. When Bea called me with the news that you were pregnant with my children, I walked away from the career I spent years building to come back to you."

"I didn't ask you to do that," Joy snapped.

"It's what I wanted. When I saw you pregnant with the babies we created, my heart overruled my brain and I walked away from my dream job and life in China to be here for you. Have you ever done anything like that for me?" He chewed his bottom lip as he stared at her. The pain on her face broke his heart, but he needed to tell her the truth.

"I'm sorry." She searched her memories for a time when she put him first and she couldn't think of anything. He had always given her what she needed, but she took his love for granted because she knew he would be there for her no matter what. Realizing he was right, she felt nauseous.

"You're not perfect, Joy. We all make bad choices. When I proposed to you, you turned me down because of your mother, and then a few months later, you went against her and married a god-damn psychopath."

"That was a mistake," Joy whispered.

"I know! I got the scar on my chest to remind me every day of your mistake." Allen pulled his shirt over his head, tossed it on the table, and pointed at the scar left by Dean's bullet. "I'm not obsessing over this because as long as you and the twins are alive and safe, I'm grateful."

"I'm sorry I'm the reason that happened to you." Joy sat at the kitchen table, put her head down, and cried uncontrollably. When Allen touched her, she pushed his hands away. He went in the bathroom to get her some tissue and a washcloth. When he returned, she straightened up and he wiped her face. There was so much she wanted to say, but she couldn't.

"Me getting shot wasn't your fault. I was just a man protecting his family from an unstable person. I love you and our children." He tried to kiss her lips, but she turned her head.

"You should've thought about me and our children while you were sticking your tongue down Diana's throat and jerking off to her emails in the hospital." Joy rolled her eyes at him.

"Do you ever think about me? How do you think I felt when you called me in the hospital to tell me that Bea wants you to take your last two classes online?" Allen stared at her with a hardened face. "I suggested online classes to you when I proposed and asked you to move to China with me, but you didn't even consider it."

Joy stared at him in stunned silence because he was right. She realized she was one of those women Gabby talked about who put everybody and everything before her man. Now she understood why he turned to Diana, but she still couldn't forgive him. She didn't know if she would ever be able to forgive him for hurting her.

He put his forehead to hers and held her face between his hands. "I don't wanna lose you. I wanna come home so we can work through this together. Tell me what I need to do to make this better, baby."

"I don't know. I was wrong for putting Bea and my girl-friends first, but I never put another man before you. Never! I don't think I can be with somebody I don't trust." Joy shook her head.

"Don't give up on us, Joy. I can't lose you again. I just can't." He tried to kiss her lips again, but she stepped back. "What do I need to do?"

Joy shook her head and covered her ears with both hands. "I can't decide this right now! I need time!"

"Time apart is not the answer. We need to be together to work through this," Allen pleaded.

"I'm tired and I don't want to talk about this anymore. Just leave and call me tomorrow. The door self-locks." She walked out of the kitchen, went upstairs to her bedroom, and stretched across her bed.

Allen walked in her room a few minutes later and lay beside her. "I'm not leaving you like this. We can work this out."

"I don't want you here right now," Joy said softly.

They lay facing each other on the bed. Joy touched his scar, and tears trickled down her face. She wondered if the same guilty feelings would surface every time she saw that scar. She leaned over and kissed it. Allen moved closer to her and kissed her gently on her lips.

"No, don't. You did that to her," Joy softly protested.

"But I don't love her. I love you and I need to feel you. I wanna make love to you and watch you fall asleep in my arms." He placed small kisses from the corner of her mouth, down her neck to her chest. He pulled her shirt up and unhooked her bra. She arched her back and moaned while he sucked her breasts and pinched her nipples. She enjoyed it, so he took his time giving them his undivided attention.

"I want you so bad right now," Joy whispered.

He pulled her maternity jeans down while she wiggled out of them. After quickly removing his jeans, he tossed them on the floor and kissed her belly. She smiled and rubbed his bald head affectionately. Moving his head between her legs, he licked her clitoris quickly and passionately until she climaxed. He guided her to a kneeling position on top of the bed and entered her from the back.

"Oh, baby. You feel so good." With each stroke, he groaned and panted loudly. Joy stroked his organ and moved in rhythm with him. During his climax, he moaned Joy's name and fell on the bed, gently bringing her down beside him. Pulling her back to his chest, he wrapped his arms around her and rubbed his cheek against hers.

"I love you, Joy." He kissed her cheek.

She took his arms from around her and stood up. "I still want you to leave. The whole time you were inside me, I wondered if you did the same thing to her."

"Don't do this. I didn't sleep with Diana. We just made love to each other, Joy. Diana had nothing to do with it. That was nothing but love between us. I know you felt it. You can't deny that. C'mon, baby," Allen begged.

"It was nothing but sex to me. It felt like a booty-call. No love at all. Now get your shit and get out of my house!" Joy glared at him.

"If you kick me out, I'm not coming back. You'll be in here pregnant and alone." Allen got off the bed and pulled his pants up.

"I'm fine with that. It's what I had planned before Bea called you. Now get the fuck out." Joy went in the bathroom, locked the door, and turned on the bathwater.

Allen kicked the door. "You're not willing to forgive me after all the sacrifices I made for you. I went against my bosses and took a leave of absence from my vice president position to be here for you. I was your dirty little secret for years and remained faithful to you the entire time. One goddamn slip-up and you write me off. Fuck you, Joy! I'm out of here." Allen took his gym bag out of the closet, stuffed it with as many of his clothes as he could, then stomped out of the house.

$\mathscr{C}$hapter 16

Light snow fell as Maxine pulled into the parking lot at Maxwell's daycare. It was Valentine's Day. She thought about how miserable and lonely she felt as she pulled into an empty parking space. After she stepped out of her minivan, she buttoned her long, puffy coat and began her short walk across the lot.

A squad car pulled in front of the daycare as she approached the building. She smiled when Christian LeBlanc opened the car door and got out. He was perfection and it didn't go to his head. He had the sexiness of Idris Elba and the swagger of Denzel Washington all rolled into his ripped and chiseled milk-chocolate body. They had become good friends over the past few months because Maxwell and Christian's son, Shane, were the best of friends. It used to make Trent crazy with jealousy when Christian called her to schedule a play date for their boys. Now that she didn't have to worry about Trent anymore, she was looking forward to catching up on some play dates. She thought a fine brother like Christian was out of her league, but it didn't stop her from fantasizing about him.

"That's not fair, Officer LeBlanc. You get to pull right in front of the school while I had to park all the way over there and walk in the cold. Shame on you," Maxine joked.

"Hi, Maxine. I'm sorry, but I'm running late for work. I'm on the night shift this week. Shane stayed with my parents last night and they kept him home with them today."

"Oh, no. That means Maxwell is gonna be in a bad mood because he didn't see his best friend today. Lucky me." Maxine sighed and frowned.

"Shane has been driving my parents crazy all day asking if they can take him to see his brother, Maxwell." Christian laughed.

"Awww! Now that I'm single and my calendar is open, can we schedule a play date for the boys? I'm sorry for postponing, but I've been going through a transition. If you're not comfortable with Shane coming to my house, maybe we can meet at Chuck E. Cheese's or one of the local bounce houses," Maxine suggested.

"Oh, your house is not a problem. I just have one condition," he said with a serious expression.

"Sure. Anything. What is it?" Maxine asked with raised eyebrows.

"While our kids are having their play date, we should have a date of our own. Is it alright if I stay and keep you company?" Christian asked with a bright smile.

Alright now! Hell, yeah! "Sure, I would like that." Maxine blushed. "Why are you here if Shane didn't come today?"

"It's Friday. Tuition is due, remember?" Christian laughed.

"Oh, crap! I left my checkbook in the minivan. I'll call you over the weekend. Don't be late for work and Happy Valentine's Day." Maxine waved goodbye as she ran back to her van.

"Happy Valentine's Day to you too, Maxine!" Christian laughed and shook his head as he walked into the daycare.

Maxine felt as if she was floating on air as she walked back to her minivan. All of the daycare mothers, married and single were after him, but he asked her out. She planned to schedule that play date as soon as possible.

Grabbing her checkbook out of the glove box, she locked her doors, and turned to walk back to the school. Without warning, Trent stepped from behind the car she was parked beside. She gasped, dropped her checkbook, and froze. His face was twisted with anger and his breathing was labored. He had something in his hand pointed at her. She was too afraid to look down. Fearing it was a gun, she kept her eyes on his.

"I saw you flirting with that cop, you whore!" he shouted.

"We're getting a divorce, Trent. I can flirt with whomever I like. It's not your weekend with the boys, so you need to leave," Maxine warned. Her whole body shook as she locked eyes with him.

"I'm not gonna let you keep disrespecting me. I came here to make sure another man never looks at you again!"

"Why would you want to do that, Trent? Hurting me would hurt your sons." Trent turned his head when he heard a car pull out of the parking lot. While he was distracted, she squeezed past him and ran as fast as she could toward the daycare. The heavy, puffed coat and slippery ground slowed her down. Right behind her, Trent reached out and grabbed the hair on the top of her head. She screamed for help, but he yanked her back and put his arm around her neck to silence her. Fighting back only made him tighten his grip around her throat so she stopped. The minute he swung her around, she tried to kick him between his legs, but her coat was too long so she swung her arms at his face and yelled for help. Using one arm to block her, he raised his fist and punched her nose hard. Blood gushed down her face as she fell to the ground.

She tried to scream again, but every time she opened her mouth, it filled with blood. She was groggy, but she could see Trent standing over her. He was spraying something wet on her. *Is he urinating on me?* A strong odor burned her eyes and throat and made her gag. She turned on her side to get up, but he kicked her hard and she fell back. He was holding something over her. He dropped it on her coat and walked away.

What's burning? Are those flames? Oh, my God! I'm on fire! He set me on fire! "Help! Help me!" she screamed. *What am I supposed to do? I forget. I'm on fire! I need to do something!*

The heat from her burning coat licked her face. The flames had already spread to her arms. She was too afraid to move. The sound of the material crackling from the heat echoed in her ears. She heard voices and wondered if it was God calling her home. She closed her eyes and prayed. "No! I don't want to die yet, God! Please, my boys still need me."

A white cloud engulfed her. The heat from the flames went away. She opened her eyes when she felt someone lift her from the ground. Her arms and torso jerked as someone ripped her smoldering coat from her body. She still couldn't see anything. *Am I blind?*

"Maxine, you're safe! Open your eyes!" Christian ordered.

I thought they were already open. Maybe that's why I can't see anything. "Am I dead?"

"No, you're alive. A little banged up, but you're still here," Christian said.

She opened her eyes and looked around. She lay on the carpeted floor in the daycare's office. Christian was on his knees beside her, examining her body for injuries. The daycare director, Mrs. Carter, was standing on the other side of her crying. Maxine could hear sirens as the fire truck and ambulance pulled in front of the school.

"My husband set me on fire!" Maxine cried with tears streaming.

"I know, but you survived it. You're a survivor." Christian held her in his arms.

"That's what people said the last time he almost killed me." She buried her head in his chest and sobbed. "I should've learned my lesson. Where did I go wrong again?"

Minutes later, paramedics entered the office and examined her. Surprisingly, she wasn't burned and didn't have any life-threatening injuries. Other than a bloody nose, which the paramedics stopped, and sore muscles, she was fine. The paramedics suggested she go to the hospital for a more thorough examination, but she refused. She wanted to get her boys and go home.

Christian took his jacket off and wrapped it around her as she spoke with the police. They watched the daycare's security footage. The cameras captured everything. It felt like déjà vu for Maxine to sit in the office and watch what happened to her on the small monitor. Trent had been sitting in his car in the parking lot waiting for her. She was glad she forgot the checkbook and didn't have Maxwell with her when it happened. Trent didn't look like himself on the monitor. He was smiling and laughing like a deranged lunatic when he sprayed lighter fluid on her and used a cigarette lighter to ignite the piece of paper he dropped on her coat. Even the police officers gasped when they watched her go up in flames. She thought she was burning for a long time, but seconds after Trent walked away, Christian ran out of the building and pulled a fire extinguisher out of his squad car. He ran to her and sprayed a white chemical from the extinguisher over the flames. He picked her up and Mrs. Carter ripped the burned coat from her body and threw it on the ground.

Although she was still shaky, Maxine stood and hugged Mrs. Carter. "Thank you for helping me."

"You're welcome. I'm glad you're okay." Mrs. Carter brushed off the fire extinguisher powder that had been transferred to her clothes during the hug.

Maxine looked down at her bloody shirt and the white powder on her clothes. "My gym bag is in the back of my minivan. Can you get it for me? I don't want my boys to see me like this." Maxine gave Mrs. Carter her car key.

"Of course."

When she left, Maxine looked at Christian and smiled. "Thank you!"

"You're welcome." Christian pulled his cell phone out of his pocket. "Do you want me to call your family?"

She shook her head and took his phone from him. She thought about whom to call. She didn't want to upset her friends again, especially after they had all warned her about Trent. She called her parents. It was the first time she had talked to them since her father told her to leave his house. They became hysterical when she told them. After Christian reassured them she was fine, she called Joy. She didn't answer, so Maxine left her a message without any details.

"I need to wait for my girlfriend, Joy, to call me back because I can't drive and I need to get TJ from aftercare at his school." She handed Christian his phone.

Christian took the phone, put it in his pocket, and held her shaking hands between his. "I can drive you to get TJ and stay with you and your sons until he's caught."

"Don't you have to go to work?" Maxine looked up at him with glistening eyes.

"I'm not going in tonight." He put his arms around her

trembling shoulders.

"Thank you." Maxine nodded and breathed a sigh of relief.

After she changed into the sweatpants and T-shirt from her gym bag, they got Maxwell and left. Christian arranged to have another officer drive his squad car to Maxine's house while his partner followed them. When they walked outside, she saw fragments of her burned coat on the ground and a cold chill went through her.

Christian turned her head away and helped her into the van. While Christian put Maxwell in his car seat, her son repeatedly asked Christian about Shane, which made Maxine smile. She looked at Christian as he got in the driver's seat of her minivan and pushed the seat back to allow room for his long legs. She leaned over and kissed him hard on his lips.

He stared at her in confused silence.

"I just realized that life is too short to play it safe. I like you, Christian. Thank you for saving my life and I hope this won't make you cancel our date." She smiled and squeezed his hand.

"You can't get rid of me that easily, and you don't have to keep thanking me. They say when you save someone's life, you're responsible for that life forever." Christian kissed her lips gently. "I'm here for you as long as you need me."

$\mathcal{C}$hapter 17

Later that evening, a million thoughts played through Gabby's mind as she sat on Maxine's couch and gently rubbed the back of her friend's hand. *What if Trent had killed her? Why did I stop speaking to her? I should've done more to keep her away from Trent.* Her stomach knotted and gurgled as she thought about Maxine being set on fire.

"I'm sorry, Maxine. What can I do for you?" Gabby asked with tears welling.

"I'm fine, girl. I'm happy to see you. I missed you." Maxine hugged Gabby then took Nadia from Gabby's lap. "Come to Auntie, big girl. I missed you, too. Look how big you are." Nadia babbled happily as Maxine bounced her on her lap.

Bea walked downstairs and sighed. "Maxine, your boys are bathed and finally asleep after I read them two bedtime stories. I almost fell asleep on the second one myself." She laughed, then plopped on the sofa beside Joy. "I put Maxwell in TJ's room so I can sleep in his bed tonight."

Joy gave Maxine the I-told-you-so look. Bea had a way of taking over your life whether you wanted her to or not. When she found out Maxine's parents were in Richmond, she decided to step in and fill their parental shoes until they returned.

"Oh, you don't have to stay, Bea. The police found Trent at his apartment and arrested him. We'll be okay. Besides, Christian offered to stay with me and the boys tonight." Maxine looked at

Christian sitting across the room and smiled.

Bea, Joy, and Gabby narrowed their eyes on him like laser beams.

Christian cleared his throat and pointed at the couch. "I was gonna sleep there."

"Um-hum, do you think that's a good idea, Maxine?" Bea asked suspiciously.

"Of course it's not a good idea. Officer LeBlanc, we appreciate what you did for Maxine, but that doesn't entitle you to her body or give you access to her bed. I'll stay with her." Gabby looked at Christian with a suspicious scowl.

"I can stay, too," Joy added.

"I don't need any of you to stay with me. Christian is staying, and after the day I've had, if he wants to share my bed with me, I'm alright with that, too." Maxine looked at her girlfriends and Bea with an angry expression. "End of discussion."

"Okay... it's your house and your decision." Bea stood and removed her coat from the closet. "I'll be back in the morning."

"Thanks for all your help tonight, Bea. I appreciate it, but I'm fine. You don't have to come tomorrow." Maxine gave Nadia to Gabby and stood to walk Bea out.

"No, I'm coming back. I promised your parents I would look after you until they return," Bea explained. She buttoned her coat, put on her gloves, and picked up her purse.

"Okay." Maxine knew it was a waste of her breath to argue with Bea.

Bea turned to look at Christian. She pointed her gloved index finger at him. "Let me give you a bit of advice from the wise and all-knowing Beyoncé. She said put a ring on it. If you happen to make it upstairs to Maxine's bed tonight, put a condom on it."

"Bea! Oh, my God!" Maxine covered her face.

Christian laughed. "Thanks for the advice, ma'am, but I plan to stay on the couch tonight."

Gabby and Joy looked at each other and shook their heads.

Bea caught them giving each other funny looks. "I think all three of you girls need to take a break from men for a while. Maxine, your husband almost killed you twice, and Joy, your husband almost shot you and my grandchildren. Then you break up with their father after he saved your life." She put her hat on and shook her head. "Learn to be more like Gabby. She had a husband who didn't try to kill her."

"That's because she killed him," Joy mumbled.

Maxine gasped.

"Awww, Gabby, Joy said it, not me," Bea explained quickly because she knew how upset Gabby got whenever somebody mentioned William's suicide.

"She did what?" Christian asked with a confused expression.

"My husband suffered from a mental illness and he committed suicide," Gabby said, looking Christian directly in his eyes.

"Um-hum," Bea grumbled. "Goodnight, everybody." She looked at Maxine, clutched her chest, and sighed. "Thank God!" She hugged Maxine again, and then left.

"Officer LeBlanc, if Trent is behind bars, why do you need to stay with Maxine?" Gabby asked, full of attitude.

Maxine walked back into the living room. "Because I asked him to." She put her hands on her hips, cocked her head to the side, and locked eyes with Gabby.

Gabby ignored her and focused her attention back on Christian. "Maxine is kindhearted and trusting. People take her kindness for weakness and I'm gonna make sure that never happens again."

"It seems to me like we're on the same team, Gabby. We both care about Maxine and want to protect her." Christian looked at Maxine and smiled.

"Let me decide if we're teammates. You seem older. How old are you? And what's your status? Married? Divorced? Children? If so, how many and what type of relationship do you have with the mothers of your children?" Gabby was determined to find something wrong with Christian. Maxine was a terrible judge of character when it came to men. Gabby planned to stop Christian before he had a chance to hurt her friend.

"I'm thirty-eight and a widower. My wife died of breast cancer two years ago. I have one son, Shane. He's three and goes to school with Maxwell. I own a house in Laurel and I'm assigned to the Forestville station. I have excellent credit and don't believe a man should *ever* hit a woman." Christian looked at Gabby with furrowed brows.

Gabby crossed her arms over her chest and frowned at Christian. "You're all tight T-shirt and muscles. You wouldn't happen to be one of those down-low brothers, would you?"

"What!" Christian snapped.

Maxine gasped. "You don't have to answer that, Christian. Stop it, Gabby!"

Maxine liked Christian and could definitely see herself in a relationship with him. If Gabby did anything to ruin her chances with him, she would never forgive her.

Joy and Gabby looked at Maxine and then at each other. They knew their friend was already planning her future with this man she barely knew. When was she ever going to learn?

Chapter 18

A week later, Gabby sat across from Rayshawn in Hooters at the Baltimore Harbor. When he wasn't staring at the waitresses in their skimpy uniforms, he was glaring at Gabby.

"Rayshawn, thanks for agreeing to see me. When I found out you were in town, I had to come talk to you." Gabby stared at Rayshawn with pleading eyes.

"I didn't agree to see you. You said you was bringing my daughter to see me. I should've known your ass was lying." He gave her an evil look as his lips twitched. "I should smack your ass for spitting in my mother's face."

Gabby cleared her throat. "I'm sorry about that. Things between us got out of control." Gabby picked up her cell phone and looked at him with sad eyes. "Do you want me to call her and apologize?"

"Hell no! I'm out of here! I'll see your ass in court!" Rayshawn stood to leave.

Gabby grabbed his arm. "No, Rayshawn! Wait! Please!"

An attractive waitress with large breasts and a big butt stopped at the table across from theirs. Rayshawn sat back down and stared at her. He licked his lips and smiled as he thought about how much fun he could have with her.

"Rayshawn." Gabby raised her voice to get his attention.

"What! Damn, you irritating as hell!" Rayshawn watched the waitress's butt as she walked away.

"Please don't take Nadia away from me. I need my daughter in my life. Here are some pictures of our new house. We just moved in last week, but I'm getting it together. Look at this picture of our daughter's room. It's all pink, just like you wanted." Gabby held the picture inches from Rayshawn's eyes.

"How I know that's her room for real? You probably went in a model home and took some damn pictures. You do dirty shit like that." Rayshawn pushed Gabby's hand out of his face.

"I didn't. Honest! Work with me on this, Rayshawn." She put the pictures in her handbag and touched his hands across the table. "I'll do whatever you want. Just tell me."

"Don't think I wanna fuck you, 'cause that's not happening." He stared at her cleavage.

"What do you want then? I'll do anything. Just don't take Nadia away from me. I'm begging." Gabby put her hands in prayer position under her chin.

"Oh... it's happening. My lawyers already got everybody lined up to testify against you. You brought this shit on yourself, so now you gotta live with it," Rayshawn bragged with an arrogant smirk. He enjoyed watching Gabby beg.

"Gabby! Gabrielle Roché! OMG! I can't believe it's you, girl!" The woman was so loud, people stopped to look at her.

Rayshawn and Gabby turned their heads to look at the exotic and shapely Asian woman standing beside their booth. She wore a strapless pink and black corset dress that emphasized her narrow waist. The dress clung to her hourglass shape like a second skin. She stood tall and sturdy in a pair of five-inch pink and black ankle boots, and her hair was cut into a short bob. Sparkling diamond jewelry covered her ears, neck, wrists, and fingers.

"Osaki?" Gabby stood and hugged her. "I haven't seen you in years."

"I know." She stepped back and walked around Gabby, moving her eyes up and down Gabby's silver open-backed dress. "I heard you had a baby, but you still look damn good, momma."

Gabby rubbed her hands over her flat stomach. "You know me. I gotta keep it tight and looking right."

"I hear you," Osaki agreed and laughed out loud.

Rayshawn cleared his throat.

"Oh, I'm sorry. Osaki, this is my daughter's father, Rayshawn Robinson." Rayshawn stood, stuck his chest out, and shook her hand. "How you doin'? I'm R&R, quarterback for the Baltimore Ravens."

"Hey, R&R!" Osaki shook his hand, then quickly slid in the booth beside Gabby and put her evening bag on the table.

Rayshawn sat back down with his eyes glued to Osaki.

Gabby covered her mouth and turned her head to avoid laughing at him. The only thing he had going for him was his title and he used it every chance he could. She glanced across the table at him, and he was actually flexing his chest muscles trying to get Osaki's attention.

"Football, huh?" Osaki laughed. "I always wanted to fuck in one of those locker rooms. My pussy gets wet just thinking about it."

"Girl, I see you haven't changed." Gabby sighed and shook her head.

"And never will. So what you up to tonight? I'm looking for some fun." Osaki brushed her chest against Gabby's arm. "Gabby, you know I always had a crush on you. Why wouldn't you ever let me eat your pussy? I always think of you as the one who got away."

"I told you before, I'm not into women, Osaki. It was nice seeing you again, but I'm trying to discuss something important with my daughter's father."

Osaki pouted and stuck out her bottom lip. "I understand. Baltimore is so boring. I can't find anybody to fuck. I'm going back to D.C." She took her card out of her evening bag and gave it to Gabby. "Keep in touch this time, bitch, and if you change your mind about letting me eat you, you wouldn't have to return the favor." She laughed out loud, drawing more attention to their table.

Gabby gagged and tossed the card to the side. "Bye, girl."

Osaki stood and leaned over to Rayshawn. "Bye, bye, baby daddy. Too bad you fucked my girl. I would've had some fun with those big hands." She ran her tongue across Rayshawn's lips, bit his ear lobe, and walked away.

119

He whipped his neck around and watched Osaki until she disappeared.

"Sorry about the interruption. Do you think we can work this custody issue out before we go to court?" Gabby crossed her arms over her chest and sighed.

"How you know, um, Osaki? Y'all go to college together or something?" He rubbed his erection under the table.

"No, I met her before college. We used to club together when I was a teenager. I cut her back when she tried to get me to have a threesome with her. You know that's not my thing. Stay away from her, Rayshawn, she's bad news." Gabby picked up her business card and ripped it in half.

"Hold up! Don't do that!" Rayshawn took the ripped card from Gabby and put the two halves back together on the table in front of him. "Maybe we can work something out."

"Like what?" Gabby asked with arched eyebrows.

Rayshawn leaned across the table. "Call your girl back. We can go across the street to my loft and have some fun together. You know I always wanted to do a threesome."

"You haven't done that yet? That's hard to believe." Gabby rolled her eyes.

"These females don't be trying to share me with another bitch. They want me all to themselves." Rayshawn rubbed his chin and chuckled.

Idiots. "I'll consider a threesome as long as the third person is a man. What about your backup quarterback? Now that man is fine." Gabby closed her eyes and moaned.

"Fuck, no! No men in my bed!" Rayshawn protested.

"No women in mine!" Gabby countered.

They shot evil looks across the table, waiting for the other to give in.

"Okay... if you do this for me, then I'll drop my custody case as long as you agree to lower the child support and give me a visitation schedule."

"I'll agree on a set visitation schedule. You can't just pick her up whenever you want. And I'll drop the child support to $10,000 a month."

"That's too much. My ex-wife hitting me for child support on two and she agreed to less than that. What about $5,000 a month?"

Gabby covered her mouth as she yawned and looked down at the table, thinking about Rayshawn's offer.

"Hurry up! Osaki might be halfway to D.C. by now."

"Since I'm going back to work, Nadia needs a nanny. I'll accept $5,000 a month if you pay the nanny's salary."

Rayshawn extended his hand across the table. "It's a deal. Now call her."

Gabby shook Rayshawn's hand and smiled. She frowned as she picked up the ripped business card and called Osaki. She hadn't left the restaurant, so she returned to their table within minutes, excited about their offer.

They walked across the street to Rayshawn's loft. As soon as they walked in, Osaki took off her shoes and walked around barefoot, oohing and ahhing over Rayshawn's awards. His erection and ego were about to burst all over his loft. Gabby stood back and let Osaki and Rayshawn get acquainted.

"Where is the music, R&R?" Osaki had a way of whining with her Asian accent that made men jump to attention.

"I got it!" Rayshawn went to his sound system in the corner of the room and took his iPod off the docking station. He searched through his playlist for a song. He smiled seductively as he returned the iPod to the docking station and turned on the surround-sound speakers.

Osaki put her arms in the air and started moving her hips to the beat of *Lil Freak* by Usher. "Come dance with me, Gabby. Let's give baby daddy a show before we fuck."

"I'm good." Gabby rolled her eyes and sat on the couch.

"Oh, R&R, Gabby's no fun. Maybe this was a bad idea." She stopped dancing, put her hands on her hips, and poked her lips out.

"Get your ass up and dance with her or our agreement is off," Rayshawn ordered.

Gabby shot daggers at him with her eyes. She put her purse on a nearby table, then took her coat off and threw it at him. He caught it before it hit his face and tossed it on the couch. Osaki danced over to them, grabbed Gabby's hand, and pulled her off the couch. They gyrated and ground against each other to the music. Rayshawn's eyes bulged and he chewed his lower lip as he watched them with his erection straining to get out of his jeans.

"Come, R&R. Join us, baby." Osaki extended her arm to Rayshawn.

He danced over to them, completely off beat, and put his arms around their waists.

"I'll be back." Gabby removed Rayshawn's arm from around her waist and walked down the hall. She entered the bathroom and locked the door. Her plan was to stay in the bathroom until they finished. She knew Rayshawn wasn't going to wait until she returned, and he definitely wasn't going to last longer than a few minutes. She gagged when she heard Osaki laying it on thick with her compliments to Rayshawn.

Back in the living room, Osaki moved closer to Rayshawn when *Chocolate Legs* by Eric Benet came through the speakers. She turned her back to him and started rubbing her butt against his erection.

"Gabby need to come back in here so we can get this shit started." Rayshawn craned his neck around Osaki and looked down the hall.

"She can join us when she comes back." Osaki turned around, dropped to her knees, and unbuttoned Rayshawn's jeans. Slowly, she pulled them and his Baltimore Raven's boxers down.

"Naw, she need to be in here. We had a deal. Gabby!" Rayshawn looked down the hall for her again.

"Oh, my! Look how big you are. Gabby, you a fool to give this up," Osaki whined.

"You like that, huh?" Rayshawn forgot about Gabby and thrust his erection in Osaki's face.

"Can I taste it first, Gabby?" Osaki begged as she sneaked a condom from between her breasts and opened it. She slid the wrapper in a pocket in her dress.

"You don't have to ask her shit. Go 'head," Rayshawn ordered.

"Okay, R&R." Osaki put the condom in her mouth and skillfully rolled it down Rayshawn's manhood without him realizing it. She moved her mouth around his shaft and he started screaming louder than the music. Osaki gripped his butt cheeks and pushed him deep down her throat. Minutes later, he let out a loud grunt as his knees buckled and he exploded into the condom. Osaki quickly rolled the condom off, tied it and stuck it in her pocket. He fell to the floor panting like a dog on a hot summer day.

"Oh, R&R! You taste good, baby, like sweet salt-water taffy." She giggled.

"Damn, that was good. You swallowed my shit?" Rayshawn looked at Osaki with pure admiration.

"Of course, baby. Oh, R&R, you don't like that? I'm sorry. Will you forgive me?" Osaki curled up beside Rayshawn on the floor and wrapped her arm around his chest.

"No, I like it. Most chicks don't do it, but you got skills." Rayshawn laughed.

Gabby laughed and clapped her hands as she walked back in the room. "I knew you weren't gonna last long enough to handle two women. That's why I always kept my vibrator nearby. So after I had sex with you, I could finish what you couldn't. He's done for the night and so am I. My lawyer will contact your lawyers Monday morning."

"You didn't keep up your end of the deal, so don't waste your time calling your lawyer. I wasn't gonna drop my case against you anyway. You not the only one who can lie around here." Rayshawn laughed. "Now leave me and my baby alone."

Your baby? "I should've known better. You're not getting custody of my daughter, especially with this crazy chick around." Gabby grabbed her coat off the couch and her purse off the table.

"Watch me!" Rayshawn stared at her with narrowed eyes.

"Ugh... I hate children!" Osaki interjected with a frown. "R&R, I have some other friends I can call. I hope you don't mind that I like a man and a woman in my bed when I fuck. Some men can't handle it."

Rayshawn sat up with his eyes bulging. "No, baby. As long as it's another woman, I don't mind at all. Call your friend and invite her over."

"You two freaks deserve each other." Gabby opened the door to leave.

Osaki jumped up. "Gabby, don't be mad because I take care of your baby daddy better than you! Get the fuck out!"

Rayshawn rolled on the floor laughing.

"You can have him!" Gabby left.

Osaki stuck her head out the door and watched Gabby walk down the hall. "I'll take real good care of your baby daddy for you, bitch."

"Have fun!" Gabby waved her hand in dismissal and sashayed down the hall.

Chapter 19

With her eyes still closed, Joy reached for the phone on the table beside her bed and answered in a groggy voice. "Hello."

"Joy? I'm sorry. May I speak to Joy, please?" a woman asked nervously.

"Speaking." Joy opened her eyes and yawned.

"Oh, good." She cleared her throat. "Joy, this is Allen's girlfriend, Diana."

Joy rolled over and sat on the edge of her bed with her eyes bulging. "Who?"

"Let's not play games. You know who I am," Diana replied apprehensively.

"I don't give a damn who you are. Why are you calling me?" Joy shouted into the receiver.

"Allen gave me your number after I told him we needed to have a woman-to-woman chat since we're both in love with the same man." Diana exhaled loudly.

"Bitch, you have lost your goddamn mind! There can't be that much love between you and Allen or he wouldn't be blowing up my damn phone or knocking on my door every day begging me to let him come back home." Joy stood and started pacing back and forth around her bedroom.

"You don't understand why he's doing that? It's not you he wants, it's his children. You know Allen is a good man. When your mother called him in China, he walked away from me and his career to be a father, not to be with you. He's with you out of obligation, not because he loves you." Diana spoke loudly, as if trying to be strong, but her voice cracked so much it was hard for Joy to understand her.

"Oh, my... You're threatened by me. You don't believe Allen is with me out of obligation any more than I do or you wouldn't have stolen my phone number off his cell while you were playing nursemaid to him in the hospital." Joy laughed.

Diana cleared her throat. "Um, I didn't have to steal it. Allen gave it to me after I asked."

"Yeah, right. You thought just because Allen kissed you in the hospital, y'all were gonna live happily ever after. Bitch, please. I know Allen. It didn't go any further than a couple of kisses because he's not attracted to you. You see, he never just kissed me and stopped. One kiss between us *always* led to so much more. You can't say that, can you?" Joy stopped pacing and looked at her angry reflection in the mirror.

"Well, um, you know we..."

"We what, Diana? I watched your sex tape with Allen, all six minutes of it, from beginning to end. That wasn't my man screwing you. He looked robotic, like a man just trying to bust a nut and get it over with. Hell, he spends six minutes just licking my pussy, so I wasn't impressed." Joy sighed and shook her head.

"I always heard you Latinas were freaks. When Allen's with me, he's excited to be with a real, classy woman," Diana stated confidently.

"Diana, in case your momma didn't teach you this, real classy women don't need to take naked pictures of themselves and email them to men for attention." Joy smacked her lips and sighed to show her disappointment.

"Those pictures were a motivational gift for my man. Something for him to look forward to when he got out of the hospital," Diana teased.

"Oh, okay. Well, the picture with the cucumber or zucchini sticking inside of you, that was real classy. You should send that one to 'White Girls Gone Wild.' They might give you a couple hundred for it." Joy laughed out loud.

126

"Funny! What are you? Some kind of comedian? Well, the joke will be on you when the paternity test comes back and shows Allen he's not the father of your retarded twins," Diana countered.

"You just earned yourself an ass-whipping talking about my children. Pregnant or not, if I ever see you again, I'm gonna whip your ass." Joy imagined the phone was Diana's neck as she gripped her fingers around it tightly.

"I have never fought a woman over a man and I'm not going to start now. The purpose of my call was to ask you nicely to stop making Allen feel guilty about your bastard children. If they *are* his, I'll make sure he drops a child support check in the mail to you every month; just leave us alone," Diana demanded in a high-pitched tone.

"You should hear how desperate you sound. No matter how hard you try, you'll never take my place in Allen's heart. My spot there is permanent and that's why he left *you* and his *career* behind in China, not out of obligation, but because he loves me. Bye, bitch!" Joy ended the call and threw the phone on the bed.

She walked around her bed with her chest heaving, trying to catch her breath. Her whole body shook with anger, and her head felt like a jackhammer was doing construction on her brain. She lay on the bed to calm herself. Within minutes, she flowed a river of tears that left a puddle on her comforter. Hatred for Allen and Diana coursed through her body. She grabbed her phone and dialed Allen. After a few rings, his voicemail came on. She hung up and dialed Tyesha's house number.

"Hello," Tyesha answered.

"Tyesha, is your piece-of-shit brother there? It doesn't matter. Just tell him to stay the fuck away from me and if his girlfriend calls me again, I'm going to hunt that bitch down and choke the life out of her ass," Joy screamed with tears flowing.

"Joy, what happened?" Tyesha asked in a panic.

"Just give him my message, Tyesha!" Joy hung up.

Seconds later her phone rang. "Hello!"

"Hey! I'm sorry I missed your call. I was in the bathroom. I'm glad you called me, baby. Are you ready to sit down like an adult and talk?" Allen asked full of hope.

"Fuck you, Allen! After this conversation, I never want to talk to you again." She could hear Tyesha in the background telling him about her call.

"Who called you, Joy?" Allen asked anxiously.

"Your girlfriend, Diana, called me. The bitch had a nerve to call my children retarded. I hate you right now! We're through! Diana can have your lyin' ass." She hung up the phone.

Within seconds, her phone rang again. She ignored it and went into the bathroom. The pain in her head wouldn't stop. The room looked like it was spinning out of control. She sat on the floor in front of the toilet and held her head in her hands. To stop her dizziness, she closed her eyes. Her stomach was twisted in knots and doing somersaults. She turned her head to the toilet and vomited again and again until her stomach cramped. The phone rang again. She stood and tried to take a step to the door, but a sharp pain in her stomach made her drop to her knees. She grabbed her stomach and groaned as she bent over in pain.

"Get it together, Joy. You can do this," she said to herself.

She took slow deep breaths as she crawled to her bed and dialed 911.

"911, what's your emergency?"

"I'm home alone, pregnant with twins, and I think I'm in labor." She gave the 911 operator her address and took several deep breaths when she felt a sharp contraction.

She held the phone to her ear and listened to the operator try to help her remain calm.

Minutes later, Allen and Tyesha shouted her name as they banged on the front door and rang the doorbell. She wanted to open the door for them because she didn't want to be alone, but her pain wouldn't allow her to walk downstairs.

Before long, she could hear sirens in the distance. Because she was unable to open the door, the fire department raised a ladder to her bedroom window. Joy hung up with the 911 operator and took deep breaths as she crawled to the window. Using the wall to pull herself up, she unlocked the window and two firefighters climbed through. One went downstairs to open the door for the paramedics while the other helped Joy get comfortable on the floor.

"What's your name?" the firefighter asked.

"Joy Marshall," she said through deep breaths.

"When is your due date?"

"March twenty-sixth."

The paramedics entered the room with a stair chair and medical equipment. Allen and Tyesha entered next, looking terrified.

"I'm her boyfriend. Can I be with her?" Allen asked one of the paramedics.

"No!" Joy screamed. "Tyesha, you come! Keep him away from me!"

The firefighters and paramedics looked at Allen accusingly.

"Joy, you need to remain calm. Do you take medication for high blood pressure?" the paramedic asked.

"No," Joy answered.

"It's 160 over 100," the paramedic said to his partner who was writing everything down. "The rest of her vitals are normal."

"Everything's gonna be okay! I love you, baby!" Allen declared as he stared at her with tears in his eyes.

Joy ignored him and looked at Tyesha. "It's too early. I still have seven more weeks. I'm scared, Tyesha. I don't want to lose my babies."

"I know you're scared, but you need to be strong for them. They need all your positive energy. Right?" Tyesha held her hand while the paramedics continued their exam.

Joy nodded as tears flowed down her face.

The paramedics secured her on the stair chair and took her down to the ambulance. Allen and Tyesha followed them. While they were transferring her to the stretcher, Allen's phone rang. He answered it quickly, like he was expecting a call.

"Hello," he yelled.

There was a brief pause.

"Shut the fuck up, you stupid bitch. You gonna make me forget I don't hit women. Why did you call Joy?"

There was another pause.

"Bullshit! You're gonna make me hurt you, Diana. I'm

watching paramedics put her in an ambulance right now because of your stupid ass. I told you what happened between us was a mistake. I love Joy! I don't want you!"

He punched the air as he listened.

"No, you don't care about me because if you did, you would know hurting Joy is like hurting me. She's a part of me and when she hurts, I hurt. You know why I was in the hospital. I was willing to die to protect Joy and my children, so be warned, I'm willing to kill to protect them from anybody who tries to hurt them. Stay the fuck away from us or you'll regret it." He threw his phone against the brick garage.

"Allen, you need to keep it together. You got cops out here listening to you," Tyesha warned him.

"Who's riding with Joy?" the paramedic asked.

"Here I come. Meet us at Southern Maryland Hospital." Tyesha gave Allen her car key, hugged him, then ran to the ambulance.

Allen watched in disbelief as the ambulance pulled off without him. He always thought he would be by Joy's side when she gave birth to their children. He jumped in the car and quickly followed the ambulance, praying the entire ride.

An hour and a half later, Joy was resting comfortably in her hospital bed. The medicine she was given when she arrived stopped her contractions and she felt much better. Tyesha sat in a chair near her bedside and held her hand while she stared at the monitors for the machines attached to Joy's belly. Allen sat in a chair in the lobby of the Labor and Delivery ward because seeing him still upset Joy.

Bea burst into Joy's room in a panic. "Joy! Oh, my God, baby! Are you okay?" She rushed to Joy's bed and wrapped her arms around her daughter.

"Mom," Joy whispered and hugged Bea tightly with tears in her eyes.

"Are you in labor? What did the doctor say?" She looked at Tyesha. "What happened?"

"Where were you?" Joy asked angrily.

"I went to see the new Tyler Perry movie and had my phone turned off. I came as soon as I got the messages." Bea hated herself for not being there for Joy when she needed her. "Tell me what happened."

"Tyesha, can you give us some privacy?" Joy half-smiled at her.

"Sure, I'll go give Allen an update." Tyesha squeezed her hand and smiled.

"An update? Why isn't Allen here?" Bea scrunched her face at them, wondering what was going on.

When Tyesha left the room, Joy gave Bea a play-by-play of what had been happening between her and Allen lately. Bea's caramel complexion turned an angry shade of red and her breathing became labored. Joy stared at her mother, waiting for her to explode.

"I can't believe this! I knew something was going on between y'all, but I tried to stay out of it, hoping you would work it out, but you made the right decision to end it. Once a cheater, always a cheater," Bea said.

Joy nodded, unable to speak.

Bea sat in the chair beside Joy's bed and held her hand until she fell asleep. Then she left the room to find Allen and Tyesha. They were sitting down the hall from Joy's room.

Allen stood, looking nervous, when he saw Bea stomping down the hall with a mixture of disgust and hatred on her face. She got close to Allen and pointed her finger inches from his eye. "I'm not gonna go off on you like I really want to because Joy has been through enough tonight. All I need to say to you is stay away from my daughter. She's done with you."

"That's Joy's decision, not yours. I'm in a relationship with her, not you," Allen responded.

"Not anymore!" Bea turned and looked at Tyesha. "We've been best friends for a long time, and we've both been cheated on by enough no-good men to know how much pain Joy's in right now. I'm asking on our friendship to please keep your brother away from my daughter."

Tyesha looked down reluctantly and nodded.

"This is between me and Joy! We're adults and we'll work it out. Stay out of it!" Allen snapped as he glared at Tyesha and Bea.

Tyesha gripped Allen's chin and forced his face to hers. "Allen, Joy said it's over. Respect that. You screwed up so leave her alone."

Allen stepped back from Tyesha and looked at them angrily. Bea put her hands on her hips and shot him an evil glare. He looked at Tyesha for support, but she rolled her eyes and shook her head disapprovingly. He sat back in his chair, put his elbows on his knees, and dropped his head in his hand. A feeling of dread swept over him as he realized his relationship with Joy was definitely over.

Chapter 20

After a long, hot bubble bath, Maxine stepped out of the tub, dried her skin, and wrapped her silk robe around her body. She walked into her bedroom, sat on the side of her bed, and took a sip from her wine glass. The sweet taste of Moscato filled her mouth and tickled her taste buds. She closed her eyes and savored the feeling of it going down her throat. After enjoying two more glasses of wine, she eased back on the bed, let her body melt into the mattress, and closed her eyes. Her boys were asleep, the house was quiet, and this was the most relaxed she'd felt in a long time.

Three weeks had passed since Trent attacked her. The State of Maryland had formally charged him with first-degree attempted murder. He claimed he didn't remember leaving work, driving to the daycare, and setting her on fire. An hour after he had attacked her, the police found him at home eating a submarine sandwich and watching television as if nothing happened. No one from the district attorney's office believed his lies. The prosecutors thought it was part of his plan to use an insanity defense. It didn't work. Yesterday, he was denied bail and transported to a maximum-security prison in Baltimore until his trial in October.

Her cell phone vibrated on the nightstand. She sat up and answered it. "Hello, handsome."

"Hi, Maxine. Are you alright?" Christian's deep, sensual tone made chill bumps pop up all over her body.

"I'm fine, just happy to hear your voice." She lay back on

the bed, closed her eyes, and imagined his sexy smile. Since Trent's attack, he had been her rock, and a true gentleman. On the nights she was afraid to be alone, he slept on her couch while his son, Shane, shared Maxwell's room. He helped her when no one else could and he was by her side for every meeting she had with the prosecutors handling her case.

"I'm always happy to hear your voice, too." He chuckled. "Is Shane ready?"

"He's knocked out. It's late, let him stay here tonight." She had offered to watch his son so he could work tonight to make up some of the time he had taken off to be with her.

"Okay, call me in the morning when you're ready for me to scoop him up."

"Can you stay with me tonight?" She opened her legs and imagined him on top of her.

"You don't need me on your couch tonight. You're safe. Trent is locked up. He can't hurt you," Christian said reassuringly.

"I know that. I'm asking *you* to stay with *me* tonight." Maxine giggled. "I'm horny, Christian. It's been a long time for me and my vajayjay needs some attention."

"Your vajayjay?" Christian let out a deep belly laugh. "Have you been drinking?"

"I had some wine. A couple of glasses." She sat up and held the wine bottle up to the light. "Oh, I had half the bottle." Now she understood why she was speaking so freely to Christian.

"I would love to come over and give your, um, vajayjay some much-needed attention. It's been a long time for me, too, but I don't think tonight is the night."

Maxine gasped. "I can't believe this. I just offered you my good stuff and you turned me down. Alright, Christian. I'll call you tomorrow when Shane's ready," she stated in a quivering voice, then pushed the End button and slammed the phone on the night-stand. Her face felt flush from embarrassment.

Her cell phone vibrated again. She picked it up, pushed the Ignore button, and turned it off. She was too embarrassed to talk to Christian and the thought of seeing him tomorrow almost had her in tears. She poured herself another glass of wine and finished it in one swig.

The doorbell rang a few minutes later. Her stomach tightened into a painful knot because she knew it was Christian. Reluctantly, she left her bedroom and went downstairs. She flipped the switch for the front porch light and looked out the peephole. Christian stood in front of the door dressed in his navy-blue police uniform with a duffel bag over his shoulder. She unlocked the door, opened it, and stepped back to let him in.

Without saying a word, he closed the door, dropped his bag on the floor, and pulled her into his arms. "Come here. Mmmm, you smell so good."

"Thank you, but I'm so embarrassed." She stepped back and covered her face with both hands.

"No need for that." He pulled her hands away from her face. "Maxine, I want your vajayjay and all your good stuff."

She looked up at him with watery eyes, then smiled.

"You've been drinking and I don't want you to wake up tomorrow morning full of regret." He kissed her lips gently. "I like you. A lot. And if you're sure this is what you want, then I'm yours."

Maxine put her arms around his neck and kissed him passionately, letting her tongue explore his mouth.

He pulled away from her, gasping for breath. "Maxine! You're in rare form. I've never seen you like this." He licked his lips and shook his head.

"Let's go upstairs so you can meet the other side of Maxine. She's fun and will make you feel real good." She drew imaginary circles over his chest and fluttered her eyelashes.

"I can't wait." He picked his duffel bag off the floor. "Um, I've been on duty for twelve hours. Is it alright if I take a shower first?"

"Sure." She winked and took his hand. "I'll give you everything you need to get ready for me."

He grinned and a low growl escaped his throat as he followed her upstairs.

Maxine stopped halfway up the steps and turned to look at him. "Are you hungry? While you're in the shower, do you want me to fix you something to eat?" She pulled her robe back and exposed her right thigh. "Or do you plan to just eat me all night?"

"I like that." He licked his lips as he stared at Maxine's thigh.

"I thought you would." She turned around and continued walking upstairs, thinking about all the fun she was going to have with him tonight.

Christian kept his eyes focused on her butt as he followed her upstairs.

They walked into her master bathroom. She gave him a towel and a washcloth, then closed the bathroom door to give him some privacy.

While he was in the shower, she finished the rest of the wine, removed her silk robe, and rubbed peach-scented lotion all over her body. As she put her robe back on, she fantasized about him using his handcuffs to tie her up and torture her with his dick. She was already dripping wet just thinking about it, and her hard nipples ached as they poked against her robe. Her pulse raced at the thought of having Christian's sexy ass in her bed.

Minutes later, while she was returning the lotion to the dresser, he entered the room and sat on the edge of her bed wearing a pair of blue boxer briefs. His chiseled, brown biceps were calling her name. He lay back on the bed and rubbed his hands over his tight six-pack. Maxine's eyes landed right on his cock. It was soft, but still provided a large bulge in his briefs. She was so excited, she thought she was going to have an orgasm right where she stood.

He got up and looked at her with a concerned expression. "Are you sure you're ready for this?" His serious tone caught her off guard.

She moved toward him until she could feel the heat from his breath on her face. "I've never been more sure about anything in my life. I need to feel your hands on me. I want to know what it feels like to have every inch of you inside me," she whispered between kisses.

Removing her robe, he kissed her mouth and worked his lips down her neck. She tilted her head back and moaned. The feeling of his lips on her skin made her whole body tingle with pleasure. She rubbed between his legs and purred as his penis swelled from her touch. With her eyes glued to his flat stomach, she pulled his boxers down and pushed him back on the bed. He pulled her on top of him and put one of her breasts in his mouth while he squeezed the other. The feeling of his penis pressing against her clitoris sent electric jolts through her body.

"I want to feel you inside me," Maxine moaned.

He took his lips off her breast and looked into her eyes. "Touch where you want me to put it," he whispered.

Maxine rolled onto the bed and put her fingers on her clitoris. "Right here."

He put his fingers on top of hers and moved them in a circular motion. She never knew touching herself like this could feel so good. He put his mouth around her breasts again and sucked them as if his life depended on it. She arched her back and moved her hips back and forth.

"Oh, Christian! I'm coming!" She screamed.

"Shhhh." He put his lips on hers to silence her.

While she lay on her back and tried to catch her breath, Christian moved to the side of the bed. She wondered what he was doing until she heard him rip open a condom packet. She watched his back move side to side as he maneuvered to put the condom over his penis.

He lay back and pulled Maxine's petite frame on top of him. With her legs straddled over his body, she shivered with anticipation. Her juices dripped on his hand as he guided his manhood inside her. The pleasure she felt when her vaginal walls swallowed his cock was pure ecstasy. While holding the headboard, she bounced up and down on top of him. He gripped her hips and thrust himself in her continuously until they both climaxed. Out of breath and spent, she collapsed onto his chest. He laid her beside him, kissed the top of her head, and held her close until she fell asleep.

The next morning, Maxine yawned as she walked downstairs with bloodshot eyes and heavy eyelids. Thanks to Christian, she had a restless night's sleep. He stretched his long limbs across the bed like she wasn't there and almost kicked her out of bed twice. He was definitely used to sleeping alone. But his snoring was what really drove her crazy. When he slept on his back, he sounded like a freight train barreling through the room. When he slept on his side, he squawked like a bird and let out a high-pitched whistle every few minutes. She had never heard anything like it and never wanted to hear it again.

She leaned against the wall for a few minutes before she entered the kitchen. Thanks to the bottle of wine she drank last night, the smell of bacon cooking made her nauseous. It was the most alcohol she'd ever consumed in her entire life. The way she felt was a sure guarantee she'd never do it again.

In the kitchen, Christian stood at the stove taking bacon out of the frying pan and putting it on a paper-towel-covered plate. The boys sat at the kitchen table and played with their *Hot Wheels* cars.

"Mommy!" Maxwell ran and hugged her leg.

She smiled as best she could, picked him up, and kissed his cheek. "Good morning, baby!" She walked to the kitchen table, sat Maxwell in a chair, and hugged TJ and Shane.

"Hi, Mommy. You sick?" TJ dropped his two cars and looked up at her with a taut expression. He was very observant for a five-year-old.

"I'm not sick." She tickled his stomach to play off the pain. "If I was sick, could I do this?"

TJ screamed and laughed, making her headache vibrate even more.

"Hi, Ms. Maxine." Shane waved at her with a bright smile on his cute, dimpled face. "Daddy is taking us to the Spy Museum today. Yayyy!"

Not today, Maxine thought as she cringed from Shane's yelling.

Christian finally turned away from the stove to acknowledge her presence. "I hope that's alright with you, Maxine. Since we're both off today, I thought we could take the boys out for a day of fun."

Her heart skipped a beat. Christian was a good man, a terrific father, and a great provider. On the nights he slept on her couch, they always woke up to a big, hearty breakfast waiting for them. Last night was so good, her complaints about his loud snoring seemed insignificant. They could work on their sleeping arrangements. Maybe her alcohol-induced stupor made sharing a bed with him seem worse than it actually was. She walked to Christian at the stove, rested her head on his back, and put her arms around his chest. He turned the stove off and turned around to look at her.

"A day of fun sounds like a plan to me." She reached up to kiss his lips, but he turned his head.

"Not in front of the boys," he whispered.

"Mommy, is Mr. Christian your boyfriend?" TJ asked.

All three boys stopped playing and turned to look at them.

"What about Daddy?" Maxwell pouted and folded his arms over his chest.

Christian gave her an I-told-you-so look, then grabbed a plate stacked high with pancakes and a plate of bacon. He took them to the table and put them down. "We'll talk about that later, guys. It's time for breakfast now so move your toys off the table."

Before long, they were sitting around the table eating. The more Maxine ate, the better she felt. The boys were talking excitedly about visiting the museum. Between bites of food, Christian smiled at her from across the table. He looked like he wanted more of what she gave him last night, and she couldn't wait to give it to him.

"Christian, since we're spending the day with you at the museum, why don't you and Shane go to church with us tomorrow and then come back here for a big Sunday dinner?"

Christian's smile disappeared. "We'll come over after you get back from church."

"Are you worried about having to sit through a long, drawn-out first Sunday sermon? We won't be there all day. Minister Miller is preaching tomorrow and he's short and to the point. We'll be out of there before you know it and Shane can go with the boys to Sunday school."

Christian put his fork on his plate and looked at Maxine with a hardened expression. "We're not going because I don't believe in God, Maxine. Between serving in the military, losing my wife, and my job as a cop, I've seen too much evil in this world to believe there is some supernatural being that protects us if we just close our eyes and pray." He looked at Shane. "I don't want my son growing up with false hope. Believe what you want, but to me God is on the same level as the fat man in the red suit that comes down the chimney or the Easter Bunny."

Pump the brakes. Not believing in God was a definite deal breaker for Maxine. *How could I have slept with a man who doesn't believe in God?* She could hear Gabby chastising her for not asking Christian more questions or getting to know him better before she started planning their future together. She kept her eyes downcast, unable to respond to what he had just revealed. She wanted to end this pronto, before it went any further. *How do I break up with a man who saved my life and has feelings for me?*

$\mathcal{C}$hapter 21

The following Saturday, Bo's heart stopped when he opened his front door and saw Gabby standing in front of him. She was dressed in a purple stretch lace dress, black-leather crop jacket, and black-leather ankle boots. She adjusted her handbag on her shoulder, tilted her head to the side, and smiled innocently.

"What the hell are you doing here?" Bo whispered through clenched teeth.

"I came to tell your wife I'm tired of you getting out of my bed at two o'clock in the morning to rush home to her. It's interrupting my beauty sleep, and we need to do something about it," Gabby whispered back, then giggled.

"Bo, who's at the door?" his wife, Peaches, asked as she approached them from inside the house.

Bo tried to swallow the lump forming in his throat as he glared at Gabby. His mind went blank as he tried to come up with an excuse for Gabby being there.

Peaches snatched the door open. "Why you bein' rude, Bo?" She waved her hand for Gabby to enter. "I'm sorry. You can come in."

"Thank you." Gabby ignored Bo and entered the house.

Bo watched with his mouth hanging open as his wife and mistress walked into his living room together.

"What's wrong with you, Bo? I hope he didn't have you standing out in the cold too long," Peaches apologized.

"Huh?" He was frozen with fear and couldn't think of a single word to say.

"Oh, it's no problem. We've seen each other over the years since I've known Joy, but we've never officially met each other, so he was probably a little shocked to see me here." She extended her hand to Bo. "Hi, I'm Gabrielle Roché, but you can call me Gabby."

He cleared his throat as he shook her hand. "Hi. Bo."

Peaches shook Gabby's hand as soon as Bo let it go. "Hi, Gabby, nice to meet you. I'm Peaches, Bo's wife."

"Nice to meet you as well, Peaches. I hope I'm not the first one here." Gabby smiled as she removed her coat.

"You're fine, girl. It's just family, Tyesha, my sisters, and a couple of Bo's brothers' girlfriends. We all love Joy and wanted to plan this baby shower for her." Peaches took Gabby's jacket and gave it to Bo to hang up.

"Thanks for letting me come in Bea's place. She wanted to stay with Joy." She turned to Bo and gave him a seductive smile.

"No problem, I understand. I'm glad Joy's doing better." Peaches unconsciously adjusted her outfit. "You can follow me to the den. We're discussing themes for the baby shower and we got plenty of food to eat." She turned to walk toward the back of the house.

"Sounds like fun. Bye, Bo. It was nice to finally meet you." Gabby blew him a kiss, then followed Peaches.

"Yeah, you, too." Bo was able to breathe for the first time since he saw Gabby at his door.

Gabby looked Peaches over as she followed her to the family room. For a woman in her mid-forties who had birthed three children, she still looked good. She was a curvy size ten with a cute face. Gabby could tell by the way the house was decorated and the outfit she had on that Peaches had some style. Her weave made Gabby wonder if it was really her hair, which meant she spent a lot of money on the high-quality hair and paid the right person to put it in correctly.

When Gabby entered the family room, she spoke to everyone and gave Tyesha a hug. Tyesha pointed for Gabby to sit in a single chair near her. There was an unspoken bond between them since they were held hostage by Dean. There were eight women sitting around discussing Joy's surprise baby shower. Gabby didn't understand why they were going through so much trouble trying to keep it a secret. Gabby had already decided to tell Joy because she didn't think it was a good idea to surprise a woman pregnant with twins. A room full of people screaming "Surprise!" and Joy's water breaking would definitely ruin the party.

Their pitiful ideas for Joy's shower prompted Gabby to suggest they rent the Sunset Room at the National Harbor. The place was elegant with a beautiful view of the Potomac River, and they had on-site caterers. When she told them the price, they ignored her and went back to planning it at a nearby community center. When someone suggested they hang pink and blue paper babies from the ceiling and going potluck on the food, Gabby actually broke out in hives. This baby shower was going to be a disaster, and she didn't want her name associated with it. She wasn't going to waste her breath on this tacky group of women. They were already looking at her sideways, like she didn't belong, and she couldn't agree more. She didn't belong with them; she belonged with Bo.

"Gabby, what's going on between Joy and Allen?" Peaches looked at Gabby with questioning eyes. "Poor Allen. He left the hospital and went straight into the dog house."

Gabby turned her head and mumbled, "That's what happens when you cheat on your pregnant girlfriend."

Tyesha shot her an evil glare. She was still upset and embarrassed by what Allen did with Diana. She felt guilty, too. If she had taken off work and not depended on her stupid brothers to be with Allen when he was in the hospital, his cheating with Diana would've never happened.

Peaches sat on the edge of her seat. "Whatever is going on between the two of them, I just want them to fix it and get back together before the twins are born. I'm thinking about inviting them to dinner, so Bo and I can help them work things out."

"Stay out of it. If they're meant to be together, they'll work it out," Tyesha snapped, then stood and left for the bathroom.

Peaches rolled her eyes at Tyesha. She loved her sister-in-law, but sometimes she was too damn moody.

"I guess we can eat now since we have everything planned," Peaches announced as she stood.

Gabby noticed two women waiting to use the restroom after Tyesha.

"Peaches, is there another bathroom I can use? I've been holding it since I got here and now I feel like I'm gonna explode," Gabby exaggerated. She crossed her legs together and wiggled in her seat.

"Let her use the one downstairs," one of the women suggested.

"Oh, hell no! Bo Junior moved down there and I know it's a mess." She pointed upstairs. "Use the one at the top of the steps on the right."

"Thank you." Gabby practically ran upstairs with a big smile on her face.

As she reached the top of the stairs, she saw Bo go into the bathroom in his master bedroom. She tiptoed into his room, opened the bathroom door, and eased in.

"What the fuck!" Bo turned around to see who it was. He stopped urinating midstream.

Gabby locked the bathroom door and turned to face him. "Finish what you're doing because I need to use that."

"You better get the fuck outta here. My wife is downstairs," Bo whispered through clenched teeth.

"I told you before, I don't care about your wife, but I do care about you." Gabby wrapped her arms around his neck and kissed him.

He pushed her away and shook his head. He knew she was going to be trouble when he opened his front door. After he finished urinating, he shook his penis a couple of times, put it back in his boxers, and zipped his jeans. If Peaches suspected anything between them, her and her crazy-ass sisters would happily beat Gabby within an inch of her life, and he cared too much about her to let that happen.

He washed his hands, then dried them on his wife's decorative towel. He turned around and glared at her. "This shit is not cool," he barked.

"I know. It's hot. I want you to make love to me with your wife downstairs," Gabby ordered with her hands on her hips.

Bo put his hand around Gabby's neck and slammed her back against the wall. "Don't play games with me! Go home and I'll try to come by later."

"No." She removed Bo's hand from her neck and kissed him passionately. "I don't want to wait until later; I want you now."

Bo stepped back with a hardened face. "You trippin'. I'm not fucking you in my house with my wife and family downstairs. That shit ain't happening."

"Ohhh, baby, I'm drippin' wet from you talking about it." She pulled off her black lace thong and twirled it around her finger playfully.

"I'm not doing this shit with you here. C'mon, baby, I'll come over later. I promise." Bo tried to grab her thong to put it back on her.

Gabby giggled and pointed at his erection. "Are you gonna let your wife and family see you like that? You know it's not going away on its own."

Bo looked down and sighed. "Shit! I don't have a condom."

"I'll take care of it." She licked her lips. "I haven't tasted you in a while."

Bo kissed her as he unzipped his jeans and slid them down his legs. He grabbed a handful of Gabby's hair, pulled her dress up, and bent her over the sink.

"Now I know why you like to pull my hair." She laughed out loud. "Can't do that with Peaches, can you? You'll pull her weave out."

"Be quiet." Bo moaned as he slid himself inside her and started stroking.

Somebody turned the door handle, then knocked on the door.

"What?" Bo asked as he gasped for breath.

"Have you seen Gabby?" Peaches asked.

"I told her ass to go back downstairs, and don't send no

more strangers up here, Peaches," Bo snapped. "Damn, a man can't shit in peace in his own goddamn house!"

"Alright. I'm sorry," Peaches yelled back. "When you finish, wash your hands and come get a case of water out of your junky-ass garage."

"Alright," Bo moaned.

They heard Peaches walking down the steps.

Gabby laughed. "Isn't this fun?"

"Shhhh." Bo put his hand over her mouth. "Don't let me come in you."

He closed his eyes and enjoyed the feeling of her warm wetness around his manhood. The more he moved, the more he felt his release coming. Gabby cried out as waves of pleasure caused her body to quiver uncontrollably.

"I'm gettin' ready to squirt my shit all in you," Bo groaned.

Gabby pushed him back and dropped to her knees. She wrapped her hands and mouth around his cock, then sucked and stroked him until his salty juices shot into her mouth. She swallowed quickly and kept him in her mouth until he was soft and limp.

Bo helped her to her feet and stared into her eyes as he gently put his lips on hers. "You are so fuckin' bad for me, but I love you," he whispered.

"I know," Gabby replied as she pulled away and put her thong back on.

"You wanna wash up before you go back downstairs?" Bo turned on the faucet, wet a washcloth, and cleaned his privates.

"No, I want to keep your smell on me as a reminder that your wife might have you by her side, but I have you inside me." She opened her mouth and stuck out her tongue.

Bo shook his head and laughed. "I don't know what to do with you."

"You can spank me later." Gabby stood in the mirror and raked her fingers through her hair.

"Let me go out first." He kissed her again. "I might see you later tonight." Bo peeked out the door, then left.

Gabby checked her reflection in the mirror again. Bo told

her he loved her. She knew it was coming. Lately, he'd been spending more time with her and Nadia than with his own family. Sex with him was addictive and she could talk to him about anything. She didn't have to pretend to be somebody else with Bo. He never judged her, even after she told him about her past. He accepted her for who she was and that's what she always wanted in a man. She had even decided to overlook his criminal past. She loved him, too, but wasn't ready to tell him yet. She was saving that for a special occasion like when she was ready for him to leave his wife and move in with her and Nadia.

She opened the bathroom door and tiptoed back downstairs.

"Gabby, where you been?" Tyesha asked as she eyed her suspiciously.

"Oh, I stepped outside to call and check on Nadia," Gabby answered.

"I hope my evil-ass husband wasn't too rude to you," Peaches said as she piled some tuna salad, chicken wings, and meatballs on a paper plate.

Before Gabby could answer her, Bo walked in the back door carrying a case of bottled water.

"Oh... no, Peaches. Bo wasn't rude to me at all. I would feel the same way if he walked upstairs in my house." Gabby coughed and cleared her throat. "Bo, may I have one of those waters, please. I swallowed something a few minutes ago and it left a nasty taste in my mouth."

"Yeah." Bo bit his bottom lip to stop from laughing. He used a knife to cut the plastic off the case of water, took one out, and gave it to Gabby.

She smiled and touched his hand as she took the water from him.

Tyesha watched the interaction between them. She shook her head disappointedly and shot Bo an I-know-you're-not-doing-what-I-think look. He ignored her and kept sneaking looks at Gabby.

Peaches walked across the kitchen and gave Gabby the plate of food she fixed.

"For me? Thank you, Peaches. That was so nice of you,"

Gabby said, faking her excitement.

"You're welcome." She pinched her lips at Bo. "It's the least I could do."

Gabby put a forkful of tuna salad in her mouth. "Um-um! This tuna salad is so good."

"It's my specialty. I might fix a tray for Joy's shower," Peaches stated proudly.

"Please do. My daughter would love this. Can I come over one day so you can teach me how to make it?" Gabby looked at Bo and smirked.

He stared at her with squinted eyes. The veins on the side of his head were jumping and beads of sweat formed on his forehead.

"Yeah, girl. I'll give you my cell phone number so you can call me." Peaches smiled at her guest, oblivious to what was happening between her husband and Gabby.

"Okay... Thanks. I'll call you next week." Gabby set her plate on the counter. She went to Peaches, hugged her, and planted a big kiss on her cheek.

Tyesha gave Gabby the evil eye. She thought Gabby was smart. She'd soon realize getting involved with Bo was the biggest mistake she'd ever made. It was going to end badly and she didn't want any part of it. Bo's and Allen's recent behavior made Tyesha appreciate being single.

Chapter 22

Joy sat on her couch with her feet propped up on an ottoman in front of her while she sorted through a week's worth of mail. She was happy to be back home.

"Are you having any contractions, Joy?" Bea asked as she walked into the living room looking concerned.

Joy looked at her and half-smiled. "No contractions. I'm fine."

"I was going to cook you some dinner, but you don't have enough food to fix a decent meal," Bea complained.

"Yeah, I know. I had planned to go to the grocery store, but I ended up in the hospital." Joy hunched her shoulders. "There are some carry-out menus in the drawer beside the refrigerator."

"You need a home-cooked meal. Will you be okay if I run around the corner to Giant? I won't be long."

"I'm fine, Bea, but you don't have to do that. I was gonna order something to eat, take a shower, and just go to bed."

"The last thing you need is to get food poisoning from one of those dirty carry-outs. I'll be here the rest of the weekend and I plan to cook my own food, not eat carry-out crap." She put her jacket on and grabbed her purse off the table.

Oh, lucky me, Joy thought. She smiled at Bea and then looked at the large suitcase Bea brought in with her earlier. She wondered how long her mother really planned on staying with her.

"I'll unpack my clothes when I get back. I won't be long.

Keep your phone beside you." Bea put Joy's cordless phone in her hand and kissed her goodbye.

She watched her mother leave, then returned to her mail. A large pink and yellow envelope caught her attention. It was from Allen. She opened it and smiled when she saw a greeting card. The cover had white Calla Lilies and yellow roses. She opened it and read:

I'm sorry for the mistake I made that caused you so much pain, but that had never been my intention. I'm truly begging for your forgiveness.

There was a handwritten note on the other side of the card.

Joy,

I'm lost without you. I love you more than words can say. I know I hurt you, but it doesn't compare to how hurt I am without you. I would give my life to be in the hospital with you right now. Knowing you're going through this because of my immature actions is tearing me up. The thought of not seeing my children come into this world is scaring me more than anything I've ever experienced. Please forgive me. Don't give up on us.

Love,

Allen

She wiped the tears from her eyes and closed the card. She knew exactly how he felt. If it weren't for Bea standing guard at her bedside, Joy would've called him. He sent a beautiful bouquet of flowers to the hospital. As soon as the nurse brought them to her room, Bea read the card and took them out. Joy knew they were from Allen because of the scowl on Bea's face. Although he was wrong and she didn't trust him anymore, she still loved him and wanted him by her side when the twins were born.

Her doorbell rang. She pushed the pile of mail to the side and grunted as she got up from the couch. Bea probably rushed Poppy or Tyesha over to babysit her while she was at the grocery store. When she opened the door, Allen was standing there with a dozen long-stemmed, pink roses in a crystal vase and a box of her favorite chocolate-dipped strawberries.

Joy looked at him with an angry expression.

Allen handed her the box of strawberries. "Please don't ask

me to leave. I haven't seen you since they put you in the back of that ambulance. I'm sorry for everything."

"You should be sorry, Allen. How is Diana?" Joy flinched and rubbed the side of her belly where one of the babies kicked her hard.

"What's wrong? Was that a contraction?" Allen asked nervously.

"Just a kick." Joy closed her eyes, took a deep breath, and exhaled loudly.

He looked relieved. "Oh, okay. Um, I haven't talked to Diana since the night she called you. I broke my phone that night and just got a new one today." He bit his lips as he pulled out his new phone to show her. "She keeps calling and she left all these crazy messages, but I have nothing to say to her."

There was an uncomfortable silence between them as they stared at each other.

"I miss you. What do you want me to do, Joy? Tell me what to do and I'll do it." Allen stared at her with watery eyes.

"Let me go." Joy looked down and swallowed hard.

"I can't do that." He raised her chin to see her eyes.

Allen's cell phone rang. He held the vase in one hand and pulled his cell out with the other. He looked at the phone with a creased forehead. "It's her. Why is this stupid bitch calling me?"

"I wanna hear it," Joy stated firmly as she stepped back to let Allen in.

"I don't wanna upset you." Allen looked at her with pleading eyes.

"It won't upset me, but if you have something to hide, then leave, Allen," Joy stated angrily, then began to close the door.

"Okay. I'll answer it." Allen answered the phone and put it on speaker. "Didn't I tell you never to call me again?"

They walked in the house and sat at the dining room table. Allen placed the vase on the table and Joy put the box she was holding on the table in front of her.

"How dare you tell me to stay away from you! I told Joy the truth and you should be grateful," Diana screamed. "Allen, how could you want her? I was there for you in the hospital. She didn't even care about you. Every time she called you, it was about her and her mother and friends. She never cared about you." She sobbed loudly.

"I love Joy, not you. We need you to understand that so we can move on with our lives and prepare for our twins' birth," Allen said.

"*We?*" Diana laughed. "Did she take you back? You're only with her because of those babies. I'll have your babies if you want me to. As many as you want, just don't leave me."

"Damn, Diana! What happened to you? You sound straight-up crazy!" Allen shouted.

"*You* happened to me, Allen. I was there for you. I love you and I thought you loved me, too. When you caught that bad infection, I stayed with you all night until your fever broke. Even after your family left, when you were delirious and asking for *her*, I stayed by your side. She doesn't love you like I do. She never will," Diana cried.

Joy looked at him, wondering why this was the first time she heard about him having an infection in the hospital.

"No matter what you do, you can't make somebody love you," Allen said calmly.

"I hate Joy and I hate you for loving her! That bullet to your chest should've killed you! I would rather you die than be with her! If you go back to her, I'll kill you myself, then I'll kill her and your half-breed babies!"

"Bitch, if you come anywhere near me, Allen, or our children, you will die an instant death and I'll make sure of it!" Joy threatened her.

"Oh, my God! You have her listening to our conversations now, Allen? I don't want to hear anything you have to say, Joy! The next time you see me, you won't be so lucky! Instead of a bump in the elevator, I'm going to knock those special-needs babies right out of your goddamn stomach," Diana screamed.

Allen spoke furiously. "Shut the fuck up, bitch! I warned you before about threatening my family! You better stay away from them, and if I ever see your ass again, I'm gonna choke the life out of you! Don't call me again!" Allen was dead serious.

"Wait! I'm sorry. I know that sounded crazy and I didn't mean to say it. I love you, Allen, and I would never hurt you. I promise to stay away from you and Joy. I leave for a new play in London next week. You'll never hear from me again. I promise. Bye." She ended the call.

Joy put her elbows on the table and massaged her temples. Diana's conversation alternated from crazy to sane, and it gave Joy an instant headache. Maybe it was her pregnancy hormones, but she actually felt sorry for Diana. She sounded so desperate for Allen's love.

Allen caressed her arm. "Are you okay?"

"Why didn't you tell me you caught an infection? That was one of the things the doctors were worried about after you got shot. How could you not tell me that?" Joy stood and rubbed a cramp out of her back.

"I didn't wanna worry you. You were on bed rest recovering from a concussion. Knowing I had an infection was the last thing you needed to deal with," Allen explained as he got up and stood in front of her.

"I'm sorry I wasn't there for you. The problems between us weren't all your fault." Joy wrapped her arms around his neck and rested her head on his chest. "Dr. Fields wrote a letter to Dean's parents explaining the date of my conception, which was before I knew Dean, so there won't be a paternity test."

He kissed her and enclosed her in his arms. "Thank you, baby. That means a lot to me."

"I'm worried about you. You look so skinny." Joy looked up at him.

"I'll be okay. It's hard to eat when the only information I get about you and the twins is when I eavesdrop on Tyesha's phone calls. I heard her talking to Bea this morning. That's how I found out you were coming home today." He looked down at her stomach. "Can I touch them?"

Joy nodded and put his hand on her belly. "They're okay. Healthy, strong, and staying where they need to be."

"Good." He dropped to his knees, raised Joy's shirt, and put his face on her belly. "I miss you guys. I'm sorry Daddy screwed up, but I never stopped loving you."

"Did you feel that?" Joy giggled.

"Yeah! Was that a kick?" Allen rubbed his hands over Joy's belly like it was a magic ball.

"Yep! They're trying to kick some sense in their father's head." Joy looked down at Allen with a deep frown on her face.

He stood up and stared into her eyes. "Message received loud and clear. I'm sorry. It'll never happen again."

"I know and I'm sorry, too." Joy caressed his face lovingly.

"I need to be with you, Joy. So much is going on with me." He kissed her lips, then rested his forehead on hers. "I miss you so much it hurts. I can't even breathe sometimes."

"I know." She kissed him passionately. "I miss us, too. How did we let things get this bad between us?"

"Can I come home? Please, baby? I have so much I need to tell you. I need you." He held her head between his hands and kissed her repeatedly.

"I can't have sex, Allen. Dr. Fields..."

"I don't want sex, I want you. Do you want me?" He kissed her softly.

Joy nodded. "Yes."

"I love you, baby," Allen confessed.

"I love you, too." Joy smiled.

They looked into each other's eyes. She touched his cheek and gently ran her hand down his neck, never taking her eyes off his. He slid his hand around her waist and pulled her closer to him. He placed his lips on hers and they kissed passionately.

"You can come home. I have to tell Bea. She planned to stay with me this weekend," Joy said between kisses.

"Okay, but you know your mother hates me now." He kissed her and smiled.

"I know. You hurt her daughter and that's unforgivable in Bea's eyes, but give her time."

"That might take a lifetime," Allen joked.

Bea walked in the house with two hands full of plastic gro- cery bags. Allen went to assist her but she pulled away and rolled her eyes at him.

"I got it! Why are you here?" she snapped.

Joy cleared her throat and shook her head to warn Allen not to answer. "Allen, can you wait in the living room while I talk to Bea, please?"

"Sure." Allen walked into the living room and sat down.

Bea eyed the vase of flowers and box of chocolate-covered strawberries on the table. "Hmm," she grumbled as she headed for the kitchen.

Joy followed her. "I need to talk to you about me and Allen," she said with a smile.

"What's going on?" She didn't try to hide the disapproval in her voice as she set the bags on the countertop.

"I realized that we both made mistakes in our relationship and we need to try to fix this. We love each other and we want this to work."

Bea thought for a minute before she spoke. "Sweetheart, you're twenty-seven and you've only been with two men. One tried to kill you and the other one slept with another woman while you were carrying his children. I can see how lonely you are, but don't let it cloud your judgment when it comes to Allen Johnson. He's not worth it."

"We love each other and we want to be together. I need you to understand that." Joy stood in front of Bea so she could see her serious expression.

"I understand he's gonna hurt you again! When a man cheats on you and you forgive him so easily, there is nothing stopping him from doing it again and again and again. I don't want that for you. There are more men in this world than Allen Johnson. You can do better."

"Bea, all my life I've done everything you wanted me to do," Joy said in a soft tone.

"No, you haven't. You married Dean when I begged you not to because I knew it was gonna end badly. This is the same thing. I'm begging you not to take Allen back. He's gonna hurt you again and I want better for you." Bea grabbed Joy's arms. "Love opens you up to pain already, but when you love a cheating man, it leaves you broken and bitter, unable to trust a decent man when he comes your way."

"Don't say that. I know he learned his lesson from this. He knows if he does it again, it'll be the end of us forever." She pulled away from Bea's grip.

Bea sat at the kitchen table and started crying. "I didn't raise you this way. It's not okay to let a man treat you any way he wants to. If you take Allen back, you're saying to him he can cheat on you and you'll always take him back. Don't do it." Bea buried her face in her hands and cried like a baby.

Joy sat in a chair beside her and held her weeping mother in her arms. "I'm sorry. I didn't mean to upset you."

Allen walked in the kitchen. Joy jumped up and pushed him back into the dining room.

"Hey, beautiful! I just wanted to let you know I'm going back to Tyesha's to get my clothes. You want me to bring you anything back?" Allen's smile was as bright as a child's on Christmas morning.

"I'm sorry, baby, but you can't come back home right now," Joy explained, full of disappointment.

"What do you mean I can't come back home right now?" Allen hissed.

"Bea is upset so I'm going to let her stay with me for the weekend and then you can come home Monday after she leaves for work."

Allen turned his back to her and threw his arms in the air. "It's the same shit with you, Joy!" He turned back around to face her. "Why do I even try? Huh?"

"Allen, stop being so dramatic. I didn't say you couldn't come back home. I said not tonight." Joy hugged him. "Baby, don't be mad. She's my mother and she's upset and crying."

"Crying goddamn crocodile tears to keep you right where she wants you, away from me and with her. I'm out of here. Maybe if Bea had a man, she wouldn't try to come between us. Bye, Joy." Allen stomped out of the house.

Joy walked back in the kitchen with her shoulders slumped over. Bea's tears were now replaced with a bright smile. She hummed as she put the groceries away. Joy was quickly reminded of why she had kept her relationship with Allen a secret all those years. Bea had a way of manipulating her to get what she wanted, and she wanted her daughter away from Allen Johnson. Joy knew if she didn't put an end to her mother's meddling, the next woman Allen kissed might be the one to take him away from her forever.

Chapter 23

It was Monday morning. Joy nibbled on saltine crackers covered with peanut butter as the news aired on her living room flat-screen. The television was on, but she wasn't paying it any attention. Not hearing from Allen since he stomped out of her house on Saturday had her in a bad place. She couldn't stop thinking about him or wondering what made him change his mind about moving back in with her. Maybe choosing Bea over him again was the final straw. She wanted to call him for answers, but her pride wouldn't let her. It was best for her to get used to not having him around. After Bea left for work, she was able to shed the tears she'd been holding back all weekend.

The doorbell rang.

Joy grumbled. *Lord, help me keep my sanity through the rest of this pregnancy. Knowing Bea, she had a group of people lined up to stop by and check on me all day. All I want is to be left alone to wallow in my misery. Is that too much to ask?*

She wobbled to her front door prepared to get rid of her guest as soon as possible. When she opened the front door, her knees buckled. Allen stood on her doorstep. A duffel bag was on his shoulder and his laptop bag was in his hand. How could he look so damn good dressed in a pair of jeans, a black hoodie, and sneakers? The dimpled smile he showed whenever he was in her presence made her heart skip a beat. She had an instant desire to run into his arms and cover him from head to toe with loving kisses. Instead, she yelled, "What the hell are you doing here?"

159

His smile disappeared immediately. "It's Monday."

"And? You stomped out of here Saturday with an attitude and I haven't heard from you since. And now you just show up with your luggage ready to move back in. I don't think so." She tried to close the door but he stopped it with his foot.

Determined not to let Allen upset her, she ignored him, walked back in the house, and sat on the couch.

He came in behind her and put his bags in the foyer. With his droopy mouth and sad eyes, he followed her into the living room. "Baby, what are you talking about?"

"Is Diana back in town? Did you spend the weekend with her or some other chick? Trying to get your last fuck in before you move back in here with me, knowing I can't satisfy your needs right now?"

"C'mon. Trust me, baby. I wasn't with another woman. I kissed Diana when I was in the hospital. It was a stupid mistake that will never happen again. My promise to you."

She looked at him with tears welling. "Just leave. I was stupid to think we could go back to the way we used to be."

"Don't say that." Allen looked like someone had knocked the wind out of him.

"Bye, Allen." With her eyes on the television, she picked up the remote and turned up the volume.

He took the remote out of her hand and turned the television off. "I could beg you to forgive me again if that's what you want, but everything I've done since I left here Saturday has been for us. I went back to Tyesha's and packed my stuff because I wanted everything to be ready to go this morning when I came back to you."

With a questioning expression, Joy turned around and faced Allen. "Really?"

"Yes, baby. Yesterday, I woke up and asked Tyesha to take me to the car dealership. I spent most of the day there. Let me show you." Helping Joy up, he escorted her to the living room window and pulled the curtains back. He pointed at the shiny, black Range Rover in Joy's driveway.

With her mouth wide open and her hands clutching her

chest, Joy asked, "You bought a new truck?"

He stood behind Joy and wrapped his arms around her. "Not that I have anything against your Toyota Corolla, baby, but we needed something a little bigger so I leased this. It has plenty of space for us, two car seats, and everything we'll have to carry for the twins." He kissed her neck.

She turned around and faced him. "Why didn't you tell me?"

"Babe, I've been calling you all weekend. Didn't Bea give you any of my messages?"

Joy was speechless. *How could Bea not tell me Allen called?* She wasn't surprised though. Taking over her daughter's life must be coded into Bea's DNA. She couldn't help herself. In Bea's mind, she had it all planned out that she would move in with Joy until the twins were born. When she mentioned it, Joy blew it off. It was bad enough having her mother invade her space the past few days, but the next few months would irritate Joy and make her go into early labor for sure.

"Bea didn't tell you I called, did she? Of course she didn't. I left at least five messages with her, not to mention the texts I sent." He looked at Joy. "Check your cell phone."

"I will." Joy was too embarrassed to say she hadn't seen her cell phone since she got home from the hospital. Whenever she looked for it or asked her mother about it, Bea changed the subject, which meant she probably hid it somewhere. It was her mother's way of maintaining control and keeping them apart. She should've known better. "Let me deal with my mother. She's gonna keep trying to come between us until she gets what she wants, but we can't let her."

"Yeah, okay. She's relentless. Like a goddamn tiger mom and lioness rolled into one." The more time he spent on the receiving end of Bea's wrath, the more he understood why Joy had wanted to keep him a secret from her mother for so long.

"Can we make a promise to leave the past in the past? No more talk of Dean or Diana and whatever Bea hits us with, we deal with it together."

He crossed his arms around her neck and put his forehead

to hers. "That sounds like a plan. You and the twins are the best things that ever happened to me. I love you." Without taking his eyes off hers, he covered her lips with his.

Joy closed her eyes and enjoyed the tenderness of his soft, full lips on her mouth. Moments like this made her realize how much she really loved him. She wasn't going to let her mother's hatred for Allen or his fling with Diana decide the fate of their relationship. In her heart, she believed their love was deep enough to handle anything. And she had a strong feeling they had a few more challenges coming their way before they could begin to relax and be truly happy.

Chapter 24

Gabby was already dreading her day. Sadness overcame her as she walked into the Muscogee County Superior Courthouse. Not having a relationship with her family usually didn't bother her, but today she felt like the loneliest person in the world, even with Maxine, Nadia, and her nanny at her side. Yet, she knew in her heart the one and only person she could ever count on was working hard to keep her and Nadia together. She was counting on that for a positive outcome.

When she entered the courthouse lobby, Maxine pulled her to the side. "Joy wanted us to call her before your hearing."

"I can't be late, Maxine."

Maxine waved her cell phone in the air. "It won't take long. It's already ringing." She pushed the speaker button for Gabby to hear.

Gabby's cheeks turned as red as the devil because she was ready to find her assigned courtroom and get this over with. She ordered Nadia's nanny to take her to a nearby restroom and check her diaper while she talked to Joy.

"Hello," Allen answered.

"Good morning, Allen," Maxine sang into the phone, smiling ear to ear. "Joy wanted me to call her before we go inside for court."

"Wassup, Maxine? Hold on a sec and I'll get her for you."

Maxine covered the phone with her hand. "I'm so glad

they're back together."

Gabby rolled her eyes and puckered her lips. "Ummm. Until he screws up again."

Maxine looked Gabby up and down, shaking her head disapprovingly. She usually avoided Gabby when she was in one of her nasty moods, but today, she couldn't abandon her friend. If the shoe were on the other foot, Maxine knew she would be just as hateful. The possibility of losing custody of your child could make a saint snap.

"Gabby? Maxine?" Joy's voice echoed through the lobby.

"I'm here! Make it quick, Joy! I have to go!" Gabby snapped.

"Hi, Joy," Maxine greeted in a happy tone.

"Hi, Maxine. Gabby, you need to calm down! I wanted to talk to you before you went to court. Rayshawn'll probably have all his family there, but don't let that intimidate you. Maxine will be there for you. I tried to get Bea to come, but she doesn't want to leave me and Poppy is still in Puerto Rico with my sick grandmother." Joy smacked her lips and exhaled. "I almost asked the Johnson brothers to come. You know they'll come deep, but they'll probably hurt your case more than help it."

Gabby thought about Bo and couldn't hold back her smile. He stayed with her the entire night before she left to come here. They had sex all night and even squeezed in a quickie before she left for the airport yesterday afternoon. He hardly ever mentioned his wife to her anymore unless he was complaining about something stupid she did. Gabby was tired of her role as his side chick. It was time for him to leave Peaches and be with her permanently or until she got tired of him. "I'll be fine. At least *one* of my best friends is here with me," Gabby said sarcastically.

"I know you weren't expecting my fat ass to be there. I can barely walk to the bathroom without feeling like I need to take a nap," Joy replied with an attitude.

"Joy will be with you in spirit. Now let's pray," Maxine suggested.

"Thank you," Gabby replied anxiously.

"Everybody close your eyes and open your hearts. Father

God, we pray that the truth will come to light and..."

"What! Don't pray for the truth!" Gabby shrieked.

"Maxine, you must've forgot who you were praying for, girl." Joy laughed.

"Oh...You're right. I'm sorry, let me do it again," Maxine stuttered.

"*No!* Just forget it. Let's go." Gabby walked away.

"I'll call you as soon as it's over, Joy." Maxine hung up and ran to catch up with Gabby.

Gabby's attorney, Jim, met them after they went through security. He escorted them to the third floor and proceeded down the hall to the courtroom where Gabby's custody hearing was scheduled to take place. Her heart thumped when she entered the courtroom and saw Rayshawn talking quietly with his three lawyers. His mother, dressed in a loud purple pantsuit and matching hat, sat directly behind him. Osaki sat beside her, looking bored and frustrated. As the rest of the witnesses came in, Gabby pointed them out to Maxine.

Jim left to sign in with the courtroom clerk. Rayshawn strolled over to them with an arrogant smirk. He took Nadia out of her stroller and talked to her in his stupid baby voice, while making the ugliest faces. Nadia leaned back in his arms and stared at him with a blank expression.

"Osaki, come meet my daughter, Nadia Rae Robinson," Rayshawn ordered, then looked at Gabby and smiled. "I'm changing her last name today. She's a Robinson."

Gabby intentionally ignored Rayshawn, which infuriated him.

Maxine sat on the bench behind Gabby's attorney. She observed the interaction between Gabby and Rayshawn. Osaki took her time getting up to join them. She was dressed in a black, sequined tube dress with black platform shoes. She looked like she was going out for a night of clubbing, not going to a custody hearing. When Nadia saw Osaki, she became excited and jumped in her arms. Maxine was amazed because Nadia wasn't the type of child who just went to anybody. She had been in her life since the day she was born and she would only come to her if Gabby was nearby or Maxwell and TJ were around.

"She likes you, Osaki!" Rayshawn exclaimed.

Frowning, Osaki gave Nadia back to Rayshawn. "I don't like babies," she whined. "I'll be back."

"Where you going?" Rayshawn asked anxiously, handing Nadia to Gabby so he could follow Osaki.

"Can I go to the restroom?" She pouted like a young child and walked away. Her platform shoes made a loud clicking sound with every step she took.

A few minutes later, a social worker came out and informed them that she needed to take Nadia with her until the judge made a ruling. Maxine got up from her seat and joined Gabby. She knew this was going to be hard on her friend.

Gabby sat on a wooden bench behind her. With tears in her eyes, she held Nadia in her arms and whispered, "Mommy loves you and I hope one day you can forgive me for what I'm getting ready to do." She kissed Nadia's cheek.

The social worker took Nadia from her arms and the baby immediately started crying. She reached her arms out for Gabby, crying, "Mama." The social worker turned and walked away.

"Wait!" Gabby shouted. "I'm not sending my daughter off with a complete stranger."

"Gabby, we discussed this," Jim interjected while approaching them.

"I understand, Jim, but I still have full custody of my daughter and I want her nanny to stay with her until this is over," Gabby stated angrily as she shoved Consuela toward the social worker. Nadia stopped crying when Consuela took her and the social worker agreed to let the nanny join them. They left the courtroom through a side door.

Maxine fought back her tears as she hugged Gabby and rubbed her back.

Gabby pulled away and regained her composure. "I need to go to the restroom before this starts." She picked up her purse and walked to the back of the courtroom.

"I'll go with you." Maxine grabbed her purse and followed Gabby.

"Maxine, I need a few minutes alone." Gabby half-smiled and rubbed Maxine's arm.

"Oh, okay. Sure." Maxine went back to her seat behind Jim.

Gabby left the courtroom. When she reached the hall, she practically ran to the ladies' room. Osaki was standing at the sink drying her hands with a brown paper towel. Gabby locked eyes with her. "The social worker just took Nadia and I almost lost it. I don't think I can do this." Gabby looked at her with tears welling.

Osaki gazed at Gabby with sympathetic eyes. She hadn't seen her look this uncertain and afraid since she took Gabby in when she was a dirty and confused teenager with no place to live. She pulled Gabby close to her and held her while she cried. "I know it's hard, but you can do it."

"What if it doesn't turn out the way we planned? I could lose her," she wept.

Osaki stepped back, raised Gabby's chin, and smiled at her. "Do you trust me?"

Gabby wiped her tears with the back of her hands and nodded. She trusted Osaki with her life. When everybody else had turned their backs on her, Osaki stepped up and took care of her. They became family. After Gabby left for college, Osaki preferred to stay in the background. She didn't want people judging Gabby because of her line of work. Gabby didn't like it, but she learned how judgmental people were and went along with what Osaki wanted. Even though out of sight, Osaki remained a part of Gabby's life and was still there whenever Gabby needed her, like now with Rayshawn.

Gabby's phone rang. She smiled when she saw Bo's name on the screen. She walked over to the sinks and leaned against the wall. "Hi, I can't talk long. It's almost time."

"You sound kinda shaky. Is your girl there like we planned?"

Gabby turned around and looked at Osaki. "I'm okay and she's right here with me. She got Rayshawn whipped already. He practically threw Nadia at me when she left to go to the bathroom."

"Good. I gotta go, but call me as soon as it's over. I love you." Bo kissed her over the phone and hung up.

Gabby put her phone back in her tweed suit jacket, took some make-up out of her purse, and touched up her face.

"You talking about Rayshawn being whipped. Look at you! Who is this man and why isn't he here with you?" Osaki stood beside Gabby and looked at their reflections in the mirror.

"It's complicated." Gabby avoided looking at Osaki in the mirror as she combed her hair.

"No, it's not. He's married." She grabbed Gabby's shoulders and turned her around. "The first rule I ever taught you was never, no matter what, never fall in love with a married man." She shook Gabby's shoulders in frustration. "They never leave their wives, Gabby, and you know this."

"He spends more time with me at my place now than he does with her. I love him and I think he's ready to move in with me. We're just waiting on this custody issue with Rayshawn to be resolved."

"Give that dick-swinging motherfucker back to his goddamn wife. You got a nice bank account and a daughter to think about. End it, Gabby." She flung her hand in Gabby's direction and paced back and forth. "I'm fucking Rayshawn, dressing like a crack whore, and doing all this freaky shit with him so you can keep custody of Nadia. Don't let an affair with a married man jeopardize everything."

"I appreciate everything you've done for me, but Bo's different," Gabby explained with pleading eyes.

"Yeah, right. If I had a dollar for every time I heard that one." Osaki frowned.

"Let's talk about it later, Osaki. I need to deal with the custody hearing first." Osaki had a lot more to say about Gabby's married boyfriend, but she didn't want to make her more upset than she already was. Gabby didn't want to admit it, but she was more vulnerable than Osaki had seen her in a long time. The Gabby she knew and loved wouldn't give a married man a second glance unless he had something to offer her, and this guy sounded like a total loser. Married or not, if he cared about Gabby, he should've had his ass in court today. One more lie wouldn't hurt his wife. Her female intuition warned her that this man was bad news.

"It's time. You ready to do this?" Osaki asked through clenched teeth.

Gabby hugged Osaki and said, "I'm ready." She released her, then left the bathroom.

Gabby sashayed back into the courtroom feeling more confident, thanks to Osaki and Bo. She stood near the door and looked at the number of people who had appeared while she was in the bathroom. Rayshawn's side of the courtroom was full; even a couple of his teammates showed up. There wasn't a single seat available. Maxine was the only person sitting on her side, but she didn't let it bother her. She took a deep breath and headed to her seat.

Halfway down the aisle, her former sister-in-law, Phyllis, stepped over several people and jumped in front of Gabby.

"Oh, your day has come, bitch!" she yelled at Gabby.

Gabby tossed her hair over her shoulders and smiled. "I didn't think you could get any bigger. How much can human flesh stretch? You look disgusting."

"I'm pregnant!" Phyllis shouted and lunged at Gabby.

Phyllis's husband, Sam, leaped over the crowd and put his arms around Phyllis to hold her back. "Phyllis, I knew this was a bad idea. I'm not gonna let you hurt my baby, woman."

"Sam! Oh, sweet Sam! You look good. Have you lost weight?" Gabby touched her cleavage and gave him a seductive smile.

Sam took his arms away from Phyllis, stuck his chest out, and tucked his shirt into his pants. "Yeah, a little bit. You can tell?"

"Of course, I can." Licking her lips, Gabby rubbed his big beer gut. "Umm."

Phyllis smacked her hand away before Sam blocked her.

Gabby whispered in Sam's ear, "I bet you were thinking about me when you climbed on that elephant and made that baby." She blew him a kiss and walked away to her seat.

"What did she say, Sam? That's alright. I hope I'm the first one to testify to get that innocent baby from her lying ass and into her daddy's arms where she belongs." She balled her fist at Gabby. "You killed my brother, took all his money, and burned his body like he was a piece of trash. Today is payback, slut."

"Good luck with that, Sis," Gabby teased. She took her seat beside Jim and pinched his cheeks.

Sam pulled Phyllis back to her seat seconds before the judge entered.

Osaki gave Gabby the finger as she returned from the bathroom and went back to her seat behind Rayshawn. He looked relieved to see her. Laughing out loud, he wanted Gabby to know he enjoyed watching the interaction between her and her enemies. He leaned his chair back on two legs, looked around at his lawyers, and winked at her.

The bailiff entered through a side door. He was a large Hispanic man, bald on top with his side and back hair pulled into a long ponytail. Judge Evelyn Bollinger came in, put on her robe, and surveyed the room. She was a petite white woman, with long straight blonde hair and a face full of deep wrinkles. She took her seat, removed her eyeglasses, and shot the lawyers and their clients a warning look before she proceeded. In a booming voice, the bailiff called court into session.

Jim stood. "Your honor, if I may address the court, please."

Judge Bollinger cleaned her glasses, put them back on, and said, "You may."

Jim helped Gabby to her feet. "Your honor, my client, Gabrielle Roché, would like to relinquish custody and parental rights of her and the plaintiff's minor child, Nadia Rae Roché. She is requesting the plaintiff, Mr. Rayshawn Robinson, be granted sole and permanent custody of the minor."

Rayshawn fell out of his chair and hit the floor, face first.

Chapter 25

"Gabby, what are you doing?" Maxine screamed, jumping up from her seat.

Gabby forced her eyes to look everywhere except at Maxine. The pain on her face would be too much for Gabby to bear. While Rayshawn's lawyers helped him off the floor, Osaki screamed her frustration at Rayshawn, then stormed out of the courtroom. Rayshawn's mother ran up and down the aisle, shouting and testifying like she was at Sunday morning service. People in the courtroom clapped, cheered, and chanted "R&R" repeatedly.

"Order!" The judge banged her gavel several times. "If I witness any more disrespect in my courtroom, some of you will be going to jail for contempt of court."

The judge's stern tone and threatening expression were enough to quiet the courtroom immediately.

"Gabby," Maxine whispered, but she was ignored.

"Counselors, I want to see you and your clients in my chambers now," the judge ordered.

Maxine reached out and grabbed Gabby's arm before she left. Gabby turned her head to look at her. Tears streamed from Maxine's eyes as panic and uncertainty covered her face. Gabby shot her a guilty look, then followed Jim to the judge's chamber.

Jim noticed tears in Gabby's eyes. "It's not too late to change your mind." He reached in his pocket and gave her his handkerchief.

"It's done." Gabby snatched the handkerchief and dabbed at her eyes.

Rayshawn and his lawyers walked ahead of them. He was on his cell phone begging and pleading for Osaki not to leave him. She kept hanging up and he kept calling her back. When she stopped answering his calls, he turned his anger on his lawyers and threatened to fire them if they didn't fix this.

Watching Rayshawn in panic mode made her smile. Bo was right. Giving him what he wanted didn't include being a full-time daddy to Nadia. What he really wanted was to be a full-time freak with Osaki. She wondered what he was going to do when this was all over and Osaki disappeared. Gabby almost burst out laughing thinking about it. After what he put her through, he deserved every bit of the heartbreak coming his way.

They entered the office they were directed to and waited on instructions from the judge. She pointed at seats around a large conference table and told everybody exactly where she wanted them to sit. The judge took her seat directly across from Gabby. She steepled her fingers together and placed them under her chin.

"What kind of games are you playing, Ms. Roché?" the judge asked.

"Your honor..." Jim started.

She pointed her index finger at Jim. "I'll let you know when it's your turn to speak, counselor." She pointed the same index finger at Gabby. "Right now, I want to hear from your client."

I would get a Judge Judy wannabe. "I can assure you, Judge Bollinger, that giving up my parental rights is not a game. I thought long and hard about this before I made my decision."

Rayshawn's cell phone rang. He looked at the screen and smiled when he saw Osaki's name. "Excuse me, but I need to take this."

"What is more important than discussing the custody of your daughter, Mr. Robinson?" the judge inquired with an arched brow.

Rayshawn frowned when he realized how badly that made him look in the judge's eyes. "I'm sorry, Your Honor. Nothing is more important than my daughter."

"Good to hear it." She pushed her glasses up on the bridge of her nose. "Now, back to you, Ms. Roché. Are you certain about your decision to relinquish your parental rights?"

"Don't I have some say-so in this?" Sweat trickled down Rayshawn's face. He removed his jacket and revealed two large stains under his armpits.

"If you don't mind, Rayshawn, I was going to answer the judge's question." She shot him a hateful frown. "Your Honor, being a single parent is very hard. Nadia relies solely on me for everything. Since my husband died, all of my time is spent taking care of my daughter. I had three job interviews in the past month and only made one because Nadia was sick with another ear infection. I don't have the luxury of hanging out with my friends or dating like Mr. Robinson."

"Hmmm, yeah right," Rayshawn mumbled.

"If Rayshawn thinks he can do better than me, then let him try." Gabby crossed her arms over her chest and sat back in her chair.

"Naw, see, I ain't sayin' I could do better than you. All little girls need their mothers. She always look good whenever I see her, but I just don't get to see her as much as I like and, Judge, she knocking me over the head with child support." Rayshawn used his hands to wipe the sweat dripping down his face, then rubbed his hands on his slacks. "And since her husband died, I got proof she's been hanging around some criminals and possibly involved in some illegal activity. That shit, I mean, I'm sorry, that stuff got me concerned about my daughter's safety."

Gabby's stomach turned inside out. She hoped Rayshawn didn't start pulling out pictures of her and Bo at the Red Roof Inn. That could open doors she needed to remain shut forever.

"It sounds to me like you're not interested in full custody of your daughter, Mr. Robinson. What you really want is a visitation schedule, to pay less child support, and to control who Ms. Roché has around your daughter. Is that correct?"

"Yes, ma'am." Rayshawn looked down at his vibrating cell phone. Osaki was calling him again.

"In the future, don't waste my time or the county's resources by suing for something you're not serious about." She scanned through a pile of documents in front of her. "Other than a few ear infections, there is nothing in your daughter's medical records that concern me, and I don't see any criminal record for Ms. Roché. I'll grant you a visitation schedule and lower your child support payments, but the last time I checked, this was a free country and Ms. Roché can spend her time with whomever she wishes."

Rayshawn nodded his head at Gabby in a teasing fashion. "From now on, I wanna approve the men in her life to keep my daughter safe. I have proof of her hanging out with criminals that could put my daughter's life in danger."

"You sound dumber than you look, but two can play that game." Gabby glared at Rayshawn. "I don't approve of your bisexual, freaky girlfriend. I don't want *her* around my daughter."

"See, there you go!" Rayshawn flipped her the bird. "Osaki might be her stepmother one day."

"Enough! This is a free country and you're both free to date whomever you like without getting permission from the other." The judge stood and tucked their file under her arm. "Stay seated until the custody terms have been typed and signed by both of you. Any questions?"

"No," they said in unison.

The judge's clerk arrived twenty minutes later with documents for both of them to sign. Gabby read over her copy first, then gave it to Jim, whereas Rayshawn's lawyers read his and then explained every detail to him. He shot her a winning smile across the table like he had just hit the jackpot. He was too dumb to realize it was the same thing they agreed to at Hooters the night he met Osaki with the exception of him paying the nanny's salary. He would get to see Nadia every other weekend and pay $5,000 a month. Since Jim had no changes, she signed the document, got a copy for her records, and left the courthouse with Nadia in her arms. Everything had gone just as Gabby had planned it.

———

Later that night, Bo pulled his Suburban in front of Gabby's house and rolled down the window. He took one last puff of his cigarette and flicked it out the window. While he sat and thought about the best way to deal with Gabby, he opened a pack of gum and put two pieces in his mouth.

The thought of driving away and never coming back crossed his mind a couple of times, but he knew that was the wrong thing to do with a woman like Gabby. His other side pieces knew their place and didn't expect any more than he gave them, but not Gabby. He could tell by the way she'd been acting lately that she was ready for more.

He made the mistake of spending more time with her than he should have over the past couple of months, but he had to do it. She was the only person he didn't trust who knew the truth about Dean's murder. After Bo killed Dean, his brother Chuck got one of his dope boys, Peanut, to confess to the murder. He agreed to do it since he was going away to do some serious time anyway, plus nobody turned the Johnson brothers down and lived to tell about it. In exchange for helping them, the Johnson brothers promised to take care of Peanut's mother while he was locked up.

Bo thought everything was a done deal until Gabby contacted him about the pictures Rayshawn's private detective took. Chuck thought she was a loose end and wanted to kill her, but Bo couldn't do that to Joy or leave Nadia without a mother. His plan was to help her deal with Rayshawn to keep the pictures out of the cops' hands, but they started sleeping together. That was a stupid move on his part. He wasn't expecting sex with her to be that good, but she was addictive. Whenever he screwed somebody else, he found himself fantasizing about Gabby and he hated it. Falling in love with her was clouding his judgment. He didn't want any woman to have that much control over him. It was time for him to do something about her.

Gabby looked out her window when she heard Bo's truck door close. She knew he was out there smoking, but she wasn't going to complain about it tonight. She wanted him, smoke breath and all. Maxine agreed to babysit Nadia. Gabby wanted her and Bo to have the house to themselves so they could celebrate freely. She ordered a couple of steak and lobster dinners from Bo's favorite restaurant and even stopped at the liquor store and got him a bottle of his favorite drink, Hennessy X.O.

When she heard him using the spare key she put under the mat, she lay back on the sofa and prepared to greet him with his first surprise of the evening. Bo walked in the house and locked the front door. He went into the living room when he saw the lights shining in the usually dark room. Gabby was lying on the sofa ass naked with her legs open, showing her fresh Brazilian wax. Her long curls hung loosely around her shoulders and she looked exquisite without any makeup.

Bo felt himself becoming aroused and forced himself to stay focused on what he was there to do. He picked her nightgown off a nearby chair and threw it over her body. "Where the papers from court at?"

"What is your problem?" Thinking he had somebody with him, Gabby quickly put on her robe.

Bo didn't respond. Papers on the coffee table caught his attention. He picked them up, sat in one of Gabby's white armchairs, and read them thoroughly. "You signed it so you good with this?"

"Of course I am. I already told you that when I left the courthouse." She got up and sat on Bo's lap. "It's over. Let's celebrate. I have dinner and your favorite drink, but first I want this." She rubbed between his legs.

He grabbed her wrist to stop her. "I'm not staying. Now that this shit is over with your baby's daddy, we're through. Get up." He pushed Gabby off his lap, making her stumble to her feet.

Her eyes flew wide open and she looked livid. "Men don't leave me until I'm through with them! We're through when I say we're through!"

Bo chuckled. "I told you when we started this you were gonna get hurt, but you didn't listen. I became who you needed me to be to get you through this and to keep me and my brother out of jail. This shit is finally over, so I don't have a need for you anymore. Shit, my other side chicks require a lot less attention than your ass."

Gabby smacked him hard across his face with her open

hand. "I hate you!"

"I'll give you that one, but if you do it again, I'll hit your ass back. I never had a problem beatin' a bitch's ass." He walked to the dining room and took one of the containers of food. "Thanks for dinner. I'll take mine to go. I'll leave the liquor for you. You look like you'll need it more than me."

Gabby snatched the container out of his hand and threw it at his head. The food hit his face and leather jacket, then dropped to the floor. He reached out to grab her robe. She backed away, picked up the other container of food and threw it at him. Steak, lobster, potatoes, and broccoli covered the dining room floor. She ran around the table, grabbed a bottle of Coke, and threw it at his head. He ducked, causing it to hit the wall and splatter. The dark soda dripped down the eggshell white wall.

"Get out or I'll kill you!" Gabby fell to her knees clutching her stomach. "I can't believe this! You were playing me the whole time. Why did I let myself fall in love with you?"

Bo became overwhelmed with guilt as he watched Gabby lose control. He went in the kitchen, got a glass, and poured some Hennessy in it. He helped her to the sofa and tried to get her to drink the strong liquor. She pushed it away and kissed him.

"Don't do that," Bo warned. He set the glass on the table and stood to leave.

"I know you love me. You told me. So why are you doing this?" Gabby sobbed.

"Never believe what a man says when he's about to bust a nut or try to get between your legs." He looked at Gabby's tear-stained face. Her robe was partially open, revealing her perky breasts. He felt himself getting hard. "I told you in the beginning I'm married and I ain't leaving Peaches. So what you want from me?"

Gabby looked up at him with hope in her eyes. "I want you."

"I know." Bo pulled her up and removed her robe. "I want you too, baby." He covered her mouth with his and inserted his tongue.

Gabby removed his jacket and unbuttoned his jeans without

taking her eyes off his. His face had softened and his touch was gentle. She was beginning to see the man she had fallen in love with. She helped Bo pull his jeans down to his ankles. He helped her to the floor and lay on top of her.

"Is this what you want?" Bo asked as he guided his erection inside her.

Gabby purred with pleasure. "Yes. I want you." She crossed her legs around his back and moved in rhythm with him, raising her hips off the floor. Bo wouldn't even look at her. Her tears started flowing again because she knew it was over between them.

He wasn't inside her for long before she felt his body tense. He pulled out and sat on top of her chest. While stroking his man-hood, he shot his cum on her face. She was too shocked and humiliated to move.

"You like that don't you, whore?" He laughed as he wiped the head of his penis on her lips, making sure every drop of his semen was on her face.

"Get out," she whispered through her sobs. She hadn't felt this low and degraded since she was raped by the man her mother sent her to live with.

Bo stood, pulled his pants back up and gulped the glass of liquor he'd poured earlier. He took a wad of cash out of his inside jacket pocket and rolled off five one-hundred-dollar bills. "Every bitch got a price. Yours is money." He dropped each bill on top of her, one at a time. "Fucking you was worth every penny." He walked to the door and looked back at her.

Gabby lay on the floor curled in a fetal position, sobbing.

Bo wanted to turn around, pick her off the floor, and hold her until she stopped crying, but he didn't. Falling in love with her was a mistake; continuing a relationship with her would be stupid. He forced himself to open the door and walked away with no regrets. Gabby cried as her mind raced with questions. *How did I not see that he was using me? How did I let myself fall in love with somebody so cruel?* A clear image of William's face popped in her head. She wondered if he asked himself the same thing before she hurt him so badly that he took his own life.

178

Chapter 26

Allen rushed into the bedroom with the cordless phone in his hand. He gently rubbed Joy's shoulder. "Babe, wake up. Gabby's nanny is on the phone. She said it's an emergency."

Joy blinked her eyes a few times before she opened them and looked at Allen's worried expression. *Emergency?* Panic shot through her when she realized she hadn't seen or talked to Gabby since she returned from her custody hearing almost a week ago. She snatched the phone from Allen. "Consuela, what's wrong?"

"Ms. Gabby, she sick. She stay in the bed, won't eat or drink, and when Nadia cries for her, she don't want her. I been here all week, but I need to go home and check on my mother. She say to call you to come get Nadia," Consuela explained in her thick Hispanic accent.

"Okay, I'm on my way." Joy hung up and tossed the phone on the bed beside her. She rolled over and stuck her arms out for Allen to help her.

"What's up?" Allen asked with concern.

"Gabby's sick and Consuela needs to go home. I have to go get Nadia." Joy rubbed her aching back as she wobbled to the bathroom.

"Naw, you stay here. Give me the address and I'll go get her. I don't want you to get sick, too." Allen was already dressed in a pair of loose-fitting jeans and a sleeveless white T-shirt. He sat on the side of the bed and put on his Timberland boots.

"I'll be okay." She watched him from the bathroom as she brushed her teeth. His freshly trimmed goatee, deep dimples, and smooth bald head made her insides flutter. She smiled when she saw the cross tattoo on his arm with her name inside it. No matter how hard she tried, she just couldn't stop loving Allen Johnson. Her heart and soul belonged to him and there was nothing she could do about it.

"If that's what you want, babe." Allen stood and adjusted his jeans over his boots.

"Can you call your brother and find out if he knows what's wrong with Gabby? I have a feeling Bo has something to do with her sickness." Joy massaged a foamy cleanser over her face.

"Oh, so now you believe me." Allen entered the bathroom and looked at Joy with raised brows. For the past month, he had been trying to tell her Bo and Gabby were messing around, but she didn't want to believe him.

"It's not that I didn't believe you. I was just shocked when you told me." Joy knew Gabby, and she didn't do thugs or criminals. Bo Johnson was the biggest thug and career criminal Joy knew. He had been in and out of jail since he was a teenager, had never held a real job, and was a high school dropout. That was three strikes against him, according to Gabby's standards. It wasn't until Tyesha told Bea what she saw happen between Bo and Gabby that Joy realized it was true.

Forty minutes later, Allen parked in front of Gabby's house. He got out, opened Joy's door, and helped her out. "Do you want me to go in with you?"

"No, I won't be long." She kissed his lips and proceeded up the porch steps. Consuela was at the door waiting. "Hi, Consuela."

"Hi, Joy. Thanks for coming so fast. I fed Nadia breakfast and now she's down for her nap." Consuela picked her bag off the floor and swung it over her shoulder. "My mom is waiting for me. I'll be back Monday."

"Okay, Consuela. I'll let Gabby know. Thanks for your help." She locked the door and went upstairs to Gabby's room. The musty smell of armpits and body odor made her gag. She opened the bedroom windows to let some air in.

"Gabby." Joy stood over her and shook her shoulder.

"Leave me alone," she muttered. "Take Nadia with you."

"Are you sick? Do you need to see a doctor?" Joy shook her shoulder even harder this time.

"Stop. I'm not sick. I just want to be alone. I'll come get Nadia in a couple of days," Gabby mumbled through her dry, cracked lips. Her skin was pale and she had dark circles under her bloodshot eyes.

"Okay." Joy walked downstairs feeling frustrated. She had gone through the same thing with Gabby when William committed suicide, but she wasn't in the mood for it this time. She opened the front door and walked to the Range Rover. Allen got out smiling ear to ear when he saw her.

"That was quick." He opened the passenger's side front door for her.

"This is gonna take longer than I thought." She moved as close to him as her belly would allow, crossed her arms around his neck, and kissed his lips. "I'm sorry. You want to go back home and I'll call you when I'm ready?"

"Alright." Allen's smile was replaced with a blank stare. Once again, he would have to push what he had arranged for them aside so Joy could be there for her friend.

Joy walked back in the house feeling guilty. She knew Allen had planned a special day for them, but what could she do? Bea and Maxine were at work and Gabby didn't have anybody else. She went in the kitchen, fixed two slices of cinnamon raisin toast, and took two bottles of water out of the refrigerator.

Walking back upstairs, she thought about her conversation with Bo on the way to Gabby's. When he confirmed their affair, it broke Joy's heart. Bo wasn't Gabby's type at all. She must've been in a bad place emotionally to start sleeping with him. Joy knew the only way to snap Gabby out of her depression was to tell her the truth about Bo. It was going to hurt her even more, but she needed to know in order to move on with her life. Gabby was still in bed when Joy returned. She set the plate of toast and water on the table beside the bed and pulled the covers back. "Get up, Gabby! You need to eat and then wash your body."

"Do you understand English? Get out of my house!" Gabby turned her back to Joy and pulled the covers up to her shoulders.

Joy got one of the bottles of water and opened it. "Here, drink this," she ordered firmly.

"No!" Gabby pushed the water bottle away.

Joy pulled the covers back and poured the bottle of water over Gabby's face.

She jumped up coughing and gagging. *"Are you crazy?"* Gabby screamed as she tried to catch her breath.

"Yes, I am and I don't have time for your bullshit. If you get back in that bed or any other bed in this house, I'll bring a hose up here and spray your ass until you get your shit together," Joy threatened with fire in her eyes.

"If you knew everything I'm going through right now, you would leave me alone and let me get myself together," Gabby sobbed.

"We're all going through a lot right now, but we're dealing with it. Damn, Gabby, Maxine was set on fire by her husband on a Friday evening and Monday morning she was back at work like nothing happened. My husband tried to shoot me in the head and kill my babies but ended up shooting the man I love. The guilt alone could've shut me down, but I didn't let it. And let's not forget Allen's fling with Dirty Diana. It hurt me and I'm still trying to forgive and trust him, which isn't as easy as I thought. Did you see me or Maxine crawl in bed and shut down? Hell, no!" Joy was so close to Gabby she thought her friend's body odor was going to make her vomit.

"I fell in love with somebody and I'm..." She sat on the wet bed, unable to say anything else.

"I know, Gabby, but Boaz Vaughn Johnson is not worth it. Trust me." Joy picked up the other bottle of water.

Gabby looked at Joy with water dripping from her hair. "Who?"

"Bo. The married man you've been screwing since January. That's his real name." She took the top off the water and gave it to

Gabby.

Boaz? That's the perfect name for him because Bo is an ass. Gabby took a sip of water and her empty stomach growled for more. "I don't want to talk about him." She stood to go in the bathroom but Joy stopped her.

"You don't have to talk, but you will listen to me. Bo played you, Gabby, and you fell for it. He's a dog and everybody knows it, except his stupid wife, Peaches. He's been sleeping with her sister since he's been with Peaches, and everybody knows the little boy she had a couple of years ago is Bo's child. He looks just like him, but Bo knows how to handle Peaches so she won't suspect a thing. He's the best con artist around, and he's got a different woman for every day of the week and just as many children outside of his marriage. You should've told me about you and Bo. I could've saved you from a broken heart." Joy sat on the bed and put her arm around her friend.

Rage fueled Gabby as she thought about all of Bo's lies. "I can't believe this happened to me."

"Payback is a bitch, girl. Look at how you used dumbass Rayshawn and gullible William. Let's not even mention all the other men you've used over the years." Joy sighed.

"It doesn't compare to what Bo did to me." She burst into tears.

Joy went into the bathroom and got some tissue. She sat beside her friend on the bed and wiped her face. "You can compare your lying and cheating to Bo's all day long, but the bottom line is you were fucking somebody's husband, and that's wrong no matter how many excuses or reasons you come up with."

"Okay... You're right," Gabby agreed and then hugged Joy.

"I know I am. Now go wash your ass so we can finish this conversation when you smell better." Joy laughed.

With every step toward the bathroom, Gabby felt better. The love she felt for Bo was quickly replaced with hate and disgust. Thanks to Joy's news about him, Gabby's dream of her, Bo, Nadia, and the baby she was carrying living together as a happy family was now a nightmare. There was no way she was going to have his baby and add to his litter of illegitimate children. She was

183

going to make an appointment to terminate her pregnancy as soon as possible and then take care of Bo. He must've forgotten who he was dealing with if he thought he could just hurt her and walk away.

Chapter 27

Maxine dropped Joy off at home shortly after eleven o'clock. After she heard Joy's message about Gabby's drama, she came over after work with her boys. It was the first time since Dean held them hostage on Christmas Day that they weren't arguing with each other about something. It felt like old times. They cried together after Gabby told them about her family and Osaki. They joked about Gabby falling in love with Bo. Out of all the successful and financially stable men she had dated over the years, an ex-con was the one who turned her out and broke her heart. Even Gabby laughed about it, but she stunned them when she announced she was having an abortion because she was pregnant by Bo. Maxine spent the rest of the evening trying to convince Gabby to have the baby and let her raise it or give it up for adoption. Joy didn't say a word, because she knew Gabby's mind was already made up. By the time they left, Gabby was doing better and not trying to force anybody to take Nadia off her hands.

Joy walked in the house feeling intoxicated from the good time she shared with her girlfriends. Allen was sitting in the living room watching a Lakers game.

Joy sat beside him and kissed his cheek. "Hi, baby."

"Wassup," Allen replied with his eyes glued to the television.

"Maxine's friend, Christian, you know the cop we met, he invited us to his son's birthday party on Saturday. I told them we'll

185

be there." Joy took off her coat and tossed it over the arm of the sofa.

Allen turned off the television and gave her the evil eye. "You can go. It's supposed to be warm on Saturday so I'm thinking about borrowing Chuck's bike and going for a long ride to clear my head."

"What's wrong with you?" Joy asked, completely shocked by his attitude. He knew she hated it when he rode his brother's Harley or any other motorcycle.

"What's wrong with me? What the hell's wrong with you?" He threw the remote on the coffee table in front of him. "I dropped you off at Gabby's at ten o'clock this morning and it's going on eleven-thirty."

"Well, damn, I didn't know I had a curfew," Joy stated sarcastically.

"Naw, you don't, but you could've called instead of texting me to let me know you and the twins were alright." He picked up his cell phone and pointed it at her. "You were too busy to answer my calls? Your due date is in three weeks and you pull some shit like this. I can't believe you."

"I'm sorry, but you act like I planned this. You know Gabby had an emergency." Joy tried to hug him, but he pulled away from her.

"She ain't have no damn emergency. She was sleeping with my married brother and he broke it off. I told you last night I had something planned for us today and that we needed to talk. Once again, you chose your friend over me. Same shit, different day." Allen stood and shook his head at Joy.

"I couldn't let her go through that alone. She was there for me when I was hurt after finding out about you and Diana." Joy gasped, regretting what she said. They had made a promise to not discuss Dean or Diana once Allen moved back in. It was their way of putting their past mistakes behind them. "I'm sorry."

"Don't be. You just reminded me again that I'm the only one committed to this relationship. Now that you're home safe, I'm going to bed." He went upstairs.

Joy hated herself for bringing up Diana and not calling

Allen while she was at Gabby's. She had gotten used to it being just her; now she needed to remember she was in a relationship again. It wasn't like she was avoiding him. They were having so much fun at Gabby's house, she didn't realize how late it was until TJ and Maxwell started whining about being sleepy. She turned off the lights, turned on the alarm, and went upstairs to apologize and give him some attention.

Her blood boiled when she saw the guest bedroom door closed and the lights from the television flickering under the door. *Oh, he's too mad to sleep in the same bed with me? Fuck him. I'm not apologizing and he can take his ass back to his sister's house as far as I'm concerned.* She went to her bedroom, took a shower, and got into bed.

After tossing and turning for close to thirty minutes, she took off her nightgown and lay there, blaming Allen for the heat coursing through her body that made her sweat. She missed him, but her pride wouldn't let her go to him in the guest bedroom. She took a picture she kept of him from her nightstand and stared at it until her eyes closed and she fell asleep.

When Allen felt himself dozing off, he turned off the television and went to his and Joy's bedroom. He was upset and wanted to put some distance between them before their arguing caused her to go into labor. All the lights were on when he entered the room. Joy lay naked on her side with her nightgown on the floor and the comforter partially covering the bottom half of her body. He picked up her nightgown and tossed it over the hamper in the corner. The picture of him in her hand made him smile. It made him happy to know she couldn't sleep without him either. He took it out of her hand and put it on the nightstand.

After he showered and brushed his teeth, he got in bed with Joy and pulled the covers over them. She kicked them off, exposing her butt and the tattoo on her lower back with his name in it. He ran his fingers across his name and caressed her butt cheeks. His erection was instant.

Joy opened her eyes, elated that Allen was back in their bed. "I'm sorry," she said, enjoying his hands on her body.

"Me, too. Don't go that long without talking to me. I love

187

you, baby, and I need to know you're okay." He rubbed Joy's large belly. "I would die if anything happened to you or the twins."

Joy turned on her back and pulled Allen's bald head to her so his lips were on hers. They kissed passionately with their hands exploring each other's body and their tongues touching inside each other's mouths. She put both her hands around his manhood and stroked it.

"It's been a long time. Is it safe? The babies?" Allen could barely catch his breath.

"The doctor said it's okay. The twins are strong enough to survive if they were born now." She ran her tongue over his lips. "Can you handle it? It's gonna be warm, juicy, and very tight in there and I need you to move slow."

"Damn, baby! I might not even make it inside you if you keep touching me and talking like that." He stuck two fingers inside her to see if she was ready. Her juices drenched his fingers.

Joy removed her hands from his manhood when she felt him leaking pre-ejaculate. She turned on her side and stuck her butt out. He moved close to her in a spooning position and raised her leg, then slowly inserted himself inside her. They moaned with pleasure. Joy put her leg down and squeezed them together while rocking her hips back and forth.

"Don't do that yet, baby! Wait! You gonna make me come too soon," Allen pleaded.

Joy didn't care. Every nerve in her vaginal area felt a heightened sensitivity to Allen's touch and she was having short, multiple orgasms. Allen moved deeper inside her and pinched her nipple. Joy moaned when he hit her spot, causing her to squirt her juices on him and down her inner thighs. The warmth from Joy's fluids made Allen's body quiver as he released. He fell back on the bed completely spent.

"What the hell was that?" Allen asked.

"Pregnancy sex," Joy bragged. She had read about it in some of her pregnancy books, but to experience it was blowing her damn mind.

"Are you okay?" Allen propped himself up on his elbow and moved his eyes up and down her body.

"Yes, baby. I'm fine." Joy rubbed his face to put him at ease. "I love you."

"I love you, too. Do you need anything?" He moved his fingertips over her belly making imaginary shapes as he thought about seeing his children soon. "Anything you want and I'll get it."

"Since you're offering, can you write this paper I have to turn in for school next week?" Joy laughed.

"Naw, but I can pay somebody to write it for you." Allen joked.

"You're going to be a terrible role model for our children." Joy smacked her lips. "Please go get me some water so I can replenish my fluids. Our babies are thirsty."

"Now, that I can do." Allen kissed her before he went downstairs.

Shortly after two o'clock in the morning, Joy woke up with a dry cough. She sat up, turned on the lamp, and looked beside her for Allen. His side of the bed was empty. She put on her robe and went downstairs to get something to drink. When she reached the bottom step, she heard Allen in the kitchen talking to somebody. His tone was harsh and confrontational. She stood outside the kitchen door and listened.

"I already told you, it's over and I'm not coming back," Allen said aggressively.

There was a pause.

"Of course I want to, but I have to push what I want to the side right now and focus on my family. Can't you understand that?"

Another pause.

"Okay, do what you have to do, but I'm not leaving them. I can't do that right now. Bye."

Joy felt like someone had punched her in the stomach. *What did he mean he couldn't leave us right now? Is he planning to do it later? Why wait? He told me his friendship with Diana was over and here he is in my house having a secret conversation with the slut.* She walked into the kitchen full of rage. Allen was leaning

189

over the countertop with his head in his hands. She quietly approached him ready to rip his head off.

"You lying bastard!" She threw a punch at his face but missed. "You sneaking out of my bed to call that bitch! Just leave and go be with her!"

"I wasn't talking to Diana." He shot her an evil glare.

"Really, Allen? I heard your conversation. You have to give her up because of your obligations to me and the twins. No, baby, we'll be fine. The heart wants what it wants so go be with her. I release you." She flung her hands in his direction before she grabbed a bottle of water out of the refrigerator and took a sip.

"Don't do this right now, Joy! I got a lot on my mind and I need your support." He looked nervous as he tried to hug her.

Joy pushed his arms away from her. "Get out and go be with her! I don't want to see your cheating ass again! You're more like Bo than I thought."

"Goddamn it, Joy! I don't want Diana! I want you! I just quit my job in China to stay here with you! I walked away from my position as Junior Vice President of Finance for a Fortune 500 company because I love you and our children. Don't you get that?"

Joy gasped. She knew how much that job meant to Allen. Now everything made sense. Two o'clock in the morning here was two o'clock in the afternoon in China. *He gave up his career to be here with me and the twins.* "Why did you quit?"

"There were some problems with my project and they needed me to come back before my six-month leave of absence ended and I can't." He rubbed his forehead and sighed as he realized he was just another unemployed black man, something he never wanted to be. "It's done, Joy. I'll find a job here. As long as we keep our family together, we'll be okay."

"Why didn't you discuss this with me? Before you moved back in, didn't we promise to be open and honest with each other no matter what?" Joy held his face and stared into his eyes.

"I was going to tell you, but Gabby's fucking emergency ruined my plans. You were complaining that your back was hurting. I made an appointment for you at a spa in Annapolis to get a pregnancy massage. After that, I was going to take you to a nice

seafood restaurant on the water. I had planned to tell you everything going on with me and the job."

Shit, that's why he was so upset. "I'm sorry, baby, and
you're right, we'll be okay as long as we're together." Joy wrapped
her arms around him. She felt guilty for putting Gabby's needs before his yet again.

Allen neglected to tell her the rest of his conversation with
his bosses in China. *He hoped it would be taken care of before she
found out.* If not, it was going to cause more problems between
them and that was the last thing their still-fragile relationship
needed.

Chapter 28

The last guest from Shane's birthday party had barely left before Maxine grabbed a trash bag and started cleaning Christian's kitchen. The boys were in the family room off the kitchen, playing Shane's new Nintendo Wii, a gift from Gabby and Nadia. As usual, Gabby wanted to make sure Nadia's gift was better than the other children's presents and she succeeded. Joy and Allen had stopped by briefly and given Shane a fifty-dollar gift card from Toys "R" Us. The party Christian asked her to help with was a success and Maxine was glad it was over.

"What are you doing? I'll take care of this later." Christian took the trash bag from her hand and set it on the granite counter-top. He enclosed her in his arms and held her tight with his chin resting on the top of her head. "Thank you for organizing Shane's party. I heard him say it was the best birthday ever."

"I'm glad, and you don't have to thank me." Maxine put the side of her face on his chest and inhaled the scent of his Burberry cologne.

"We need to talk." He removed his arms from around her, stepped back, and took her hands in his. "I think now would be a good time since the boys are busy playing the video game."

Maxine's heart worked overtime in her chest. She didn't like the seriousness of Christian's tone or the way he avoided eye contact with her. The thought of him breaking up with her made her shake with fear. Christian was the epitome of a good man. He was tall, dark, and handsome, and treated her like a queen, catering to her every need, except one. He still didn't believe in God and refused to attend church with her no matter how many times she asked. It was her only serious complaint about their relationship. She enjoyed being intimate with him, but afterward, she always felt like she cheated on God. She thought long and hard about it and decided to weigh the good with the bad. She cared about him a lot, and he treated her boys no differently from his own son. They enjoyed spending time together and she couldn't have picked a better role model for her boys.

He took her hand and led her to the brown paisley sofa in the living room. They sat side by side with an uneasiness between them. He cleared his throat and tugged at the collar on his blue oxford shirt. Maxine took her purse off the cherrywood cocktail table in front of the sofa and sat it on her lap. She fiddled with the handles so he couldn't see how nervous she was.

"Maxine, you're the first woman I've dated since my wife died that I could see a future with. You're beautiful, smart, a terrific mother, and my son loves you. No matter how many times I correct him, he still calls you Mommy."

"Aww, Christian. I feel the same way about you and Shane. And I told you he only calls me Mommy because of TJ and Maxwell."

"I know." He shot her a half-smile. "Before this goes any further between us, I need to know if you plan on forgiving Trent and saving your marriage."

"What!" Maxine jumped up from the sofa, threw her purse on the table, and paced around the room with her hands on her hips. "Why would you ask me that?"

"Patricia White from the district attorney's office called me yesterday after you met with her. She was concerned about you." Christian sat back and let out a deep sigh. "Have you been talking to Trent since he was released from solitary confinement a few days ago? Patricia is under the impression that Trent might convince you to drop the charges against him or not testify. I need to know what's going on."

Maxine didn't want Christian to find out about Trent's phone calls like this. He had been calling her and leaving messages, begging her to bring the boys to visit him, but she never talked to him. Ignoring any numbers she didn't recognize, especially numbers with a Baltimore area code, had helped her to avoid him. She had met with the assistant district attorney to see what they could do about stopping Trent from contacting her. She didn't tell anybody about the meeting with Patricia White because she was tired of everybody coming to her rescue. Her family and friends seemed to think she couldn't handle anything on her own. Patricia's only suggestion was to change her numbers, which she planned to do after Shane's birthday party.

"So is it true?" Christian asked.

"Do you honestly think I want Trent back after he tried to set me on fire?" Maxine glared at Christian. She thought he knew her better.

"You took him back before. I just need to hear it from you."

"No, you don't. You believe what Patricia told you. Since your mind is already made up and you have no faith or trust in me, why are we even having this conversation?" Maxine picked up her purse and put in on her shoulder. "I'm leaving."

"What is leaving during the middle of our conversation going to accomplish?" He shook his head to show his frustration. "That little voice in the back of my head kept telling me I was walking a thin line with you, but I didn't listen to it. I'm eleven years older than you. You're dealing with issues from being in an abusive marriage. You're almost $300,000 in debt and you keep trying to change me. Asking me to go to church every week is not going to change how I feel about God and religion. Accept me as I am. I know all this about you and I still wanna be with you because I accept who you are."

Maxine stomped over to where Christian sat on the sofa and looked down at him with tears welling. "Just to set your ass straight, Patricia is wrong and I'll let her know when I talk to her again. When I left work Thursday, there was a message on my cell from Trent asking me to bring the boys to visit him. I deleted it. He called back a few times on my home and cell numbers, but I didn't answer and I have no intentions of answering any of his calls or ever talking to him again. I met with Patricia to see if she could make him stop calling me. Her only suggestion was to change my numbers, which I planned to do after Shane's party."

"Why didn't you tell me?"

"Because I need to stand on my own two feet and handle my problems myself. Now, let me respond to your doubts about me. As long as we're adults, age doesn't matter to me. I'm not gonna let what Trent did stop me from living my life so there are no issues with that. And yes, I'm almost $300,000 in debt, thanks to my husband, but my father's lawyer filed bankruptcy papers last week to take care of that. When you announced that you didn't believe in God, that little voice in the back of my head told me to end it with you, but the more time we spent together, I couldn't. I care about you, but now I see that was a mistake."

"No, Maxine," Christian protested.

"Yes, Christian. Speaking of issues, what's wrong with you? How could you not believe in God?"

Christian leaned over, placed his elbows on his knees, and shook his head. "I told you, Maxine, that the things I've seen in the Army and as a cop made me question my faith. Then when my wife died, I knew there was no God. Every day, over and over, people used to tell me to pray and I did. Through the cancer diagnosis, chemo, radiation, all of it, I prayed, but she died anyway. That was the final straw for me. What kind of God would leave a young child without a mother or take away the woman I loved more than any other?" He looked up at Maxine with pain in his eyes. "Why can't you understand that? The things I can change, I do. When you told me I snore too much, I started back sleeping in the CPAP machine for my sleep apnea. When you told me I hog the bed, I trained my body to sleep on one side, but this I can't change."

"I'm not asking you to change what you believe, but I just realized that I can't be with you or any other man who feels that way," Maxine reiterated.

"We've been dating for a month. Why now? Is this about Trent?" Christian snapped.

"This has nothing to do with Trent. It'll never work between us, because when I go through bad times, I run to God.

When you go through bad times, you run away from Him. How long do you honestly think we'll last if we keep seeing each other? I'm in church almost every Sunday and I sing in the choir. That's a big chunk of my life that I can't even share with you."

"I don't know what to say." He stood and walked around the living room shaking his head.

"You don't have to say anything, Christian. I'm leaving."

When she turned around to get the boys, they were standing in the doorway looking at them with questioning faces.

"Hey, guys! What are you doing in here?" Maxine tried to sound calm because she didn't want to upset them.

"Why you fighting?" TJ asked.

"We're not fighting, baby. Sometimes adults talk louder than they should, but we weren't fighting." She bent down and hugged each one to reassure them. "Go upstairs and get your bags and coats."

"I thought we were spending the night," TJ whined.

"Not tonight, baby. We have church in the morning," Maxine explained.

"TJ and Maxwell, you can come over tomorrow after church or any time you want," Christian added.

Maxwell and Shane jumped up and down screaming excitedly about Christian's invitation. TJ looked at Christian with a sad expression. He could sense something was wrong between his mother and Christian.

"Thank you, Christian, but we have plans tomorrow." Maxine avoided looking at him as she removed her jacket from the living room closet and put it on. "Boys, go upstairs and get your things now."

The boys ran upstairs when they heard Maxine's angry tone.

"Please, don't leave like this." He tried to hug her, but she pushed him away.

"Don't touch me." She backed away to put distance between them.

"I've never seen you act like this, Maxine," Christian whispered so the boys couldn't hear him.

"That's because you've never pissed me off before," she countered.

Minutes later, she heard the boys running downstairs. She met them near the steps, took their bags, and ushered them outside. After they were strapped into their car seats, she started her engine and sped off with tears streaming. A few blocks away, she pulled into Laurel Mall and parked. With the car still running, she laid her head on the steering wheel and came undone. Her shoulders crumpled and shook as tears rolled from her eyes. She was in a tug of war with herself. One part of her wanted to go back to Christian's house and never leave, but the other part told her to go home and put the brief romance they shared behind her because he'd never change.

"Mommy, why you crying?" TJ asked.

"I'm okay. My tummy hurts, that's all," she lied, wiping the tears from her face with her hands.

"You should boo boo, Mommy. When my tummy hurts, you make me go boo boo," TJ advised, sounding wiser than his five years.

Maxwell started singing, "Mommy got a boo boo. Mommy got a stink stink."

Her tears stopped and she burst out laughing at her sons. She reached in the glove box, got some napkins, and wiped her face. "Okay, let's go home so Mommy can get herself together."

Her cell phone rang. Thinking it was Christian, she quickly answered it. "Hello."

"I know you're not that damn busy that you can't answer my calls. Where are my boys?" Trent screamed into the phone.

The sound of his voice sent chills down her spine. "Hold on." She turned off the engine and stepped out of the minivan. "I'll be right back, boys."

"Okay, Mommy. I'll take care of Max," TJ stated.

"No!" Maxwell shouted.

Maxine closed the door and went to the front of her minivan so she could keep her eyes on the boys. She put the phone back to her ear. "Hello."

"I don't have much time so when can you bring the boys

for a visit?" Trent snapped.

"Never. Have you lost your damn mind? You won't see them until they're grown and able to decide for themselves whether or not they want to see you."

"I'm their father!" he shouted.

"You stopped being their father the second you decided to set me on fire. I'm not gonna waste my energy on you, Trent. I'm changing my numbers so you can't call me anymore. I hate you and I hope your fellow convicts rip a new hole in your ass every day you're in there."

"I'm sorry for what I did to you, Maxine. Punish me for it, not our sons. I need to see my boys," Trent begged.

"Fuck you, Trent Anderson! I don't want your goddamn apology and you won't be seeing the boys. But, you'll see me at your trial in October because I'm gonna make sure you pay for what you did to me. We're done!"

Maxine pushed the End button and smiled. Knowing that she had control over Trent seeing the boys made her feel strong. Visiting their father in jail wouldn't be good for her sons. Not seeing his boys grow into men was going to torment him and it was the best revenge she could inflict on him. Feeling victorious, she got back in her minivan and drove to the Verizon store in Clinton to change her cell phone number. It was her first step to leaving her past behind.

The next morning, Maxine looked at her reflection in her bathroom mirror and frowned. There wasn't enough concealer or powder to hide the dark circles under her eyes. She barely slept last night after spending hours on the phone with Gabby and Joy. They tried to convince her that her feelings for Christian were due to some kind of hero worship she had for him because he saved her life. They told Maxine her feelings couldn't be as deep as she thought they were because she and Christian hadn't known each other that long. Maxine knew better. The pain in the pit of her stomach and her tear-soaked pillow were proof enough that her feelings for Christian were real.

She took her choir robe out of the closet, put it over her arm, and went downstairs to get the boys. They should be finished eating the oatmeal she fixed them and ready to leave for church. She stopped and gasped when she reached the foyer. Lack of sleep must have been causing her to hallucinate.

"Good morning." Christian flashed a smile. He was dressed in a black suit with a white button-down shirt and a black, gray, and white tie with tiny circles on it. He took her breath away. "I'm sorry TJ opened the door without you. I got on him for doing that. I tried to call you, but I guess you had your number changed already..."

Maxine threw her choir robe on the stair rail and put her index finger over her lips. "Shhh." She walked to him in a dreamlike state with her eyes glued to his.

Christian picked her up and kissed her passionately.

This is real, Maxine thought as she wrapped her arms around his neck and kissed him back.

The boys walked into the foyer and laughed at them.

Maxine immediately pulled away from Christian because he didn't like for them to be affectionate in front of the boys. "The boys," she whispered.

"It's okay. They need to get used to this because I'm not letting you go." He kissed her again.

"Mommy, look," Shane said.

Maxine got down from Christian's arms and looked at Shane. He was pulling his suit jacket for Maxine to see.

"You look handsome, Shane. I like your suit." Arching her brows, Maxine bent down and rubbed the fabric.

"What about my suit?" Maxwell whined.

"All three of my boys look very handsome this morning." Maxine hugged each one.

"Daddy bought it last night so we can go to church," Shane announced.

"Oh, did he?" Maxine chuckled as she turned around to look up at Christian.

Christian laughed. "He wasn't supposed to tell you that."

"It's okay. Thank you, Christian." She stood, fixed his tie, and caressed his face.

"I can't promise this every Sunday, Maxine..."

"It doesn't matter, Christian. You're here now and that means everything to me."

"Okay. Let's go to church," Christian announced with a half-smile.

I love my life.

"I love it. I love it. I love it," Maxine proclaimed as Christian took her hand and they left for church.

$\mathscr{C}$hapter 29

Gabby picked up her gifts for Joy's baby shower and walked downstairs in her three-inch stilettos to look for a shopping bag. She glanced at the time on the microwave and became instantly irritated. Rayshawn had agreed to bring Nadia back home today so she could attend her godmother's baby shower and he was thirty minutes late. She always liked to be tardy for an event so all eyes were on her when she entered, but if she was too late, people would be too engrossed in the party to notice her.

She slid the two gift boxes with the twins' christening outfits and two five-hundred-dollar savings bonds in a Nordstrom shopping bag, then walked outside to put it in her Lexus. Rayshawn pulled up in his latest toy, a burgundy Cadillac Escalade, fully loaded, of course. She thought about all the attention she'd get if she arrived at the baby shower in that.

Rayshawn stepped out of his truck and approached her with Nadia asleep in his arms. Gabby was glad to see her daughter dressed in the outfit she sent with Rayshawn and her hair styled the way she showed him. He was a better father than she gave him credit for.

"Hey. Traffic was bad," Rayshawn stated in a gloomy tone. His eyes glossed over her brown and gold mini-dress. The front drooped down to show just enough cleavage to make him want to see more.

"Um-hum, you can bring her in," Gabby ordered as she turned and walked in the house. Her entire back was exposed with the dress's material stopping just above her butt crack.

"Damn, you look sexy! What kind of baby shower you going to dressed like that?" He followed Gabby in the house with his tongue hanging out of his mouth and his eyes glued to her butt.

"Thank you!" Her ego danced with joy. It was just the reaction she wanted.

Rayshawn laid Nadia on the couch. "Alright, I'm out. Remember, I'm taking her to Georgia with me next weekend." Rayshawn headed toward the front door.

"What's wrong with you?" Gabby asked sincerely. "You look like you lost some weight and you're not your normal goofy self. Are you sick? Oh, my God! It's not AIDS, is it?"

"I ain't got no damn AIDS!" Rayshawn shouted. Anger was written all over his face.

"Then what's wrong with you?" Gabby pulled him back into the living room. They sat side by side on her white loveseat.

"I guess I been depressed. Osaki left me and that fucked my head up for a while. I haven't been eating like I used to." He chuckled. "I fell hard for her and she just disappeared. Her number's disconnected. No address. It's just been hard. It's like I lost my soulmate."

Gabby felt Rayshawn's pain after dealing with Bo breaking her heart. Guilt gripped her for causing Rayshawn so many problems over the two years they'd known each other. Now, she felt obligated to help him and make things right. "I'm sorry, Rayshawn."

"It ain't your fault. You told me not to mess with her, but I got caught up in that good snatch. Damn, my shit get hard just thinking 'bout her and I ain't seen her in weeks." Rayshawn sighed.

"Umm, TMI, Rayshawn." She rolled her eyes at him. "Getting over somebody takes time, but you'll be okay. Trust me."

Rayshawn gave her a sideways glance. "Trust you! Yeah, right!"

"I know I've done some terrible things to you and I'm sorry. I want us to be friends and to get along for Nadia. Can we do that? I don't want to keep asking myself where did I go wrong again with you, Rayshawn. Let's show a united front for our daughter so she can know both of her parents love her and will put their differences aside to support her no matter what." Gabby held Rayshawn's hand in her palm and rubbed the back of it.

He snatched his hand away and jumped up from the love seat like it was on fire. "Hell no! I ain't falling for your games no more. I'm out. I'll be back Friday to get baby girl."

"No, Rayshawn. I'm not playing games with you. I don't want anything from you. I see how hurt you are and I want to help you through this. I know how it feels. Honestly." She got up and hugged him.

He put his arms around her waist, then slid his hand down her back, into her dress and squeezed her butt cheek. Gabby pushed him away and smacked him hard across the face.

Rayshawn rubbed his face and burst out laughing. "I'm just playing. I wanted to know how far you was trying to take this."

Gabby crossed her arms over her chest and glared at him. "Don't do that again. We can be friends and co-parents, but there will be no sex between us. *Never. Ever.* Got it?"

"Yeah, I'm cool." Rayshawn smiled and bumped her shoulder playfully.

"Good. Now, let's go get you a decent outfit so you can hang out with me and Nadia today."

"A baby shower? Hell no!" Rayshawn threw his arms in the air and frowned. "I'm going back to my loft and watch some ESPN."

"No, you're not! Get Nadia and let's go. We can stop at Bowie Town Center on the way. My treat. I can't have you looking like that while you're with me." Gabby scrunched her nose and lips together to show her disappointment in the wrinkled jeans and Baltimore Ravens hoodie he wore.

Rayshawn's eyes bulged. "Oh, you got it like that, huh? You gonna spend my money on me. Ain't that some shit!"

"It's not *your* money, Rayshawn. I use *your* money for Nadia now. The probate court determined that my in-laws didn't have a case and released the rest of my husband's estate to me. He was very generous." Gabby shimmied her shoulders and giggled.

"That's why your sister-in-law, Phyllis, hate your ass. You

know she still calling me about taking you back to court to get full custody." Rayshawn sat beside the sleeping Nadia and shook his head.

"I thought big girl would've learned her lesson by now." Gabby laughed as she thought about how the paramedics had to come for Phyllis after she found out Gabby still had custody of Nadia. While they were loading her on the stretcher, Gabby intentionally walked by her with Nadia in her arms and blew Phyllis a kiss. She became hysterical. Everybody thought Phyllis was going to lose her baby in that courtroom.

Before long, after Gabby had promised to introduce Rayshawn to some of the single women at the baby shower, he agreed to go with them. She was glad he changed his mind. The thought of walking into Joy's baby shower alone with Bo there didn't sit well with her. The date she had planned to take claimed he had food poisoning and backed out at the last minute. It was too late to find someone else, so Rayshawn would have to do.

Shortly after three o'clock that afternoon, Rayshawn dropped Gabby and Nadia off in front of the Harmony Hall Recreational Center in Fort Washington. All eyes were on them as Rayshawn took Nadia's stroller and Gabby's gift bag out of the back of his luxury truck. He left to find a parking space while Gabby put Nadia and the bag in the stroller. Since it was nice, sunny, and almost seventy-five degrees outside, she decided to wait for Rayshawn so they could walk in together. That way, all the men would get to see her walking in with an NFL quarterback and all the women would see her walking in with a millionaire.

She smiled her approval as Rayshawn strode across the parking lot with a little swagger in his step. She had to pat herself on the back for the makeover she did on him. There was no resemblance to the nappy-headed, beard-wearing caveman she apologized to earlier. Now he had on a pair of loose-fit black jeans, a silver button-down shirt, and a pair of black, pointed-toe alligator shoes. While the salesperson at Macy's steamed his outfit, she took him to a nearby barber shop and had the barber give him a low fade, shave his beard, and clip the excess hair in his ears and nose. His makeover cost her close to a thousand dollars, but it was the least she could do after what she had Osaki do to him. He looked like a different man and she could tell he felt better, too. In Gabby's mind, they were even now.

He removed his new silver Arnette shades and stuck his chest out. His confidence was definitely back. "What's up?"

"You look nice, Rayshawn. Be careful when you go in there. The ghetto-project girls at this shower are going to try to do whatever it takes to get you in their bed. Stay away from them. I don't need you having any more children cutting into my daughter's inheritance." Gabby picked a piece of lint off his shirt and brushed the wrinkles away.

"When the hell you start sounding like my damn mother? Know your place, Gabby. You my daughter's momma, not mine." He glared at her with evil eyes and then put his shades back on. "Plus, I ain't having no more children. I got a vasectomy after dealing with your ass. Now let's go. I'm hungry." Rayshawn pushed Nadia's stroller inside the building.

He's smarter than he looks, Gabby thought as she followed them. Joy's baby shower was in the first room they saw after they entered the building. Gabby was surprised by how nicely it was decorated. It was definitely Bea's style and not the Johnsons'. Gabby was happy not to see any blue and pink paper babies hanging from the ceiling. Instead, each of the twenty round tables had a pink or blue tablecloth and a basket full of baby items as the centerpiece. There were pastel balloon sculptures in the shape of animals throughout the room and two tables full of chafing dishes overflowing with food. A DJ's booth was set up in the corner. Joy was right when she said the Johnsons turned every event into a party. Joy and Allen sat on the stage at the head table with Bea and Juan beside Joy and Tyesha and Tyrese beside Allen. Gabby was surprised that Joy even made it since today was her due date. *What kind of idiot would plan a baby shower on a woman's due date? Bo's stupid wife, Peaches.*

Maxine waved at her from a table near the stage in the back of the room. Gabby waved back and headed toward her. On the way, she saw Peaches sitting alone across the room and decided now would be the perfect time to talk to her.

"Rayshawn, my friend Maxine is waving at us." She pointed at Maxine who she knew was going to keep waving until they were at the table. "It's that time of the month for me so can you take Nadia to our seats while I go to the ladies' room?"

He growled under his breath and pushed Nadia's stroller toward Maxine.

While walking toward Peaches, Gabby heard men whistling and trying to get her attention. Bo's laugh made her turn around to look. He was sitting at a table with his brother Chuck and three other guys. Chuck glared at her like he always did whenever he saw her, but the other three whistled and called her over to their table.

She made a detour and went to their table, flashing them her beautiful but deadly smile. "It sounds like somebody is trying to get my attention over here."

"It wasn't me!" Chuck barked.

"You wore that dress for me, didn't you?" Bo laughed. "Can't let go, can you?"

"Bo, I let you go when I got on my doctor's table and he sucked out that little alien you left inside of me called a fetus. Any feelings I had for you left my body with your DNA."

An awkward silence replaced the calls and whistles of moments before. Bo stared at her, his face twisted in shock and disbelief. He stood, unable to speak. They locked eyes for a few seconds before Gabby turned and walked away. With tears welling, she was more determined than ever to make him pay for hurting her. She let her tears stream down her face as she approached Peaches.

"Ms. Peaches, can I talk to you, please?" Gabby sniffed.

"Sure. What's wrong, Gabby? I saw you come in with the football player. Did he do something to you?" She stood and looked across the room at Rayshawn who already had his face buried in two plates of food.

Gabby shook her head and put her hands over her mouth while releasing more tears.

"Then what is it?" Peaches moved closer to get the scoop.

Gabby wiped the tears from her cheeks and stared directly into Peaches' eyes. "You have to promise me you won't tell Bo what I'm getting ready to tell you." She sniffed and looked down. "Usually, I would tell Joy something like this, but I don't want to ruin her baby shower."

"I won't say a word," Peaches promised as she moved in even closer to Gabby.

"I was on my way to the bathroom and your husband said he wanted to do things to me. It made me feel very uncomfortable." She pointed at Rayshawn. "I'm trying to work things out with my daughter's father and I don't want any trouble, but Bo really made me feel... dirty." Gabby let out a wail and fell on Peaches' shoulder.

"Girl, that's just Bo being Bo. Don't pay him no attention. He ain't crazy. We got kids your age, and he know I don't play that." She reached on the table behind her and got a napkin for Gabby. "Here, wipe your face and forget about Bo. Go on over there with your daughter and that fine football player."

She's dumb and blind, Gabby thought as she wiped her face.

"Wow. Bo was right. Your husband really knows you, Ms. Peaches." Gabby wiped her eyes again. "Thanks for the talk." She turned to leave.

"Wait a minute. What you mean by Bo really knows me?" She turned her lips up at Gabby.

"When I told Bo I was gonna tell you about him being disrespectful, he said you wouldn't believe me because he's been sleeping with your sister for years and you don't even know it."

Peaches felt her chest tighten and her temperature rising. She had caught Bo and her sister having sex over twenty years ago, but they both apologized and blamed it on smoking too much weed that night. She forgave them because they were high, but she always wondered if there was more to it. Her sister and husband messing around behind her back was too much to handle so she always pushed it out of her mind. They couldn't be that cruel and nasty.

"Are you okay, Ms. Peaches? I don't want to tell you any

more if it's going to upset you." Gabby put her hand over her chest and flashed Peaches an innocent, caring expression.

"What else he say?" Peaches glared at Gabby with her hands balled into tight fists.

Gabby hesitated. She didn't want Peaches swinging on her, but then she decided it was worth the risk. "He said he has a little boy with your sister and you too dumb to realize it, even though your nephew looks just like him."

Peaches stomped off with her arms swinging. Gabby stood in the corner and watched as Peaches snatched Bo out of his seat and started cursing him out. He tried to pull her to the side and calm her down, but she wasn't having it. She slapped, kicked, and punched him until Bo finally pulled her outside.

Mission accomplished.

Chapter 30

Joy rubbed her baby bump as she walked to the bathroom. The gas pains shooting through her stomach and back were unbearable. She was determined to stay and get through the last hour of her baby shower, but if another woman approached her with yarn and asked her to stand so she could guess her stomach size, Joy was going to ram that yarn down her throat. She froze when she stepped into the hallway. Gabby and Allen were standing near the front door in a heated conversation. There was barely any space between them and their facial expressions were tense with anger.

"You better not tell her about this while we're here," Gabby threatened with her finger in Allen's face.

"I won't. Do you know how much this'll hurt her? Just let me handle it. She needs to hear the truth from me." Allen's teeth were clenched and spit spewed from his mouth.

"What the hell is going on out here?" Joy asked as she approached them.

Allen stepped away from Gabby, but he didn't turn around to face Joy. Gabby flashed a phony, strained smile. Joy knew the look well. Gabby only used it when she was manipulating somebody. Joy's women's intuition rang all kinds of bells that something was wrong with this picture. These two could barely stay in the same room together and now they were up in each other's faces like long-lost lovers.

"What's wrong? Neither one of you can talk now? It

seemed like you had a lot to say when I came out here." Joy darted her eyes between Gabby and Allen, getting angrier by the second.

Allen slowly turned around.

Joy gasped and stared at him with her eyes and mouth wide open. The right side of his face was scratched and bleeding. Joy groaned, clenched her fists, and bit her bottom lip. A sharp pain shot down her stomach into her pelvic area.

"Baby, are you okay?" Allen was by her side within seconds.

"Give me a second," Joy snapped as she waited for the pain to subside. The urgency to use the bathroom was strong, but she needed to know what was going on between Allen and Gabby first.

Allen gave Gabby an I-told-you-so look and she nodded her understanding.

"This is my last time asking questions before I walk out of here and forget you two motherfuckers exist." Joy took a deep breath and rubbed her belly. "What happened to your goddamn face, Allen? And what do you two have to talk about so much?"

Christian walked in the door and announced, "She's gone. I made sure of it." When he saw Joy, he got the same stupid look on his face as Allen and Gabby.

"Joy, Allen got in between Bo and Peaches and she scratched him," Gabby interjected.

Joy's demeanor softened a little as she looked Allen over. "What! Peaches did this to you? You wait until I talk to her ass. Let's go in the bathroom and clean your face before it gets infected." She took his hand, started toward the bathroom, and then stopped. "What were you two talking about when I came out here?"

"Excuse me, I need to check on Maxine. I left her alone with three busy boys," Christian added with worry lines across his face.

"That's not a good excuse to run out of here, Christian. Handling three boys is a piece of cake for Maxine. She teaches thirty kids in public school for a living, so I wouldn't worry," Joy replied in an annoyed tone. She was in pain and everybody was getting on her last nerve.

"Oh yeah. I forget sometimes. I'll see you guys back inside." Christian left with his head down.

Anxiety flowed through Allen's body as he tried to come up with an excuse. He pulled a ring box out of his jacket pocket and showed it to Joy. "I know you said you weren't ready for this, but I was going to propose while we're here and Gabby told me it wasn't a good idea."

"And she was right. We talked about this already, baby. Not until the trust is back will I even consider marriage." Joy planted a soft kiss on his lips. "I love you, but now is not the right time."

"I understand," Allen agreed.

Gabby watched them leave for the bathroom hand in hand. She hated herself for lying to Joy, but she didn't have a choice. If the truth came out about how she and Allen screwed up, it would hurt Joy and that's the last thing either of them wanted to do.

Joy sat at her dining room table and watched Allen and his best friend, Owen, bring in the baby shower gifts and stack them in the living room. Owen had flown in from Atlanta early this morning to attend the shower and spend some time with Allen. They were roommates during their freshman year at Morehouse and continued to live together until Allen moved to China last year. Owen looked like a different person since Joy last saw him in August. His thick glasses were now replaced with contact lenses. Invisalign clear braces covered his buck-teeth, and the thick hair he hadn't cut in years was now locked into dreads. Joy wondered if all the changes to his appearance had something to do with a woman.

"Yeah, man! The game will be on in an hour!" Owen announced excitedly as he set a case of diapers on a gift box in the living room. He lived for basketball and never missed a Miami Heat game, especially when they played Allen's favorite team, the Boston Celtics.

"I got you, man. Big screen, beer, and hot wings just like we used to do it." Allen gave him the brothers' handshake. "As soon as my brothers drop off the rest of the gifts, I'll take you upstairs to the guest bedroom so you can get settled. I need to talk to

213

Joy for a few minutes, then we can catch the game." They walked into the dining room where Joy was.

"That'll work," Owen said.

Joy's cell phone rang. She reached into her handbag sitting on the table and answered it. "What's up, Tyesha?" Joy flinched as another sharp pain hit.

Tyesha cursed and yelled in Joy's ear. She couldn't understand her and was in too much pain to try to figure it out so she handed Allen the phone. The muscles in his neck tightened as he listened. When he hung up, he mumbled obscenities under his breath.

"What's wrong?" Joy asked, rubbing the side of her stomach and praying for a good fart to release some of her gas.

"My stupid-ass brothers dropped the rest of the gifts off at Tyesha's house. She was still at the community center cleaning up when they got there so they left everything on her front porch." Allen frowned and punched the air. "Dumb asses! She needs help getting the stuff in the house."

Joy shook her head and pursed her lips. They were getting high in the parking lot so she wasn't surprised they screwed up. She was thankful they dropped it off at Tyesha's house and didn't boost it like everything else they got their hands on.

"I gotta go help Tyesha, but I wanna talk to you first about what happened earlier with Gabby." Allen needed to tell Joy the truth before Gabby did because he knew she was going to blame it on him when she was just as much at fault.

"It's dark. Don't have Tyesha outside standing guard over our baby shower gifts. We can talk later when you come back. I want to take a shower and relax anyway." She stood to go upstairs.

Allen turned to face Owen. "Sorry, man, but I won't be long. Joy can show you to your room and I'll be back so we can catch the game."

"I'll come help you," Owen offered.

Allen hesitated. He could use help with the heavy items because his chest was still tender from the gunshot wound. However, today was Joy's due date and he didn't want to leave her alone. "Good lookin' out, Owen. Joy, I want you to come, too. I don't want you in here alone in case you go into labor."

"I'm tired, Allen, and I want to go to bed. I'll be okay for the next hour. You can call me every five minutes if that'll make you feel better." Joy kissed him.

Allen still wasn't comfortable leaving her alone, but he figured with Owen's help he could be back sooner than an hour. He definitely planned to call her every few minutes like she suggested. "Keep the phone near you, even when you're in the shower. If you don't answer, I'm calling 911 and coming back."

"Alright." Joy rolled her eyes to the heavens. Sometimes Allen was too overprotective and it annoyed her.

Allen pulled her in his arms. "I know I'm getting on your nerves, but do you realize any minute our lives will change forever? When you go into labor, we'll walk out of here as Joy and Allen, but we'll come back home as a family with two little people who'll depend on us for everything." He kissed her lips lovingly.

"You're right, baby." She put his hand on her belly and smiled. "Hurry back."

She locked the door after they left and proceeded upstairs. At the top of the stairs, a sharp pain in her abdomen almost brought her to her knees. *Oh, my God! I think I'm in labor.* She rushed in her room and got the stopwatch Allen bought to time her contractions. Twenty minutes later, she called Dr. Fields because her contractions were ten minutes apart and lasted for about a minute. She didn't tell Allen when he called because he was on his way back home. She took her packed hospital bag out of the closet and decided to get ready so they could leave as soon as he got back.

She turned on the shower to get the bathroom hot and steamy while she undressed. The thought of seeing her babies had her tingling with excitement. She took deep breaths and waited until a contraction passed before she got in the shower. She washed quickly and was out before the next one hit.

She heard footsteps downstairs as she dried herself. Someone walked across the hardwood floors in the living room toward the kitchen. Her heartbeat quickened because she couldn't wait to tell Allen it was time to go to the hospital. She slipped on her robe and slippers and proceeded downstairs. She stopped a few times to breathe through her contractions. A loud crash startled her. She wondered what Allen and Owen had broken as she made her way down the steps.

The sound of glass breaking and things falling made her quicken her pace. At the doorway to the living room, Joy stopped, unable to believe her eyes. The words, *whore, slut,* and *bitch* were spray-painted on the walls and fireplace. The fabric on the furniture was slashed. Cushions were yanked out. All of the accessories were broken and pieces of glass were scattered all over the hardwood floors. The baby shower gift boxes were smashed and dented. Everything in the room was destroyed. To say it was vandalized was an understatement.

Diana stood in the middle of the living room with one of Joy's butcher knives in one hand and a meat cleaver in the other.

Joy stood paralyzed with fear.

"Oh, I thought you left with Allen, but I'm glad you're here. Allen hurt me, now I'm going to hurt his precious Joy to teach him a lesson." Diana tapped the blades of the knives together.

Joy's chest tightened and her blood started to boil. "You crazy bitch! You're so desperate to be with Allen that you have to do some shit like this!" Joy grabbed the wall and moaned as another contraction hit.

"It's Allen's fault! I was in London trying to move on with my life and then he contacted *me*. I accepted his invitation to your baby shower as a peace offering and came back to attend it, but he said it was a mistake and told me to leave. He treated me like a piece of shit. And that bitch he had with him helped. I know he's fucking her!" She sobbed. "Allen's going to pay for putting his hands on me. I should've pressed charges against him for choking me. I tried to scratch his eyes out and that bitch attacked *me* to protect *him*."

Now Joy knew why Allen and Gabby were having their intense conversation. They were trying to keep Diana's appearance at her baby shower a secret from her. The house phone rang. She had left it upstairs because she thought Allen was back home.

"Diana, you got it twisted. I'm pressing charges against you

216

for breaking into my house," Joy threatened.

"You won't be able to press charges. I'm going to cut those babies out of you and make you watch me kill them and then I'm going to kill you." Diana laughed and clapped the knives together. "I can't wait to see his expression when he sees his precious Joy hacked to pieces."

From the dining room, they heard Joy's cell phone ring. Joy rushed toward it, but her contractions slowed her down. In an instant, Diana had a handful of her hair.

"Ahhh!" Joy yelled out in pain. Using her elbow, she struck Diana's stomach.

Diana stumbled back coughing.

Joy ran toward the kitchen to get a weapon.

Diana grabbed Joy's robe and snatched the belt off. While she tried to tie it around Joy's neck, Joy turned around and pushed Diana with all her strength. Diana stumbled briefly, regained her balance, and then kicked her leg, aiming for Joy's belly.

Joy turned around to block her. The kick caught her in the back, causing her to fall to the floor. She landed on her hands and knees to break the fall and protect her babies.

With anger in her eyes, Diana planted a powerful kick to Joy's side.

She fell over and rolled on her back. Her contractions were coming faster and harder now. She saw Diana walk away and tried to get up, but she was in gut-wrenching pain and couldn't move. A gush of fluid between her legs soaked her robe and the hardwood floor. Hearing movement, she looked up to see Diana rushing toward her with the butcher knife. Her eyes were wild like a madwoman. Joy put her arms up to block her and kicked Diana's leg. She tripped and landed on the floor with a loud thump and moan. She didn't move.

Seconds later, Joy heard Allen and Owen rush in the house. "Allen," she tried to scream, but it sounded like a whisper.

"What the fuck!" Allen saw Joy lying on the floor with her robe wide open and Diana's limp body beside her. He took his jacket off and laid it over Joy's exposed body. "Did your water break?"

"Yes, but please get the knife away from her before she wakes up," Joy begged in a barely audible tone. Her contractions and the pressure between her legs were too much to bear.

Joy looked on as Owen and Allen turned Diana's body over. The knife she tried to kill Joy with was stuck deep in her chest. Owen checked for a pulse. He shook his head to indicate no pulse.

Joy screamed and then everything went black.

Chapter 31

The following afternoon, Joy watched from her hospital bed as two Prince George's County police officers left her room. They came to inform her that after their initial investigation, she wasn't going to be charged with Diana's death. Allen stood vigilant by her side with a hardened look on his face the entire time the officers were there. Bea and Tyesha sat across the room holding the twins and listening to every word. They looked like they were ready to attack if the officers said anything they didn't agree with. Joy was too sore and exhausted from giving birth last night to complain to the officers for even considering charging her. What were they thinking? Diana had broken into her house and threatened to kill her and the twins.

"Don't let this worry you, Joy," Bea said in a soothing tone.

"I'm not worried, Bea. Diana snapped and tried to kill me but ended up killing herself. She got what she deserved. I'm moving on and focusing on my children, not what she tried to do to me." Joy tried to sit up, but pain shot through her body making her moan.

"Are you okay, honey?" Bea asked. "Do you need some pain medicine?"

"I'm fine, just sore and tired, but I can handle it." Although the doctors said it was safe, she wasn't comfortable taking pain medicine while she was breastfeeding.

"You sure can handle it, you big booty bad-ass! Pushing out two seven-pound babies with no drugs. Damn! You earned my respect last night, girl," Tyesha exclaimed.

They laughed out loud.

Allen smiled and kissed Joy's forehead. He was impressed by her strength after all she endured last night with Diana and delivering their twins. "You are amazing and I'm sorry, baby. I can't apologize enough." Allen sat in the chair beside her bed, pulled her hand to his lips, and kissed the back.

Bea glared at Allen. "You should be sorry. A lot of this could've been avoided if you hadn't cheated on Joy in the first place. Hopefully, it'll open your eyes to what I've been trying to tell you, Joy."

"Stop it, Bea!" Joy ordered.

Allen looked down, sighed, and rubbed his bald head. Bea had been on him like white on rice since she found out what Diana tried to do to Joy. She blamed him and badmouthed him to Joy every chance she got. She even tried to block him from being in the delivery room last night, but Joy wanted him there. He was trying to remain calm, but Bea was working his last nerve.

"I suggest both of you do a background check on your future dates. The next person you end up with might actually kill one of you." Bea scrunched her face at Allen and Joy.

"I know that's right, Bea. They broke up and started dating two mental cases." Tyesha chuckled. "I need to interview everybody you date so I can keep the twins safe."

"We're together and not dating anybody else," Allen replied angrily.

"Um-hum." Bea stared at Allen with her evil eyes and pinched lips.

Allen's cell phone beeped several times. "I need to step out and check my messages. Will you be alright, baby?"

"She'll be fine. I'll be here as long as she's here so you don't have to worry about that," Bea interjected.

"Bea, you can't stay here tonight. The hospital only allows one guest per patient and Allen is staying with me," Joy shot back at her mother with an attitude.

"Oh, I already made arrangements with your doctor and the nurses. It's not a problem. I just need to get my bag out of the car."

Bea looked down at the baby squirming in her arms, oblivious to them staring at her in disbelief.

Bea's announcement was the final straw for Allen. The thought of her staying in the room tonight with him, Joy, and the twins had his neck muscles and temples throbbing. He hoped Joy would send her mother packing before she had the chance to get her bag out of the car, but he knew it wasn't going to happen. Joy looked at him with puppy dog eyes and puckered lips. Her way of asking him to understand that her mother was staying with them tonight. There was nothing he could do. Bea had the power to change Joy's mind and have him going home tonight instead of staying with them at the hospital. With everything else going on in his life, that's the last thing he needed. He looked at Tyesha with arched eyebrows before he left the room to check his messages.

"Tyesha, did Allen tell you why he's been glued to his phone lately? When I asked him, he mumbled something about looking for a job." Joy stared at Tyesha with a puzzled expression.

Tyesha looked down and swallowed hard. "No." She hated lying to Joy but felt it was Allen's responsibility to tell Joy the truth, not hers. She gave Joy the baby she was holding and said, "I'm going downstairs to get me a soda. Do either of you want anything?"

They said no and watched Tyesha as she left the room without her purse. A few minutes later, Gabby and Maxine entered the room smiling ear to ear.

"Can we come in?" Maxine asked.

"Y'all better come in here and see my beautiful grandbabies." Bea looked down with pride at her grandson in her arms.

Maxine and Gabby rushed in. Although they were at the hospital last night when Joy delivered, they only caught a glimpse of the twins because it was late and they had to get home to their own children.

"I'm still mad at you two heifers for not telling me about Diana showing up at my baby shower," Joy stated angrily as she glared at them.

"It's Allen's fault," Gabby replied nonchalantly. "He's the one who sent her the invitation, not us."

"Um-hum... you're right, Gabby. How is she willing to forgive Allen, but be mad at you and Maxine when this is all his fault?" Bea's face was flaming red with anger.

"I'm mad at Gabby because Diana called her to RSVP for the baby shower and she didn't catch it." Joy rolled her eyes at Gabby.

"I didn't recognize her name when she called because I had a lot on my mind. Remember, I was recovering from the abortion I had thanks to Allen's trifling, cold-hearted brother," Gabby snapped.

Bea was stunned into silence for the first time since she arrived at the hospital.

Maxine went to Joy's bedside. "I'm sorry for not telling you, Joy. I didn't know what was going on until I saw Allen arguing with this white woman in the lobby and Gabby pulling her out the door by her hair." Maxine hunched her shoulders and sighed. "I tried to stop it, but things got out of control. I ran inside and got Christian because he's a cop and knows how to handle situations like that better than I do."

"I'm not sorry. If anybody should apologize, it's you and Allen, Joy. My life has been in jeopardy twice because the two of you slept with crazy stalkers." Gabby sighed. "I forgive you, now let's move on. Can I meet my godchildren now?"

"I'm not forgiving Allen for anything. As soon as my grandchildren are taken back to the nursery, I'm gonna rip him a new one and kick his cheating tail to the curb," Bea threatened.

Maxine and Gabby looked at Joy for a response.

"Bea, can you go get me something to eat from the cafeteria? The food they served me for lunch was disgusting and I'm hungry," Joy asked with a tense smile.

Bea stood, put her grandson in his bassinet, and took her purse off the back of her chair. "I'll get you a salad and a bottle of water. Don't ask for anything else. You need to start working on getting those extra pounds off." Bea left.

Joy gave her daughter to Maxine, dropped her head in her hands, and let out a muffled scream. "Bea is driving me crazy!"

"Tell us something new," Gabby replied sarcastically as she

took Joy's son out of his bassinet. She joined Maxine at Joy's bed-side so she could see both babies together.

"Wow! Look at them. They're precious and big. I thought twins were small," Maxine said. "What are their names?"

Joy laughed. "Allen named them. My baby girl is Jaylyn Hope Johnson and she was born first, weighing seven pounds, four ounces. Gabby, you're holding Allen Todd Johnson, Jr., also known as Lil' Allen. He was born ten minutes later, weighing seven pounds, six ounces."

"Whoa! Both my boys barely weighed six pounds full term," Maxine exclaimed.

"Bea said you delivered them without drugs." Gabby flinched. She remembered the pain from delivering Nadia naturally and the thought of delivering two made her contract her vaginal muscles and cross her legs.

"Yep, no drugs." Joy nodded and smiled. She had planned a natural childbirth, but after what happened between her and Diana, she had no choice. She was too far dilated to be given any drugs.

"What! I called the hospital after my first contraction to have my epidural ready and waiting when I got there." Maxine laughed as she pulled the pink receiving blanket back to get a bet-ter look at Jaylyn's face.

"You wimp," Gabby joked. "You did good, Joy. They're beautiful!"

"Thanks." Joy smiled as she watched her girlfriends taking turns bonding with her babies. They hadn't been here a full day yet, but Joy could already see a lot of Allen's features in them. They had his full lips and long limbs. The edges of their ears were already dark. They would probably be closer to Allen's milk-chocolate tone than Joy's light skin. Both twins had a head full of curly hair like Joy's. She looked forward to watching their features change, and seeing their personalities develop as they got older.

"Gabby, what's up with you bringing Rayshawn to my baby shower?" Joy asked.

Maxine tilted her head toward Gabby, eager to hear her ex-planation.

"We agreed to put our differences aside and get along for

Nadia. I brought him with me because he was depressed over Osaki." Gabby cleared her throat. "He offered to stay with Nadia last night and today so I could come here."

"He spent the night with you?" Maxine exclaimed.

"Let me find out!" Joy laughed.

"Don't go there. He slept in my guest bedroom. He knows we're friends, nothing more. I get nauseous at the thought of him doing anything to my body." Gabby turned her head and gagged to prove her point.

"Girl, we need to go," Maxine said as she put Jaylyn in her bassinet.

"You didn't stay long," Joy complained.

"We volunteered to help Juan and Allen's friend, Owen, get your house back together before you're released," Gabby explained. She gave Lil' Allen to Joy when he started to whine.

"Thank you." That explained why Poppy and Owen hadn't been back to visit her.

"Bye, girl." Maxine hugged Joy and said, "Don't blame Allen. He loves you."

"I know. I love him, too." Joy winked at Maxine to reassure her of any doubts she had.

"Remember that when Bea rips him a new one and kicks him to the curb." Gabby kissed Joy's cheek. "I'll call you later."

Gabby and Maxine left. Joy unbuttoned her gown, removed her breast, and fed Lil' Allen.

Minutes later, Bea walked in with a plastic container of salad and bottled water in her hands. "Joy, something is going on out there with Allen and Tyesha. She's holding his hand and they look like somebody died. When I asked what was wrong, they blew me off. I know Tyesha and she's worried about something major and it has everything to do with Allen."

Joy knew something was wrong, too, because Tyesha always defended Allen except when she thought he was at fault. Bea had been on a non-stop tirade against him since last night, and Tyesha hadn't said a single word about it. Joy put Lil' Allen on her shoulder to burp him and prayed for the strength to deal with whatever Allen was getting ready to hit her with.

Chapter 32

Tyesha tapped her foot and rubbed Allen's back while they sat in the lobby.

"I can't believe this!" Allen jumped up and walked around the table cursing under his breath.

"Is there anybody else you can talk to who would understand your situation?" Tyesha asked anxiously.

Allen covered his face with both hands. "They're not budging. They want me or the money back," Allen explained.

"I'm sorry." Tyesha stood and hugged him. "You need to tell her, Allen."

"I can't..."

"She knows something's up. She asked me before I came out here and I'm not gonna lie to her again, but the truth needs to come from you," Tyesha warned with a frown. "Who knows what Bea went in there and told her?"

Allen was quiet for a moment before he said, "You're right. I need to tell her."

They walked back to Joy's room. Inside, Allen took Lil' Allen from Joy and put him in the bassinet.

"I need to talk to you, baby," he stated in a serious tone.

"Come on, Bea, let's give them some privacy," Tyesha suggested.

Bea looked at Tyesha's teary eyes and Allen's somber expression. "I'm not going anywhere, especially if you're getting ready to hurt my daughter again."

"You don't have to leave. I only wanna say this once." Allen sat in the chair beside Joy's bed and ran his hands over his bald head.

"Allen, you're scaring me. What's wrong?" Joy could feel her heart pounding.

He stood and took her hand in his. "I just got off the phone with my former boss in China..."

"On a Sunday?" Bea asked with her fist digging in her hip.

"Shut up and listen, Bea! It's Sunday here, but Monday in China," Tyesha snapped.

"My former employer is suing me for breach of contract." Allen lowered his head in shame.

"Since when?" Joy asked.

"I got served a couple of weeks ago. I was wrong for not telling you, but I was trying to work things out with them first." Allen released Joy's hand and sat back in the chair.

"You love that job don't you, Allen?" Joy studied his face for the truth.

"Yeah, but I love my family more," Allen confessed.

Bea flicked her hand in the air and sucked her teeth. "I work for good lawyers and if I ask, they'll help you with your case. And you need to find another job because Joy can't raise two babies on her teacher's salary."

"I know that, Bea. I don't expect her to. I tried to find a job here, but nobody will hire me because I ruined my reputation when I broke my contract, and now the company is coming after me for close to a million dollars."

"A million dollars!" Joy was in shock.

"Um, yeah...I had a hell of a contract. My base salary was $250,000. When you include the moving expenses, my housing allowance, and all my medical bills, it adds up," Allen explained.

Joy, Bea, and Tyesha stared at each other in complete shock over Allen's salary.

Allen stood and kissed Joy on the lips. "I'm sorry, baby. I tried everything to stay here, but I have no choice but to go back to China."

"I understand, Allen." Joy caressed Allen's face and smiled at him. "When do we need to leave?"

Allen's mouth dropped wide open. "What did you say?"

"Baby, we're a family now. If you go, we go with you. Is that alright?"

"Hell, yeah, that's alright! That's more than alright!" Allen kissed Joy's hand. "Are you sure? We need to be in China by the end of May."

Joy smiled and nodded. "Okay, I just have one condition."

"Anything you want," Allen offered.

"I don't want to go with you to China as your girlfriend or your babies' mama. I want to go as your wife." Joy smiled.

"Oh, baby, of course! Do you know how long I've been trying to marry you?" Allen reached in his jacket on the back of his chair and pulled out the ring box he had with him at the baby shower. He got on his knee and took Joy's hand. "Will you marry me?"

"Yes, I will," Joy said without hesitation.

"Yes!" He slipped the ring on Joy's finger and looked at Tyesha. "I'm getting married."

Before Tyesha could answer and Allen could get up from the floor, Bea rushed to Joy's bedside.

"What the hell are you thinking? Why are you making such a huge decision without talking to me about it first? And you plan to take my grandchildren to a foreign country?" Bea broke down crying.

Joy looked at Allen and Tyesha. "Can you give me a few minutes alone with my mother, please?"

Allen held Joy's hand and looked at her with pleading eyes while shaking his head no. He didn't want to leave because he feared Bea would change Joy's mind. Tyesha had to pry his hands from Joy's and force him out the room.

Bea had her back turned to Joy with her arms crossed over her chest and tears streaming down her face. She didn't want to hear what Joy had to say because she wasn't prepared to let her daughter and grandchildren go.

"Mom?" Joy started crying when she heard Bea sniffling.

"Don't play the Mom card with me. You only call me that when you want your way," Bea snapped.

"That's not true. I call you Bea because that's what you want, but I call you Mom when I need my mother, like now. Please, Mom," Joy cried.

Bea turned around to face Joy. Her face was wet with tears and her lips were trembling. She checked on the twins in their bassinets before she got in bed with Joy. Joy cringed from her pain as she moved over so Bea could lie beside her. She held her mother in her arms as they cried.

"I know my decision hurts you, but I can't lose him again. I don't want to stay here asking myself, where did I go wrong again with Allen."

"He cheated on you!" Bea sobbed.

"And I cheated on him, too."

Bea sat up and looked at Joy with a bewildered expression.

"Not with another man, but for years I put you before him and I don't want to make that mistake again," Joy explained as she wiped her mother's tears. "You need to get along with Allen. I love him. Don't make me choose because you won't like my decision. Think about your grandchildren, too. I don't want my babies growing up seeing all this animosity between you and Allen."

"But you're *my* baby. I won't be able to see you whenever I want and my grandchildren won't know me," Bea sobbed.

"I'll make sure they know their Grand Bea. We'll Skype, video-conference, and visit each other as much as possible. I love him and I want to go with him. I want your blessing, but I'm prepared to go to China without it." Joy remembered how Bea had behaved when she married Dean and how they'd stopped talking for a while. She didn't want that to happen again, but if it did, she was willing to accept it.

"What about school? You're so close to finishing."

"My last two classes are over in May. I still need to finish writing my dissertation and submit it to my advisor. Once it's approved, I'll finally be Dr. Joy Hope Marshall like you always wanted," Joy said proudly.

"Dr. Joy Hope Johnson," Bea corrected.

Joy smiled because she knew that was Bea's way of giving her blessing. Joy squeezed her mother in her arms and planted several kisses on her face. "Thank you, Bea. Will you be able to go with us to China for a couple of weeks to help us get settled?"

Bea sat up, wiped her face and smiled. "Of course. There is a lot to do and May will be here before you know it."

"I know. Thanks, Bea!" Joy smiled because Bea loved it when Joy needed her.

Bea opened the door and invited Allen and Tyesha back in the room. Allen slowly entered, expecting the worst. Joy smiled to reassure him that nothing had changed. He let out a sigh of relief as he looked at the two-carat, princess-cut diamond ring on her finger.

Bea stood in front of Allen. "Promise me Joy will finish her Ph.D., and I'm expecting you to protect them and keep them safe." Tears welled in her eyes.

Allen pulled Bea into his arms. "I promise you, Joy will finish school and I will give my life to protect my wife and children."

"Damn, Bea! Didn't he take a bullet to the chest to protect them? What else do you want?" Tyesha snapped.

"Be quiet, Tyesha! Ain't nobody talking to you." Bea rolled her eyes at Tyesha.

"Whatever!" Tyesha gave Bea the middle finger.

"Allen, I don't know if we'll ever get along. I trusted you. When you hurt Joy, you hurt me, too." Bea put her arms around Allen's waist and squeezed him tight. "My daughter loves you, so I'm putting my doubts aside and giving you my blessing." She kissed Allen's cheek.

"Thank you, Bea." Allen returned a kiss to her cheek.

"I'm going home to get some rest. Call me there if you need me." Bea gathered her belongings and put them in a plastic bag.

"I thought you were staying here tonight, Bea?" Joy asked, completely shocked by her mother's new attitude.

"You don't need me. Allen will be here with you. You better get used to it."

Bea and Tyesha kissed Allen, Joy, and the twins goodbye.

They left together in the midst of a heated conversation about which family members the twins looked like. Allen picked the twins up when they started whining. He put Jaylyn in Joy's arms and he held Lil' Allen while he stood beside Joy's bed.

He smiled at Joy. "So, we're really doing this, huh?"

"Yep, and I can't wait to become Mrs. Allen Todd Johnson, Senior."

"Neither can I." Allen looked at Joy and his children. He felt blessed to finally have everything he prayed for.

As Joy fed Jaylyn, she thought about all she had to do. Get married, find a place to live in China, sell her house, pack, and quit her job, all while caring for newborn twins and finishing school. She knew Maxine and Gabby would help her, and that's when she realized they didn't know yet. Panic filled her at the thought of not having her best friends near her anymore.

Chapter 33

"I should take your ass back to court and sue you for full custody," Rayshawn screamed. "I should've known never to trust you!"

Gabby stood and smacked Rayshawn's face. "Try it and you'll regret it!"

Osaki jumped between them with her arms extended. She knew this was a bad idea. Nadia's first birthday was next week, Memorial Day weekend, and Gabby was planning a big birthday party for her. When Rayshawn found out, he insisted on coming, but Gabby wanted Osaki there. Gabby's solution was to tell Rayshawn the truth about her past and how she and Osaki set him up. They had been getting along, and even went on a couple of family outings together to show a united front for Nadia. She hoped their newfound friendship would help him understand and not hold any animosity toward them. She was wrong.

"Nadia is in here with us taking it all in. Is this what you want her to see?" Osaki looked at both of them with squinted eyes. "Don't hurt my baby like this."

"She ain't your fuckin' baby! You ain't no kin to her!" Rayshawn shouted.

"Gabby and Nadia are my family, Rayshawn. You don't always have to share the same blood to be family." Osaki pulled Gabby to the couch with her and sat down.

Rayshawn observed Osaki. She didn't resemble the loud and outrageous Osaki he had fallen in love with. This woman had on jeans, a Georgetown Hoyas T-shirt, and tennis shoes.

She wore bifocals and kept peeking over them when she looked at him. "You a good actress. How much Gabby pay you to sleep with me? You a hooker, right?"

"Gabby didn't pay me anything to sleep with you, Rayshawn. When she called me upset about you suing her for full custody, I offered to help her. And by the way, I'm not a hooker. I'm an escort. Entertaining men and women sexually is what I do for a living. I enjoy it. It provides me with a wonderful lifestyle and I'm not ashamed of it."

"Why is it okay for you to hire a private detective to follow me and get dirt on me, but you consider it wrong for me to call Osaki for help?" Gabby flung her hand at him.

"Did you fall in love with the private detective?"

"Rayshawn, you didn't fall in love with me. Most of my clients think they love me because I'm giving them what they want. It's a fantasy. I wear the hair, clothes, and makeup my clients want to see me in and I make them feel good for a large sum of money." She stood and pointed at her T-shirt and jeans. "This is the real me. This is who Nadia sees when she's with me."

"Well, I don't want her with you anymore. Gabby, if I find out my daughter been around a prostitute, I'm calling Child Protective Services." Rayshawn crossed his arms and nodded when he saw the frightened looks on their faces.

"You don't have to do that. I promise I'll leave and never see Nadia again. I'll stay out of Gabby's life because I don't want to make trouble for her." Osaki stood and walked toward the door.

"No, Osaki!" Gabby cried.

"Saki." Nadia stood and walked to Osaki with her arms extended.

"Oh, my God! Look, Rayshawn." Gabby clapped excitedly. She and Rayshawn had been trying to get Nadia to walk for weeks, but she would always fall after her first step.

Osaki picked her up and kissed her cheek.

Rayshawn snatched Nadia out of Osaki's arms. "Don't kiss her. Who knows where your mouth been."

Nadia started crying and reaching for Osaki.

"You are so stupid! Are you going to deprive your daughter of being around somebody she loves and who loves her back?" Gabby glared at Rayshawn.

He gave Nadia back to Osaki with a frown. "Alright, but if I find out you have her around any pimps or prostitutes, I'm calling CPS."

"Rayshawn, you..."

Osaki shook her head at Gabby for her to stop talking. "You don't have to worry about that, Rayshawn. I don't have a pimp and don't know any prostitutes. Gabby and Nadia have never been involved with what I do for a living." She gave Nadia back to him. "Take care, Rayshawn. I think I should go."

"Oh, you leaving? I guess I'll see you at the birthday party then." Rayshawn licked his lips as he looked her up and down.

Osaki reached in her purse, pulled out a card, and gave it to Rayshawn. "If you're ever interested in my services."

"Oh, I don't pay for pussy." Rayshawn cringed to show how insulted he was.

"Rayshawn!" Gabby screamed and snatched Nadia from his arms. "Watch your language!"

"Oh, my bad." He looked at Nadia and covered his mouth.

"I understand, Rayshawn. Why pay when you can get it for free?" Osaki kissed each of them on the cheek and headed toward the door.

Rayshawn followed Osaki. "So how much you charge?"

"Call me later and we'll discuss it," Osaki teased with a wink.

Gabby shook her head. She knew after the initial shock of what she did wore off, Rayshawn was going to pay Osaki to get back in his bed as soon as possible.

$\mathscr{C}$hapter 34

Allen pulled his leased black Range Rover into the parking lot of the Gaylord Hotel just before dusk and looked at Joy sitting in the passenger seat. She had her eyes closed with her head leaned back on the leather headrest. He turned off the engine and touched her arm to let her know they had arrived.

Joy opened her eyes and looked at her husband with a blank stare. They were married two weeks ago in a civil ceremony at the Prince George's County Courthouse with just a few family members and friends in attendance. Tonight was their last night in Maryland before they moved to China, and Allen wanted to make it special by taking her to the National Harbor for a romantic evening.

"What's wrong, baby?" Allen asked full of concern.

She sighed. "Everything's moving so fast. I can't believe we leave tomorrow and I haven't spent any time with Gabby and Maxine."

"What! You've seen them every day since the twins were born. I'm tired of looking at them," Allen complained.

Joy shot daggers at him with her eyes. She loved Allen, but he never understood her close relationship with her girlfriends. Sometimes his comments about their friendship pissed her off. "Um, whatever," Joy mumbled.

Allen leaned over, kissed her lips and said, "Enough about your girls. We got the night to ourselves. No twins waking up and interrupting our groove. I'm looking forward to a night of uninterrupted sex with you. I already have the key so when we get in that suite, I wanna see you wearing nothing but a smile." Allen laughed as he turned the truck off.

"Hmm, I'm tired and don't feel like smiling." Joy opened the passenger door and stepped out.

They walked to the hotel with an uncomfortable silence between them. Joy avoided eye contact with Allen as they rode the elevator to the penthouse level. When they stepped off the elevator, he reached for her hand, but she pulled away.

Allen gave Joy a seductive wink as he used the key card to open the door. He held the door open for her to walk in first. She stepped in the room, stopped dead in her tracks, and gasped.

"Surprise!" Gabby and Maxine yelled as they stood near the entrance to the suite.

Joy screamed, ran to her girlfriends, and hugged them. "Oh, my God! What are you doing here?" Joy asked.

"Allen arranged this so we could spend some time together before you leave," Maxine answered.

"You deserve a pat on the back for doing this for us, Allen. I appreciate it," Gabby added.

With her hands over her heart, Joy turned around and looked at Allen. "You did this?"

Allen smiled. "Yep. It's my going-away present to you."

"Oh... I'm sorry for being so mean, but you tricked me." She sashayed across the hardwood floor to Allen, threw her arms around his neck, and kissed him.

"It's all good. I didn't mean what I said in the car. I'm cool with you spending time with your girls. I got you for the rest of my life." Allen kissed her hard and long.

"I can't love you any more than I do right now," Joy said as she looked in his eyes.

"Ah... Should we leave?" Maxine interjected.

"I don't think so! Get out, Allen! She'll see you tomorrow," Gabby barked.

"Okay, I'm leaving. I love you, baby. I'll take care of the twins, so don't worry about them. Enjoy your girls' night out." He kissed Joy again and walked to the door. "Gabby, no strippers allowed and, Maxine, keep track of the porn you order on TV 'cause they got my credit card on file," Allen joked.

They laughed out loud as he left the room.

Joy locked the door and turned around to look at her girl-friends with a bright smile. "This is exactly what I needed!"

"I know that's right. I think I cried every day since you told me you were moving to China," Maxine said in a sad tone.

"Well, no crying tonight. We're going to have a good time like we used to in college, just in a more upscale environment," Gabby added.

Joy hooked each of her arms through one of Maxine's and one of Gabby's arms, and they walked into the living room area of the suite. The rich decor and open floor plan took her by surprise. She removed her arms from theirs and went to the floor-to-ceiling windows to look at the views of the Potomac River and historic Old Towne Virginia. She walked through all of the six rooms and each one seemed more elegant than the one before. Gabby's use of the word *upscale* to describe this suite wasn't grand enough.

After she finished touring the suite, she joined Maxine and Gabby at the cherrywood dining room table. "Okay, who's paying for this?"

"Your husband," Gabby answered.

"Yeah, we got here an hour before you did and I'm still shocked. He even got the adjoining rooms so we could all have our own beds," Maxine explained.

"Oh, wow! I know this wasn't cheap. What was Allen thinking?" Joy complained.

"Girl, please! Just enjoy it! It's the least he can do since he dragged you to that tacky courthouse to get married while you were still carrying around all that baby fat. I was embarrassed for you, but this made up for it," Gabby countered.

Joy frowned at Gabby. "Thanks a lot, Gabby."

"You said it, not me. The first time you got married, you said I'm not walking down the aisle showing. When you married Allen a couple of weeks ago, you still looked pregnant. I'm just saying." Gabby shrugged her shoulders.

"I did say that, but when you're marrying your soulmate, it

doesn't matter," Joy responded.

"All I'm saying is if you want to stay married to your soul-mate, you better lose that baby fat. My motto is keep it tight and smelling right and you'll always be in his sight. If not, he'll be looking at some other chick."

"Be quiet, Gabby! Well, I'm happy for you and Allen," Maxine said with a big smile.

"Thanks, girl." Joy smiled at Maxine and gave Gabby the evil eye.

Gabby sighed. "Better you than me. I wouldn't get married again for anything in this world. Well, I take that back. If he's rich, handsome, and didn't want to have children, then I'd consider it, but he'd have to give me my divorce settlement up front or at least put a lump sum in my bank account before we got married."

"You talking about getting a divorce before you even get married. Haven't you learned anything from this past year?" Max-ine glared at Gabby.

"No, she hasn't," Joy stated.

"What is there to learn? I mean, I married a weak man who lied to me about having a mental illness. That's not my fault." Gabby rolled her eyes.

"What about what you did to Rayshawn?" Joy asked.

"That's all in the past. We worked everything out. He even turned out to be a better father than I thought and believe it or not, we're actually friends now." Gabby chuckled. "Everything worked out for the best. When Nadia spends time with her father, I get to have a little fun of my own." Gabby fluttered her eyelashes play-fully. She had started dating again and was working with a busi-ness consultant to start her own interior design business. She had never been happier.

"Good for you. I'm glad you're not back with Bo now that Peaches is divorcing him," Joy uttered.

"Please. Bo can't compete with the men I date now." Gabby chuckled.

"Oh, I really liked the guy you went out with last week when I watched Nadia for you. He was fine and nice, too," Maxine said.

"Don't get used to any men you see me with because they're all on a short-term lease. They're just around to serve a purpose, be it sexual, financial, or whatever else I need." Gabby crossed her arms over her chest and smiled at her friends.

"Keep using men the way you do and the next one might kill your ass instead of committing suicide," Joy warned.

Gabby hunched her shoulders and said, "Whatever."

"Being single works for you, Gabby, but I enjoy being married. I pray that things work out between me and Christian, but if they don't, I do want to get married again someday."

Gabby pointed her index finger at Maxine. "Instead of planning a future with that boring, henpecked cop, get out and date. Explore. Experiment. You might find somebody a little more interesting."

Maxine smacked Gabby's hand down. "Christian is interesting enough for me. We enjoy spending time together and with our children. He's good to me and I love him."

"The more I get to know him, he seems like a perfect match for you, Maxine," Joy said.

Gabby let out a deep sigh. "Um-hum. Dull. Uninteresting. Law-abiding citizen."

"Everybody doesn't live for drama like you, Gabby," Maxine replied angrily.

Gabby looked away from her girlfriends and tapped her index finger on her temple. "Maybe being with Christian is a good idea. He definitely won't try to hurt you like Trent and that's one less thing I'll have to worry about. If you started dating again, you might end up in another abusive relationship and I can't go through that again."

Joy and Maxine looked at each other with raised eyebrows. Only Gabby would find a way to make Maxine's relationship and dating status about her.

Maxine looked across the dining room table at Gabby and said, "I wouldn't let a man hit me again or keep it a secret if he did. You don't have to worry about that. I promise."

Gabby hugged Maxine. "I'm proud of you. You're stronger than I've ever given you credit for."

"Yes, I am." Maxine stood to go to the bathroom. "I'll be back."

Joy looked at Gabby and mouthed thank you. She had had a talk with Gabby last week and asked her to stop criticizing Maxine so much about her bad decisions. Gabby's comments always hurt Maxine and she would stop talking to Gabby for a few days. Joy didn't want Maxine to feel alone during Trent's upcoming trial. She wanted to leave for China knowing Maxine felt comfortable turning to Gabby during the stressful days sure to come.

Maxine returned to the table with a chilled bottle of Risata Moscato d'Asti, Joy's favorite white wine, and three wine glasses. Maxine popped the cork, poured some wine in each glass, and gave one to each of her friends.

Gabby frowned at the wine glass. She didn't believe a lady should drink alcohol.

Maxine pointed her index finger at Gabby and said, "Get over it, heifer. You're going to drink with us tonight. This is the first time we'll be apart since we met in college, so we need to get our drink on."

Joy picked up her wine glass and held it up for them to toast. "I agree, Maxine. And keep it coming, especially since I'm not breastfeeding my greedy babies anymore."

Gabby picked up her glass and held it up to toast with her friends.

"Here is a toast to the future, a toast to the past, and a toast to our friends, far and near. May our friendship remain faithful and clear," Maxine said in a cheerful tone.

They touched their glasses together and took a sip.

"Speaking of past, how did we survive everything we went through this past year?" Joy asked as she looked at her friends.

"We survived because we're strong," Gabby responded.

"Yeah, and you can't keep a good sister down," Maxine added.

Gabby put her glass down, clapped her hands together, and asked, "Are we staying in here yapping all night or are we going out? I had one of my male friends reserve us a table in the hotel's club upstairs."

"Whew! Dancing! I want to go!" Joy screamed.

Maxine growled. "Okay, count me in." She never liked going to clubs.

"Okay, go change into something cute and we're out of here," Gabby ordered.

"Wait! One more toast, please," Joy pleaded.

They picked up their wine glasses and looked at each other.

Joy cleared her throat and tears filled her eyes. "I love you both like sisters. We accept the good and bad in each other and our most intimate secrets will always remain safely tucked away deep within us. Our different personalities make our friendship unique and special. Every day, I thank God for having both of you in my life. I know wherever we are, China, Maryland, or anywhere else, we'll always be friends forever."

They tapped their glasses together with tears streaming down their faces and said in unison, "Friends forever."